to use

MW01126593

COLD PERIL

Titles By Emily Jane Trent

The Passion Series

Adam & Ella:

Captivated
Charmed
Cherished
Craved

Touched By You:

Dark Desire
Naked Submission
The Heart's Domination
Bound By Love
Deep Obsession
Forbidden Pleasures
Raw Burn
Desperately Entwined
Fierce Possession
Intimate Secrets
Whispered Confessions
Vivid Temptation

Sexy & Dangerous

Perfectly Shattered
Perfectly Ruined
Perfectly Flawed
Perfectly Broken

Bend To My Will:

Forbidden Passion
Seductive Affair
Intimate Kiss
Deep Longing
Illicit Craving
Wicked Obsession
Luscious Sins
Sexy Addiction
Secret Torment
Daring Confessions
Eternal Love
Sweet Promise

Fighting For Gisele

UNLEASHED
UNTAMED
UNBROKEN
UNDEFEATED

Military Romantic Suspense

Cold Peril

COLD PERIL

Stealth Security

Emily Jane Trent

Cold Peril Copyright © 2016
by Emily Jane Trent

Printed in the United States of America
First Printing, 2016

ISBN-13: 978-1541355682
ISBN-10: 1541355687

Camden Lee Press, LLC
12112 N Rancho Vistoso Plaza
Suite 150-101
Oro Valley, AZ 85755

www.EmilyJaneTrent.com

To my friend Vicki for sharing the joy of creating.

Acknowledgements

No book is published in isolation. So many helped me, some in ways they never imagined. From my friends and family, my mentor, and a long list of indie authors, all have contributed to my success. Without my editor, cover artist, formatting expert, and others who played a part in making this book, I'd never be able to create these books for you like I do. I want to thank each of them for their good work.

A special thank you to all my readers: I hope you enjoy this romantic tale. It's been very rewarding to write. It's my pleasure to continue to create stories for you. I look forward to meeting you at my fan page, Emily Jane Trent Books, or at my website. My success is only because you read and enjoy these stories. I appreciate each of you.

CHAPTER ONE

If danger lurked, Marlene Parks surely wasn't aware of it. She appeared graceful, poised, and was clearly used to being in front of an audience. She seemed to glide along the red carpet without missing a step, while keeping her eyes on the fans, graciously accepting the open adoration and basking in the admiration. Even from a distance, she was radiant.

Garrett Flynn was smitten, as any red-blooded male who cast eyes on her would be. He worked his way to the front of the crowd to get a better view of the beloved movie star. He admired her support of organizations to help veterans, and this event to raise funds for wounded warriors had gotten a lot of publicity. It was at the Beverly Hilton, with the red carpet rolled out on the walkway so the throng of fans could interact with the stars in attendance for the fundraiser.

Awareness of his surroundings was second nature. Garrett's Navy SEAL training kicked in, and he took in the crowd, alert for any sign of threat. Yet he didn't spot anyone who wasn't gazing in awe at the lovely celebrity, or anyone exhibiting signs of unsavory intentions. Scanning faces and reading body language as he threaded his way through the crowd revealed no cause for alarm. But he didn't like the setup.

The fans were under control for the moment. But the excitement level was high, so the atmosphere was primed for trouble. When he made it to the front, Garrett noted where security was posted. The men were staggered along the walkway and hovering at the ropes, warning any overzealous attendee to stay back. In his estimation, security was insufficient. Technically, it wasn't his responsibility. He was off the clock, and Marlene Parks wasn't a client.

After leaving the service due to injury, Garrett had trained as a bodyguard for Stealth Security in Los Angeles. He was up to speed on the protection of celebrities. It wasn't solely about avoiding risk. If so, a high-profile personality would stay barricaded at home. That wasn't an option.

Fame had inherent risk. Social media and live events made stars accessible, raising the public's expectations. Interacting with fans, shaking hands, being up close and personal was good for sales. Movies tended to be more successful if the fans felt connected with the star—better yet, *loved* the star. Any big star was way too visible, even touchable as Marlene was now.

The crowd roared, and as if to encourage them, Marlene stepped closer to the ropes. It was a chilly February day, so she wore a white mink coat. The soft waves of her blond hair flowed over her shoulders, and her gold shoes glittered in the afternoon light. She opened her arms to embrace the crowd, and her brilliant smile held the crowd spellbound.

Cameras flashed and a cacophony of screams from fans nearly drowned out the music. Marlene beamed at the crowd, before continuing to walk toward a podium at the end of the red carpet. The news release had boasted that other major stars would perform at the main event to be held inside. But Marlene was the spokesperson, so she appeared first. With an air of confidence, she headed toward the media representatives, hovering in anticipation of sound bites that they would later quote.

Garrett assumed the other stars would grace the red carpet once Marlene got things started. This was the first time he'd seen her in person, and he hadn't expected to be so drawn to her. Seeing her on the big screen didn't do her justice. Glossy magazine pictures or glimpses of her on social media didn't capture her true beauty.

Up close, Marlene exuded warmth. Her appreciation for all the attention she garnered was evident in her demeanor. Although she had every right to be a bit arrogant, Garrett didn't observe any of that. She was the girl next door, a friend, a woman like any other. Only she wasn't.

Garrett was at the event to see her, as there was no other reason he'd participate in such a glorified affair. He much preferred the shadows to the limelight, but his goal was to make sure that Marlene was safe. Memories of a battle, bloody and deadly, pushed into his consciousness. The image of Andrew Parks dying in his arms haunted him.

Marlene's older brother Andrew had been a young marine, a brave soldier who hadn't survived one brutal battle. Now Garrett was there to see the younger sister Andrew had been close to, and make sure that she was okay. That was something her older brother could no longer do, so Garrett felt an obligation to stand in his place.

If all went well, Garrett hoped he'd have a chance to speak to Marlene. It wasn't as though he could contact her manager and make an appointment. He was a former Navy SEAL turned bodyguard. But no one she'd know. From brief talks with her brother,

Garrett knew her life was busy, and it made sense that there was a screening process for anyone who wanted to meet with her. At least, he hoped her security checked a person out before allowing access to her.

Garrett looked up at the podium swarming with press and took in the rabid fans pressing closer. His chances of meeting with her were slim at best. Maybe another time he could arrange circumstances more to his advantage. It hadn't been that great an idea to meet her for the first time at a well-publicized event, but he'd put off seeing her for long enough.

Although ever vigilant about keeping an eye on the crowd, Garrett observed Marlene maintaining control under the onslaught of fans and press. She was confident, a personality trait he admired. And she wasn't just pretty, she was absolutely gorgeous. Garrett hadn't expected her to have such an effect on him.

He felt like he knew her, and in a way he did. When Andrew had spoken of home, he hadn't failed to mention his sister. But it wasn't her fame or money that he bragged about. It was what a good sister she was. Growing up, Andrew had been close to his sister. He'd told Garrett about all the charity work she was involved in. She used her name to bring attention to worthy causes, and her passion was providing assistance to former soldiers and their families.

There was no way to look into her lovely green eyes without being assured of her sincerity. The real Marlene resembled the photo Andrew had carried in his wallet, more than any airbrushed image created for publicity. The first time Garrett had seen that photo, he'd known Marlene had a good heart. He couldn't say how he'd known, but he had.

Despite the goodness inside, Marlene was no

pushover. She bantered with the press, holding her own, without wavering. Her poise was admirable, especially to Garrett. His worst nightmare was being thrust into public view. He'd had too many years of clandestine activities and secret missions to be comfortable under bright lights. Staying in the shadows was Garrett's specialty.

Observing the crowd, he noted that they dressed rather casually in jeans, as he'd known they would. Paired with some outer garment to fend off the cold and comfortable shoes, as was common in California, the outfits were complete. He'd dressed in kind, wearing faded jeans, well-worn jogging shoes, and a brown jacket. A casual observer wouldn't pick him out of any crowd, which was his preference.

Marlene's bubbly laugh drew his attention. She seemed to glow as the press continued to barrage her with questions. Her security was closer now, yet she was still too vulnerable for Garrett's taste. A golden rope stretched along the length of the red carpet and in front of the podium. It was all that separated the adored star from the media and the fans.

The twist of rope was a deterrent as long as it was respected. So far the media had maintained decorum, and no fan had dared to leap over it. But Garrett was prepared for any possibility. He'd had to be for so many years that it wasn't something he could turn on and off. Hypervigilance had saved him or his team on too many occasions to count.

The ordeal with the press was finally over, so Marlene put her hand over the microphone then stepped away from the podium. The press continued to shout questions, but she held up her hand to signal that the interviews were over. The music volume increased and the crowd roared in unison. Garrett stood at the edge of the walkway near the rope, taking it all in. He was close to Marlene, almost near enough to reach her.

At the far end of the red carpet, a couple of other recognizable faces appeared. Garrett knew them from their blockbuster movies. As the audience focused on the new arrivals, Marlene took a step back, a gesture signifying that she was no longer the center of attention. The charming smile she'd maintained during the interviews faded. And her green eyes lost some of their luster.

She was a talented actress, and it struck Garrett that she'd put on a performance for the audience. That maybe the outward show of vibrant happiness wasn't all there was to her. She didn't think anyone was watching her particularly. And she certainly didn't have any idea that Garrett was observing. In that private moment, a fleeting second in time, Marlene's eyes revealed more of what she held close to her heart. Honest emotion showed in her expression but was gone as quickly as it appeared.

Yet Garrett noticed. It was a skill to observe reactions, one that he had honed to perfection. Now he couldn't brush aside the awareness that Marlene was sad. She took care not to reveal her unhappiness. Garrett saw that she played her role, whether in public or in a movie, showing only what she wished to. The world only saw the Marlene she created for them. But Garrett had seen beyond that.

Without being obvious, Garrett kept the throng of fans in his peripheral vision. Then he turned casually, as if looking for a friend, so no one would notice his movement. The audience was riveted on the famous figures emerging, hoping to get a good look as they became visible at the other end of the carpeted walkway.

All except for one man. Garrett noted his faded jeans with combat boots, likely purchased secondhand. The crowd had moved closer to the ropes at the far end of the walkway, to get a better look at the stars they'd come to see, leaving the combat-boots guy more in the open. For a couple of seconds, Garrett had a clear view of him.

The guy looked at Marlene, but something was off. The man's eyes were glued to her, as though he was stalking her. Any movie star had stalkers, at one time or another. Or just rabid fans that were a little too infatuated. But not all posed a threat.

Then the man's eyes went to Garrett, just before his right hand swept his long coat open. There wasn't time to consider whether the man had been looking purposely at Garrett or not. Instantaneously, the man's action was clear. Garrett saw it in his mind before it happened.

When the coat swept open, it stayed back as if the pocket was weighted. Likely the man had something heavy in there, so when the coat opened it would stay back. Garrett had done the same thing many times. The coat hid the gun, but it was important when drawing the weapon that the coat didn't flap closed and get in the way.

Then the man reached for his waistband. Garrett didn't need to watch the rest; he knew the man had a gun. But the guy was too far away to reach quickly. There were too many people in the way for Garrett to tackle him in time.

With split-second reaction time, Garrett leapt over the gold rope. He threw his body in front of Marlene, and propelled her to the ground in a fluid motion. A gunshot cracked in the air a moment before he hit the carpet, barely avoiding tragedy. With one hand on the back of her head and the other around her waist, he protected her from the fall. The padding of his coat buffered his forearms, and he took the impact on bent knees so his weight wouldn't crush her.

In the din of noise that ensued, Garrett heard screams and the general roar of all hell breaking loose. With Marlene underneath him, time seemed to stand still. She felt awfully good pressed against him. He breathed in her floral perfume and looked into her eyes.

Then he turned his head and yelled, "Shooter in the crowd!" But he didn't move immediately. It was best to shield Marlene until he knew the situation was under control. Her breathing was rapid and her eyes showed fear. But she didn't struggle against him, as she was probably in shock.

"You're okay," Garrett said. "The guy had a gun. You're safe."

Tears formed in Marlene's eyes but she didn't say anything. His hand was still on the back of her head, with a finger touching her neck, and he felt her pulse pounding. Garrett started to ease off, so she could get up. Before he could help her up, two of her security guards grabbed him. They yanked him away from her, one on each arm. And a third lifted Marlene to her feet, then stood in front of her and glared at Garrett.

Now her security was on high alert. They'd seen him jump her and assumed he was the attacker. "You're a little late, fellas." Garrett was in no mood for their antics. "Did you nab the guy with the gun?"

A muscled guard dressed in a suit strode up. "I heard the shot, but didn't see where it came from. Security is swarming the place now, but it appears the man got away."

Finally, Marlene spoke, directing her question to the guard in the suit. "Raymond, what's going on?"

When Raymond gave a disapproving look at his crew, they released Garrett's arms. "We need to get you inside, Marlene. Some guy shot at you, dammit."

Marlene stiffened. "I know *that*. I heard the shot. I could have been killed."

Raymond raked a hand through his hair and huffed. "Come on. Get her inside," he said to his team. Facing Garrett, he barked out, "And who are you?"

Marlene stepped closer to Garrett, evading her security. "This man saved my life." She put her arm through his, and he could feel her trembling.

Garrett needed to get her off this damned red carpet. He reached into his pocket and pulled out his badge. "Garrett Flynn, Stealth Security," he said.

Raymond grabbed it, took a look, then handed it back.

"I'm a professional bodyguard," Garrett said. "Lucky I was here."

Marlene wrapped her arm tighter around his and leaned her forehead on his arm. The gesture spurred him to action. Client or not, Garrett was duty bound to protect, especially a woman. He swept her into his arms to carry her toward the hotel. "I'm taking her inside. We'll discuss this later. I assume you've called the police."

Raymond followed them toward the entrance. "They're already here." Then the shrill sound of sirens confirmed that backup had arrived.

Marlene put her arms around Garrett's neck and leaned her head on his shoulder, while he carried her toward the hotel. He didn't like seeing her so vulnerable, so increased his pace. Once inside the lobby, Garrett lowered Marlene back to her feet. "I don't know how to thank you," she said, just before she was swept away.

A man in an expensive suit appeared, probably her event manager. "Marlene, are you okay?"

She was immediately surrounded by her staff and escorted to the lounge to recover from the trauma. Garrett took the opportunity to call in. The police would want to interview him, so he'd better let his boss know what was up. When the call went through, Garrett dispensed with pleasant greetings. "Get Travis for me."

Travis Hewitt was the operations manager of Stealth Security. He'd founded the company years ago, after his service in the Navy as a SEAL. When his wife had twins, he'd figured eighteen years was enough. He needed to be home with his family. So he started the company, staffed primarily with ex-SEALs like Garrett.

Now at age forty-five, he still worked full time, managing the operations and participating when duty called. In the short time Garrett had worked for Stealth, he'd come to trust Travis and the team. Travis took the call, and in his no-nonsense tone said, "I thought it was your day off."

"It was supposed to be," Garrett said. "It didn't work out that way." He proceeded to fill Travis in on the situation. "The cops will want to interview me. They're on scene now."

"Give them the stripped-down version," Travis said. "I'll handle the rest."

Garrett only knew a stripped-down version. Because he sure as hell didn't know who the shooter was, or why he'd been at the event. It wouldn't take long to tell the police that he'd spotted some idiot about to pull a gun, so he'd shielded the famous movie star with his body. He should be the hero, but likely the police wouldn't see it that way.

They'd have way too many questions. Considering his background, it made sense that if a shooter was in his field of vision he'd see him. But being at the scene would be more difficult to explain. Garrett would stick with the obvious, which was that he came to the event as a fan—like everyone else. In a way, that was true. Law enforcement didn't need to know that Garrett had known Marlene's brother. Or that he'd had any connection, no matter how insubstantial, prior to the incident. It wouldn't assist them to find the guy who'd tried to shoot Marlene, and it would only give them a reason to look closer at Garrett.

Taking the job at Stealth had been a good move. It had meant Garrett could do what he was good at, even though a civilian. And he could stay in the background. Showing up at Marlene's event had blown that out of the water. Now he was about to be questioned about the attempted shooting of one of Hollywood's biggest stars.

He'd answer a few questions and get the hell out of there before his face showed up on some newscast. It might be too late anyway, since so many fans had surely taken pictures on their phones. The unfortunate part was that it was unlikely that any of the shots were of the shooter. That would be nice, but the shooting happened so fast that no one would have even had their camera out yet.

Garrett spotted Marlene on a plush sofa in the lounge area off the main lobby. Her fur coat was draped over the back of the sofa, so he got a look at her lush figure outlined under the tight knit dress.

She appeared more composed, so maybe some of the shock had dissipated. An empty glass on the table meant that someone had thought to get her something to drink. Her staff surrounded her like an army. The police were going to have to fight their way in to see her. That made Garrett smile. There was some advantage to fame, after all.

Every instinct told Garrett to leave. The police could call him to the station for an interview, and if he was in the mood, he might just cooperate. But Marlene was in danger. Just because the shooter had vanished into the crowd, didn't mean that he wouldn't return. In fact, Garrett was positive that he would.

The guy wasn't some loser stalker. He was a killer. This time he'd missed, but next time he might not. As much as Garrett preferred to walk away, to return to the shadows where he was the most comfortable, he couldn't. Marlene's life had been threatened. He'd been there that day to make sure that she was safe. It was the least he could do for her brother, who was a hero, in Garrett's opinion.

The threat against Marlene was real. Garrett had no choice. He would protect her, no matter what. That was just how things were. So instead of slipping out a side door, he strode up to the group surrounding Marlene. When he peered around so he could see her, their eyes met. She motioned for him to come over, so he pushed through.

Marlene held her hand out to him. "Let him through. This is the man who saved me."

Just great. The last thing Garrett wanted was to be announced. This whole situation was going downhill, he could just feel it. To make matters worse, a couple of people clapped. *This isn't the stage*, he grumbled to himself. *This is real, and a woman's life is at stake.* But he didn't voice his annoyance.

Garrett walked over to the sofa, but he didn't sit beside her. Instead, he took Marlene's hand and pulled her to her feet. With her in tow, he pushed through the others still waiting to do her bidding. "Excuse me for a minute," she called back to them.

When Garrett found a quiet spot down the hall, he stopped and released her hand.

Marlene looked up at him, waiting. The need to protect her surged, and he resisted the urge to discreetly escape out of the hotel with her, right away. Let her staff deal with everything else.

Garrett wasn't in a frame of mind for public relations, not that he normally was. The circumstances were dire, and a direct approach was called for. "Ms. Parks, you just hired yourself a bodyguard."

"Marlene," she said. "You just saved me from a bullet. I think we're on a first-name basis."

"Okay, *Marlene.*"

She hesitated, but not for long. "I have a bodyguard."

Garrett raised his eyebrows. "I can't say I think much of his method of protection."

"It was his day off, and with all the security at this event I thought I'd be fine. Raymond agreed."

"That guy out there today wasn't playing around," Garrett said. "He'll be back. And I'm not going anywhere." He paused, but she didn't argue. "I'm your new bodyguard...at least until we put that shooter out of action."

A couple of seconds ticked by, then Marlene smiled. "Bossy, aren't you?"

Garrett didn't flinch. "You have no idea."

CHAPTER TWO

Marlene sized up Garrett Flynn. It wasn't every day that a man saved her life, or that it needed saving. He'd released her hand, but it still felt warm from his touch. The buff bodyguard had been on top of her less than an hour ago, his blue eyes looking into hers. She'd been aware of the strength of his body, all solid muscle, from the feel of it, and had his lips close enough to kiss.

It wasn't the sort of thing a woman should think about in the midst of trauma. But that intimate moment with his breath grazing her skin had affected her. Maybe it was the nature of the situation. She wasn't herself; she was still rattled. So Garrett looked better than he might otherwise.

But Marlene doubted it. He'd look good anytime, especially without clothes. But she was getting carried away about a man she barely knew. "I don't know anything about you." She blurted it out like a defense.

"What's to know? I am a professional bodyguard. You can check that out."

"I intend to."

"And recently an active Navy SEAL. I've been out a few months, long enough to train in the specialty of guarding celebrities."

"So it would seem."

"Not that I necessarily needed training, except for learning the protocol for guarding VIPs. I've dealt with much more perilous situations than an amateur shooter attempting to take out a movie star."

Marlene picked up on the arrogance. No, more like unshakeable confidence. From what she knew of SEALs, he had a right to be confident. She probably couldn't ask for a more fit or trained protector.

Garrett's gaze bored into her, making her want to fall into his arms. It might not be such a good idea to hire him as a bodyguard, and to have him in such close proximity. Marlene wasn't keen about being attracted to an ex-military guy. But it wouldn't matter. The arrangement would be strictly professional, since having a relationship with one's bodyguard was a situation that would turn out badly. If he worked for her, it would be hands off.

Seeming to sense her reservations, Garrett said, "You'll be in good hands. Trust me."

Marlene did trust him, so far. He had come to her rescue. That counted for a lot.

"You're hired, then." Marlene pointed a finger at him. "But don't screw this up."

Garrett's lips turned up into a hint of a smile. Marlene wondered if he smiled often, or laughed. He seemed like the serious type. Just as well. She didn't need a boyfriend, just a protector.

"There's a contract to sign."

"My manager can take care of it. I'll let him know."

Marlene had some trepidation about the arrangement. It was clear that Garrett was a man who took control. Not necessarily a bad thing, but she was used to having her way. To make it in an entertainment career it was advantageous to be strong and independent, and she was. Sparks might fly between the two of them, but she had to admit that she already felt safer with Garrett around.

She walked down the hallway with Garrett right

beside her. She was still shaken from the attempt on her life, but had calmed quite a bit. So she would demonstrate strength to her staff, as they didn't need to know how much the scare had shaken her. And whether she wanted to admit it or not, having her new bodyguard was reassuring.

The hotel was a flurry of activity, reminding Marlene that the place must be in an uproar. She returned to her staff for an update, while Garrett stood by her side. A few security guards milled around to ensure fans or press didn't intrude.

She was impressed that her attorney, Martin Clemson, had arrived and was prepared to manage any legal issues. "Martin," she said, and nodded to him. "I appreciate you getting here so fast."

"Of course, Miss Parks."

Alan Sadler, her event manager, spoke next. "With assistance from Beverly Hills PD, security is in the process of dispersing the crowd. Those that were close to the shooter have been detained for statements. Names of the rest will be obtained if possible."

"No doubt that some of the crowd made a fast exit, as soon as they heard the shot," Marlene said.

Alan nodded. "The other celebrities were swiftly escorted to their limos. They were at the end of the walkway, too far away to have seen anything. But the police will arrange to interview them later anyway."

"Do we know if anyone got a description?" Marlene said. "Surely someone must have gotten a look at the guy when he pulled a gun." She wondered how good a look Garrett had gotten of the man, but didn't want to interrogate him in front of the others. She'd ask him later, in private.

Alan shook his head. "I don't have that information

yet."

Garrett appeared to be taking everything in, but didn't comment. Marlene looked up at him, then motioned to her head of security. "You've met Raymond Mead," she said. "He is head of security for my fundraisers."

"Yes, we've met," Garrett said.

Marlene faced her security manager. "Garrett Flynn is my new bodyguard. I just hired him, so give him your full cooperation." She noted the dour look on Raymond's face, but that was too bad. He should have seen to her protection better, so she wouldn't have had to look elsewhere to improve her security.

Raymond's momentary reaction vanished, then he resumed his professional attitude. "Garrett...I'll do whatever it takes to see that Marlene is safe."

"That is my top priority," Garrett said.

A police officer was headed their way. "I've arranged a private room where the police can interview you, Marlene. I made it clear that under the circumstances, they should keep it brief. If they have more questions, an appointment can be arranged for a later date. You need to be allowed to leave and given a chance to recover."

"I appreciate that, Alan, but I'm not injured at all. Once my nerves settle out, I'm sure I'll be fine." Marlene looked at the police officer.

"Marlene Parks, may I meet with you to ask you some questions?"

"Certainly, but my attorney will accompany me. I'm sure you understand. As a public figure, I must be prudent."

The officer didn't seem pleased, but really had no choice. Marlene followed the officer to a small conference room with opaque windows, so they wouldn't be observed. Her attorney advised her to answer the questions simply and truthfully. It was an easy task, since she knew so little. It didn't take long to recite the details of standing on the red carpet one moment, then being on her back the next, with a man she hadn't met before on top of her.

"I heard the shot," Marlene said. "But Garrett Flynn was already shielding me with his body."

"You know him?"

"I do now. I hadn't met him before that moment. But he showed his ID to my head of security right after the incident." Marlene didn't volunteer that she'd subsequently hired him as her personal bodyguard. That wasn't a police matter and had no bearing on the case.

The officer didn't have any more questions.

Marlene had some of her own. "Did anyone get a look at the guy? Do you have a description?"

The officer stood to leave. "We're interviewing witnesses now. As soon as we obtain any information available, we'll make a report."

It was to be expected that the police would be cautious. A shot fired at Marlene Parks during a high-profile fundraiser for wounded warriors was newsworthy. Her celebrity status ensured that it would make the front page. Plus, the report of the incident must be all over social media already. The police would have their hands full.

After the interview, Marlene waited with her staff, under Raymond's watchful eye, while the police interviewed Garrett. It didn't take long. After all, he had no more to tell them than she had. Or so she assumed. If he had seen the shooter clearly, maybe he could give a description that would lead to an arrest. She hoped so.

Garrett emerged from the conference room, looking as unflustered as when he'd gone in. The police officer stopped long enough to thank Marlene for cooperating, then disappeared. Even though she hadn't done anything wrong, it was unsettling to be interviewed by the police. It seemed every word she uttered became public knowledge, so Marlene was reluctant to share anything private. The police weren't likely to reveal anything but the unembellished story. It was in their interest to keep things under wraps until they had more to go on.

"Let's get you out of here," Garrett said. "The sooner you're home, the better I'll like it."

"What about you?"

"I'm going with you. Until this crisis is over, you'll see a lot of me. The only option is for me to stay by your side."

Marlene widened her eyes. "I see. Well, you aren't my first bodyguard. I have quarters that will accommodate you quite nicely."

"It depends where they are and how accessible you are to me. I can't allow something to happen to you while I'm in the opposite wing of your mansion."

"You prefer something cozier?"

Garrett gave her a stoic look. "Whatever it takes."

"I'll get my things and have Alan call for the chauffeur." Then she had a thought. "Where's your car?"

"I took public transportation." When Marlene gave him a look, he said, "What do I need with a car at a fundraiser? I'd just have to find a place to park it. The subway makes more sense."

"If you say so."

Marlene wanted to get out of the hotel. It had been a stressful few hours. She'd lost track of time, but it was getting dark out. It would be good to be home and find some solitude. Although she wasn't sure how much of that she'd get with Garrett around. He was going to be a distraction. But he was easy on the eyes. Marlene would need to guard against looking at him too much, lest he get the wrong impression.

Garrett didn't like the idea of getting in a limo in front of the hotel. But the Beverly Hilton didn't have back doors. Marlene was escorted into her limo by her security team, with Garrett right behind her. Once inside, the doors automatically locked. "The windows are bulletproof," she said.

"I would hope so."

"I'm not completely without security. I am a celebrity, so I've learned the value of defense," Marlene said.

The limo pulled away from the curb, heading for Beverly Hills, and Garrett leaned back in the seat.

"I have people who look out for me, you know," Marlene said.

Garrett spoke without hesitation. "Now you have one more."

"I suppose you think you're the most important one."

"Right now, I am," Garrett said. "Security is really little more than crowd control. I'm sure Raymond doesn't protect celebrities from threats on their lives."

"No, the police do that."

"But they aren't at home with you." Garrett frowned. "By the time they'd get to you, it would be too late."

"Are you always so pessimistic?"

"I call it realistic. Defeating the enemy depends on facing the facts, understanding the reality of the situation."

Marlene studied her new bodyguard. He wasn't a

man to back down. She liked that about him. She also liked much more. Although she couldn't say much for his choice in clothing. He wore faded blue jeans that hugged his thighs. That part was nice. And he'd paired it with a beige T-shirt under a dark brown jacket. His brown hair was long enough to be trendy, but short enough to look like half the men in the city.

"If you're going to work for me, you'll have to dress better," Marlene said.

"I don't think so. It's important to blend in, and not be a target. Better to spot the enemy before they see you."

Marlene considered that, but not for long. "You're my personal bodyguard. Your days of blending in are over, for a while. My life is on display for all to see. Wherever I go with you by my side, you'll be noticed. You need to look good."

"We'll see about that."

The car phone rang. It was her manager, so Marlene hit the button to answer. Garrett would hear everything, since it was a hands-free system. "Hello, Marc."

"Marlene...I heard what happened. Are you okay?"

"Yes, I wasn't hurt, thank God. I'm in the limo with my new bodyguard, Garrett Flynn."

"New bodyguard?"

"Yes, he works for Stealth Security. So check out the company, will you?" Marlene gave Garrett a teasing look. "And handle the paperwork for me."

"Sure, I'll get back to you on that. And good to meet you, Garrett." Her manager clicked off before Garrett responded.

Marlene leaned her head against the seat. "That was Marc Goodwin. He's been my manager since the beginning. Are you insulted that I asked him to check out your company?"

"I'd be disappointed if you hadn't. I like knowing that you're cautious."

"Well, you never know." Marlene looked at Garrett. "Some fans will go to extraordinary lengths to get close to me."

"I just happened to be in the audience today, so that I could execute my plan to hire some guy to shoot off a gun while I became a human body shield? Then persuade you to hire me as your bodyguard?"

Marlene feigned innocence. "That isn't what happened?"

"If that had been my goal, there would have been much easier ways to go about it, without involving the police."

Marlene laughed. "I've been stalked before, several times, and harassed in social media. Mercilessly, I might add. I've developed a thick skin. It's the only way I can deal with all of it."

Garrett just listened.

"I confess that it was terrifying to have some stranger attempt to kill me. But thanks to you, I lived through it," Marlene said. "I don't think he'll try it again. It's too risky. I'm too big of a name."

"Oh, he'll try it again. You can count on that."

"How can you be so sure?"

"I know the type. He won't give up. If he was crazy enough to shoot a gun at a charity event, then that tells me he has an oversized ego. He'll have to achieve his goal now...couldn't take the failure."

"You seem to know a lot about killers."

Garrett turned to look out the window. When he looked back at Marlene, he said, "But I'll be there the next time he tries. And it's my job to make sure he doesn't succeed."

CHAPTER THREE

It was dark out, but Beverly Hills was well lit. The streets were lined with shops and restaurants. Pedestrians, dressed for the chilly evening, strolled along the sidewalks. Some chatted to a companion, while others gazed at the bright storefronts, slowing if a window display caught their eye. Others were glued to their phones, scrolling or texting, a dangerous way to walk the streets, as they were completely unobservant of what was around them.

Garrett watched, alert to anything out of the ordinary or any sign of trouble. But all looked calm, and the focus was on shopping or eating. No one seemed disturbed by more than daily stresses, nor were they aware of any threat. Had there been one, likely the event would have overtaken them before they knew what had hit them. It paid to be aware of one's environment, as he knew from experience.

The limo drove past the busy part of the city toward Marlene's home. On the residential streets, the mansions were tucked away behind lush trees. One was as rambling as the next, lit up like Christmas, or set so far back from the road that they weren't visible at all.

Garrett was content to sit in silence for the short trip. And Marlene appeared to settle into the quiet, with her head against the soft leather seat. The limo leisurely rolled down a winding street, and she turned to look at him. Garrett met her gaze.

"How do you know I don't have a boyfriend?" Marlene's voice was throaty, making Garrett wonder if she knew the effect she had on him.

"Well, if you do he'll get used to me being around."

"I don't have a boyfriend...which you probably knew already."

"How would I know that?"

Marlene's lips turned up in a hint of a smile. "If I was intimately involved, wouldn't I have called the guy to let him know what had happened?"

"It's good to know I won't have some guy to deal with," Garrett said. "I have a feeling you're going to be enough of a challenge on your own."

Marlene didn't reply. She looked out the window as the limo pulled into the long driveway leading up to the house. They had to pass through an iron gate with an armed guard on duty. Once Garrett showed identification, they were allowed through.

At the top of the incline was a garden surrounded by a circular drive. The two-story mansion was sandstone brick accented with ivory walls. It looked like every light in the place was on, the brightness nearly blinding.

A series of steps in a semicircle led up to a wide porch. The front entrance was etched glass framed in antique bronze, running from the porch up to the top of the second story. The scene blazed brighter than midday sun.

"Is this the only way in?" Garrett said. If by chance anyone was waiting, they'd be clear targets walking up to the front door.

Marlene spoke to the driver. "Take us into the garage, Samuel."

The driver navigated the smooth curve of the

paved drive and headed down a slight hill. A door rose, revealing an expansive garage. The car stopped at the elevator bay along one side. Garrett got out and assisted Marlene, glad to be in semidarkness while exiting the vehicle.

The interior of the home was elaborate, done in ivory and bronze with hardwood floors. Crystal chandeliers hung from high ceilings, and rich Oriental carpets decorated the hallways. But Garrett wasn't there to gawk. Scanning, he began to evaluate the place for any vulnerabilities that could be exploited by an intruder.

A butler dressed in slacks, a white shirt, and buttoned vest greeted them. "Good evening, Marlene."

"James, this is my new bodyguard Garrett Flynn. Will you show him to his suite?" Marlene shed her fur coat and tossed it over a chair. "I'm going to change and freshen up. James will see to your needs." Then she walked down a long hallway, leaving Garrett to stare after her. With each step, her hips swayed, the dress clinging to them seductively.

"Sir?" James said. Garrett turned to face the butler. "Allow me to show you where you'll be staying."

James guided him down the same hallway where Marlene had disappeared, but took a sharp left to heavy double doors. He opened the room and stepped inside, allowing Garrett to follow. "Will this be satisfactory?"

"Marlene's room is adjacent, I take it?"

"Yes, sir. The bodyguard suite is purposely near hers, for best advantage." James paused. "Is there anything I can get for you?"

Garrett declined refreshment, but proceeded to befriend the butler. He immediately gained his cooperation, and James was able to answer questions about the security of the home.

While Marlene was getting changed, Garrett assessed the security. The high-tech system included motion-triggered cameras and a state-of-the-art alarm. It was good to know that Marlene was security conscious and not one of the stars who left doors unlocked or keys under the mat. Unbelievably, some of Hollywood's elite had been negligent to that degree, and had been robbed or worse. Garrett had heard the stories, but clearly Marlene was smarter than that. She must have invested millions in her security setup.

In the morning when there was better light, Garrett would scrutinize the grounds, and the wall enclosing the property, to spot any weaknesses. That could wait for now, but a call to Stealth couldn't. Garrett returned to his room and sat in a chair by the window.

Ripley McConnell, Rip to those who knew him, tended to work around the clock, napping when he needed to, but usually available if duty called. He'd been a Navy SEAL before taking the position as security analyst at Stealth. His experience had been in surveillance and reconnaissance, so his skill with the tools of the trade made him a valuable asset. He was dedicated to the company and knew no limits when backing up his team. His brother was in law enforcement, a connection that had frequently been useful.

Garrett dialed, and his teammate picked up. "Garrett, you're working late...new assignment?"

"I need a personal security risk assessment, Rip." Then Garrett filled him in on the day's events, omitting no detail. "I'll interview the client and provide you with anything relevant. But I need you to identify any gaps in security or avenues of exploitation. Get me up to speed on the risk factors."

Rip would do a full background on Marlene in order to detail her connections, past associations, and more. He would scour the activities of those close to her, including career connections. If there was any clue as to who would want to harm the popular movie star, Rip was the guy for the job.

"And see what you can get from the police," Garrett said. "Check out ballistics. I'm sure they recovered the bullet at the scene, and I need any information they have. I can't wait weeks to find out."

"So you saw the guy. What's your take?" Rip said.

"It's the combat boots that stuck out. Is this guy ex-military, or an imposter...just some dude who likes to look tough?" Garrett said. "He's not a trained sniper, that's for sure. If he was, he would have gotten me in the back, at least. That is, if he was shooting to kill. And my gut feeling says that he was, and the reason for waving that gun around wasn't just to scare Marlene."

"Okay, let me get to work." Rip ended the call.

That was all Garrett could do for the moment, so he went to the bathroom to clean up a bit. Then he'd go out and find Marlene. His thoughts went to the shooter. He didn't like it. Stars were too accessible. At that event, Marlene had been on display, right out in the open. And the event had been well attended, since it had been publicized for months in advance.

The shooter had planned his attack and been armed. That much made sense. But Garrett needed to figure out who this guy was and why he wanted to kill Marlene. Then he'd have a grip on how to find him and take him out, before he did more damage. Or took another shot, one he might not miss. The man had to be stopped without delay. Until then, Garrett would be on duty to deflect any trouble.

Once he looked more presentable, Garrett went out into the hallway. Marlene's bedroom door was open, and a peek inside told him the suite was empty. The mansion was huge, but he recalled passing a living room not too far down the hall. He'd check there first.

At the edge of the doorway, Garrett looked in. Marlene sat on a velvet sofa by the fireplace, not yet aware of his presence. He took a moment to look at her. Dressed casually, she was just as stunning as she'd been in the designer outfit at the event. She wasn't sporting sloppy sweatpants or faded jeans, not that he expected that. Her at-home wear was a cream-colored sweater set over black tights that showed her long legs to advantage.

Marlene sipped wine from a crystal glass, while she fingered the strand of beads around her neck and gazed at the crackling fire. Watching her, Garrett's blood ran hot and he questioned the prudence of being in such close proximity to her. She might be impossible to resist.

But he was the bodyguard. That was his job. He wasn't there to socialize or to indulge in his fantasies. Marlene's life was at stake. She glanced up and saw him standing in the doorway. "You were so quiet. I didn't know you were there."

She crossed her legs and dangled a slipper-clad foot. For some reason, the delicate-looking ballet slippers turned him on. They looked so feminine. Garrett imagined removing them one at a time, and kissing her bare feet then working his way up her ankles. "I didn't want to startle you."

"Come in. I had the cook serve drinks and snacks. You're invited to dinner, of course, since you are my guest."

"Bodyguard," he corrected.

"Have it your way. But you're here, and you certainly won't abandon me to eat alone." Marlene took another sip of her wine. "What will you have to drink?"

"Coke will be fine." Garrett spotted a small refrigerator and pulled it open to find a can of his preferred drink. He popped the top then scooped a handful of nuts from a crystal dish.

"I opened a bottle of Merlot. You're welcome to share it."

"No thank you. I don't drink alcohol."

"That's too bad."

"You should be glad. You don't want your bodyguard's reaction time slowed, do you?"

Marlene smiled at him, and Garrett took a swig of his drink. He sat in a chair across from her. "How are you? I know it was a rough day."

"Not bad, considering. It's good to be home, away from prying eyes." Marlene swung her foot, tempting him with the sensual slipper. "The hotel wanted to call the paramedics, just to be safe. But I refused. It would have just been more drama, and I was sure I wasn't injured."

"I didn't see any visible signs, but I'm relieved to hear you say that."

"That can't be the first time you shoved someone out of the way of a bullet. You managed to get us both to the ground, and I didn't even have a scrape."

"That heavy fur coat you wore didn't hurt."

"True, but it was more than that. Anyway, thank you again. I wouldn't be sitting here tonight, if not for your quick reaction." Marlene sighed. "You must be aware that photos of the scene will be all over social media, so I hope you like having your picture taken."

Garrett cringed inside, but didn't let his reaction show. "If I'm lucky, they only got a view of my backside."

"And a nice one it is...just being honest." Marlene nibbled her lower lip and swirled the wine in her glass. "But there are a lot of drool-worthy men in Hollywood, so don't get the idea you're exceptional."

"Wouldn't think of it." Garrett took another swig of Coke. "By the way, I was impressed that you recognized the sound of a gunshot. Many times civilians think it's just a firecracker going off or something."

"I come from a military family. It would be an embarrassment not to recognize the sound of gunfire."

Her statement made Garrett uncomfortable. So far, he hadn't mentioned that he'd known her brother.

Marlene looked sad. "Not too long ago, my older brother Andrew died in Iraq. He was a marine." She brushed away a tear. "Sorry, it's just that I miss him."

Garrett could barely breathe.

"And when I was only six years old, I lost my dad to Desert Storm. He was a marine too. Andrew followed in his footsteps." Marlene looked at the fireplace, appearing consumed with memories. Then she looked at Garrett. "But we don't need to talk about that now."

Garrett drained his Coke and went to the refrigerator for another.

"I do feel bad for the other celebrities at the event today," Marlene said. "I'm sure what happened was terrifying. Stars are besieged all the time by fans, and there's always that fear of something happening. Most of the time, I don't think about it. I suppose I hadn't considered that some guy would *shoot* at me."

"He didn't shoot *at you*. He tried to kill you."

"You seem awfully sure of that."

"I have my team getting more information for me, but I'm certain whatever they find will support my theory that today was an attempt on your life."

"Then I'm glad I hired you."

Garrett admired her strength. Another woman might have wept with fright over a threat to her life, but Marlene met the threat with courage.

"Are your accommodations satisfactory?"

"Again...I'm not a guest. But yes, the suite is more than acceptable. Most importantly, it is close to your room so I can get to you quickly, if I need to."

"That was the idea when I arranged that suite. I've had bodyguards before you, so I know some of the requirements. And you probably noticed the intercom system?"

"Yes, that's a good feature."

"That way I don't have to scream." Marlene smiled. "I can just let you know if I need you."

The implication wasn't lost on Garrett. He wished she did need him, in the way she'd teasingly implied. But she was only flirting. They both knew the relationship was strictly professional. And he had to make sure it stayed that way, because he was responsible for her until this was over. He didn't know Marlene that well yet, and was aware that movie stars could be eccentric. Even if she was willing to stray, it didn't mean Garrett was. Although resisting her wouldn't be easy, it was his duty to ensure safety. That came first, above his carnal pleasures.

Marlene put her glass on a side table. "There's also a red panic button. So if there isn't time to warn you,

I can push the button and an alarm goes off."

"I sleep lightly, so you don't need to worry. If you're in danger, you won't have to fend for yourself."

"Also, you are welcome to the clothes in there. I know you didn't bring anything with you. But you look about the same size as my last bodyguard...about six feet tall, broad shoulders, all muscle. It must be part of the job description."

Garrett laughed. "It must be. I appreciate the use of the wardrobe. I'm not sure when I'll get back to my place."

A middle-aged woman wearing an apron entered the room, and nodded at Garrett before speaking. "Dinner is ready, Marlene. Would you like me to serve in the dining room?"

"Yes, Laura, that would be nice. We'll be right in. This is Garrett Flynn, who will join me this evening."

Garrett stood, and in the interest of good manners, offered Marlene his arm. "Mmm, I love a gentleman." She slipped her arm into his and they headed toward the dining room. The feel of her on his arm was nice, and her perfume wafted around him. Garrett had better watch it. This woman was alluring, and he was sure she knew it.

At the dark wood table, he pulled out a padded chair for Marlene. She scooted in and he sat across from her. It was a table for six, on a white wool rug over the hardwood floor. There was a bay window, with a window seat and tasteful artwork on the walls. It was a comfortable room, not as opulent as he might have expected.

"I thought you'd enjoy the smaller dining room, since there's just the two of us," Marlene said. "The larger one would just swallow us up."

"I prefer this one." Garrett was used to mess halls

or fast food. He hadn't had much opportunity for fine dining, or joining a celebrity for dinner. But Marlene didn't put on any pretense, so he felt no need to do so either.

The cook reappeared and refilled Marlene's wine glass. "What may I get you to drink, sir?"

"Club soda will be fine."

Marlene lifted her glass. "I'll have to get used to a man who doesn't drink. Normally, any guy would drink me under the table."

"Yes, well, I sincerely hope your life doesn't depend on their alertness."

Marlene motioned to the basket of bread on the table. "Please, help yourself."

By the time the meals arrived, Garrett had downed two chunks of French bread heaped with butter. The food smelled delicious, and his mouth watered when he saw that it was prime rib. He raised his eyebrows. "Just a light meal?"

Marlene giggled. "I thought you'd appreciate a hearty dinner."

The meal came with baked potato, sour cream, and grilled asparagus. Garrett was in heaven. His hunger level had risen from hungry to starving long before. It didn't take him long to work his way through half of his meal. He looked up to see Marlene carving a thin slice of her meat.

"Do you eat like this every night?"

"Oh, no. When I'm alone I'll often just have a salad or soup." There it was again, that look of sadness in her eyes. But it was gone in a flash. "It's nice to have company."

Garrett took a breath and slowed down. He kept eating but made an attempt to be more social. He commented on the home. The architecture and interior design were impressive. Marlene seemed pleased that he liked it. "I wanted a place that really felt like home. I'm glad you approve."

Then Marlene's expression turned serious. "Tell me, Garrett, did you get a good look at the guy who shot at me today?"

"I saw him, but I'm not sure how much good it will do us."

"Why do you say that?"

"The guy was ordinary in every way, almost as though he intended to be. From his haircut to his brand of jeans, he could have been anyone. Average height, average weight, and he wore a coat which covered him up pretty well." Garrett looked across the table at her. "Then there were the combat boots."

"What about them?"

"They weren't new, and it struck me as out of place. The audience wore trendy jogging shoes or styles of leather boots that are popular. But combat boots? It seemed that was a clue to the guy's personality."

"Combat boots...how can that assist the police?"

"I don't think it will." Garrett looked away for a moment, vividly recalling what the guy had looked like. "There was one thing about him I won't forget. If I saw him again, I'd know it was him."

Marlene leaned closer.

"It was his eyes," Garrett said. "He'd been looking at you, but then for a split second his eyes met mine." A chill ran up Garrett's spine. "His eyes were blue, a color so pale that they appeared translucent. And his look was vacant, yet..."

"What, Garrett?"

"I looked into those empty blue eyes; they were like ice, so *cold*...emotionless." Garrett looked at

Marlene. "I knew then. I was looking into the eyes of a killer."

For a moment, neither of them spoke. Then Marlene reached across the table and put her hand on his arm. "I know you'll protect me." That was Garrett's goal, but he knew it wasn't going to be a simple task. Only someone mentally unstable would shoot at Marlene. Such a man would be unpredictable. And that was treacherous.

After dinner, they retired to their respective suites. Marlene was exhausted, and Garrett appreciated the chance to think and plan. He entered his room and locked the door behind him. Then he removed his Glock from the belt holster and put it on the nightstand next to his wallet, phone, keys, and a spare ammunition magazine that he pulled from an inner pocket.

Garrett didn't go anywhere unprepared. He hadn't expected trouble, but it had found him. Too bad he couldn't have drawn his gun and shot the guy, before he'd pointed his gun at Marlene. But there had been too many people blocking the shot. He couldn't have taken the chance, as it would have been too likely that he'd injure a civilian.

After he showered, Garrett fished around in the apartment-sized bathroom and found all the grooming supplies he needed. As Marlene mentioned, there were plenty of clothes in the dresser and the closet. The size was close enough, if not exact. Garrett redressed in comfortable garb before reclining on the bed. If disaster struck, he didn't want to be in his underwear. It made more sense to sleep ready for action.

He thought of Marlene next door, and hoped she was sleeping well. She'd need the rest. The situation would escalate before it improved. That was just how things usually played out. He brushed aside the urge to go to her, to hold her in his arms and comfort her.

Garrett had just met her. But in a way he hadn't. In Iraq, when he'd talked to Andrew, he'd learned about his sister. It was personal stuff, not what was in the media. Marlene had felt real to him before he'd met her. Sure, he'd seen her movies and magazine photos. But that wasn't what had touched him.

It was how Andrew had talked about her. And then when Garrett had seen her at the event, it was like he'd known her already. She wasn't a stranger. Marlene was special. He'd known it before, and seeing her just confirmed that.

But there was something she didn't know about Garrett. Guilt settled in his heart, preventing him from embracing the prospect of getting close to Marlene. Once she knew the truth, she wouldn't see him the same. Now he was her protector, the ex-military bodyguard she trusted.

Yet he had been in the battle with her brother. Andrew had been a young marine, and under attack he got stuck behind a wall. He'd been hit and couldn't get out. Garrett had rushed back to drag him out, but when he got him out of the line of fire, Andrew had died.

Never leave a soldier behind. That was the motto Garrett lived by. But he'd failed to save Andrew. The rescue attempt left a sour taste in his mouth and regret in his heart, because the soldier had died. He should have noticed Andrew earlier, shoved him out of the line of fire. Something. Anything.

Andrew's death haunted him. And he'd planned to

tell Marlene when he met her. Not at first, maybe. But he wanted to tell her that he'd known her brother, a brave marine, and to repeat his last words. But it hadn't been that simple.

And Garrett couldn't tell her now. He couldn't choke out the words. Marlene had been shot at and nearly killed. He needed to reassure her, not give her another reason for sadness. Surely it wouldn't help her to know that Garrett had failed to save her brother. Later, once he made sure that she was safe, then Garrett would tell her. Unburden his conscience. But not yet. All that mattered was Marlene. That was how Andrew would have seen it too. Garrett was certain of it.

CHAPTER FOUR

The way Garrett had described the guy who'd tried to shoot her had given Marlene the creeps. It was like some kind of horror movie. Icy blue eyes. *Cold*, blank stare. She shivered and pulled the covers up under her neck. It was good to know her bodyguard was on the other side of the wall.

Marlene glanced at the red panic button just behind her lamp. She knew that she wouldn't press it unless there was a real emergency. Still it was comforting to know it was within arm's reach. The day had been a disaster, and she was more shaken by it than she cared to let on.

The event would go on the record for the sudden attack on her life and the risk posed to the other stars in attendance, leaving its actual purpose lost in the panic. It had been planned to raise a substantial amount for wounded warriors, so it was a shame that it all fell apart. She'd have her event manager reschedule it, ensuring that it was held indoors with tighter security. That was *if* any of the stars were willing to participate.

Garrett had been in the right place at the right time. She was lucky that he'd been so close, and even more, that he had such a fast reaction time. She knew enough about SEALs to know the extent of the training they went through. It was some of the toughest in the world. The job was hard and dangerous, which was probably the allure. And

Garrett seemed the type to crave that adrenaline pump.

Which was exactly why Marlene didn't intend to allow intimacy to develop between them. After losing her father and her brother, she'd vowed not to fall for any military, or even ex-military, man. She'd had enough of losing men she loved. Yet Garrett stirred sensations that were difficult to put aside.

In the privacy of her bedroom with moonlight creating shadows on the walls, Marlene took the luxury of letting images of Garrett float through her mind. He was strong, yet lean. Not hugely muscled, but solid as a rock. The feel of his hard body over hers had made her skin tingle. She'd looked into his eyes, as blue as the sky, eyes she could get lost in. He was handsome in a rugged sort of way, and his alpha male personality turned her on.

Garrett seemed smart, and was polite when the occasion called for it. Yet he took control, a personality trait she admired. Marlene was strong-willed, so not many stood up to her. She already knew that Garrett wasn't a man to cower or back down, that he'd risk her wrath to ensure her safety, if that's what it took. There was something terribly sexy about that.

But Marlene wouldn't give in to the attraction. She couldn't allow it, because a relationship with Garrett would probably destroy her more completely than the shooter's bullet. Her heart could only take so much, and when she found a man to share her life with, she vowed that he'd have a career that didn't involve being in danger's way.

The next morning, Marlene was up before dawn. She was used to being on the set early for filming. Laura brought coffee to her room, then Marlene sat at a desk by the window to check email. Most of it could wait, but she opened the one from her manager with the subject line *Stealth Security Contract*.

It appeared that Marc had looked into the company thoroughly. He had added a personal note in his email: *After looking at the background of Stealth and its staff, I recommend that you employ them. You need to take the risk to your safety very seriously, and your new bodyguard has qualifications beyond the norm.*

The company had attracted extremely qualified personnel, mostly ex-military, in particular ex-SEALs. It had been founded by Travis Hewitt after his long, exemplary career in the Navy.

Marlene read more of the company's mission statement:

If you are facing minor threats such as overzealous fans, minor street crimes, disgruntled but nonviolent ex-employees—standard bodyguards will assist you. But if you are facing death threats from criminals, terrorist activity, persistent violent stalkers, or other situations of that magnitude, then most bodyguard services will decline.

Your first option should be seclusion until the danger passes. But if you are unable to mitigate the chances of life-threatening encounters, Stealth Security will step in.

No wonder Garrett had been adamant that he should guard her, that no one else was qualified. Certainly, her former bodyguard wasn't, and would have likely resigned if she hadn't replaced him. The severity of her situation was clear. She needed an expert, a man trained in special ops to defend her against a killer.

The contract detailed the obligations of both parties.

One item under the client responsibilities section was: *The client shall allow all bodyguard personnel to undertake their activities without hindrance.* A nice way of saying that she had to do as Garrett instructed. He took control without asking permission, making that requirement moot.

Marlene opened the document and signed electronically. She wasn't foolhardy. She needed Garrett, for now. If there were no more incidents, as she hoped there wouldn't be, then she would release Stealth from the contract so her life could return to normal.

Before signing off, Marlene logged into social media. It was as she expected: photos of the red carpet scene had gone viral. News of the alarming threat to her life had spread like wildfire, with numerous pictures of her posted. It was publicity of a sort, but could hardly be considered positive.

There were photos of Garrett with her security, then carrying her into the hotel. Marlene didn't see any of his face, which was a good thing. He'd wanted to avoid the press and the cameras. Yet that wouldn't last. It was impossible to escape the onslaught of media attention once it got started. She had experience with that. Garrett didn't. She wondered if he'd seen all the comments and opinions freely offered in the threads, but it was likely he had.

Marlene showered then dressed comfortably. Her hair and makeup would be done on the set. She found Garrett in the garden breakfast nook. It was a covered atrium with a stone terrace. In the winter, it was heated, and light radiated through the thick glass ceiling. The space felt like outdoors, and Laura usually served breakfast there.

Garrett leaned against the buffet, holding a cup of

coffee. From the empty plate on the table, she could see that he'd eaten. He wore khaki pants that would normally have been nondescript, but the material clung to his muscled thighs. He'd paired it with a sandy-colored thermal shirt that stretched over his chest and biceps, making her drool.

"I see you found some clothes." Garrett's wardrobe choices were only slightly better than the day before, but Marlene declined to remark on it. He would accompany her to the set today, not to any public function. She'd fight her battles when needed. For now, she'd let it go. Besides, he looked like such a stud wearing the military-type garb.

"Yes, thank you for that. I hope you don't mind. I didn't wait for you, since Laura said you don't often eat breakfast."

"Sure, there was no need to wait. There's plenty of food from the caterers, so I eat later."

Marlene sat in the closest chair and poured a glass of juice. "We should leave soon. I'm expected on the set early." She took a sip. "And by the way, I signed your contract, but then, I'm sure you'd be informed of that."

Garrett didn't comment about the contract, but frowned. "I checked the security cameras. It's a mob scene at the front gate."

"Already? It's still dark out."

Garrett sat across from her, and Marlene caught the faint scent of musk. "The paparazzi are in wait, hoping to catch sight of you."

"I expect so, but I'm used to it. After yesterday, things aren't likely to be calm for a while."

"You should stay home today, Marlene. It's too risky out there. I don't like it."

Marlene shook her head. "I can't do that."

42

"You can. And you should." Garrett's stern look gave her pause. "It's your life that's at stake here. The movie can wait. I'm telling you to stay home today."

"You're so pushy." Marlene wasn't used to having someone pressure her. She responded better to suggestions, not demands. She did feel more secure with Garrett there, but it didn't mitigate her obligations.

"I'm pushy because you're headstrong. All I care about is that, at the end of day, you're safe."

Marlene looked directly at him. "It's not that simple. This movie means a lot to me. The cast and crew depend on me showing up, since I'm in the leading role. A production like this costs a fortune, and a day without filming is expensive."

Garrett stiffened, and she could tell that he wasn't convinced. She wasn't speaking his language, so she changed tactics. "You don't hide from danger, so why should I?"

"Your situation is different."

"I don't see how. Anyway, staying home is out of the question." Marlene took a breath. "I'm going. Are you coming with me or not?"

Garrett stood, then followed her out of the room. Marlene had agreed to allow him to undertake his activities without hindrance, but that didn't mean he could run her life. She had commitments, and she wasn't about to let anyone scare her into hiding. She was afraid, even if she didn't show it. But she still thought Garrett might be wrong, that the threat was blown out of proportion.

They'd managed to get through the mob at the gate and make it to the studio. The limo driver had edged into the crowd until they had let them through. The partition behind the driver had been raised, blocking the view into the back seat, and the windows were so heavily tinted that no one could see inside. It was annoying to have to live that way, but Marlene had long since resigned herself to the lifestyle.

The studio garage was guarded, and after Samuel pulled in, he let them out at the elevator. The elevator car was armored, and the studio had excellent security. The company the studio retained was well known in the entertainment industry. It was a multinational corporation that had been in business for over thirty years.

Security was provided as part of her studio contract, so Marlene was well informed. Entertainment security was unique in the scope of responsibilities and the breadth of working environments. The company handled safety when they were on location, as well as when in the studio.

The staff was composed of former law enforcement, ex-military, and even ex-federal agents. Garrett would fit right in, and Marlene hoped when he saw how well secured the premises was that he'd relax. The security team had a physical presence, and was capable of handling an attack. But they leaned toward being discreet over excessive displays of force.

Most of the time, Marlene wasn't aware of security at all. They did their job without intruding. When she and Garrett went inside, she introduced him to the guy in charge of security that day and motioned toward the food table. "I'll be in makeup for a while. I'll leave you to get to know your way around."

Makeup was a room lined with mirrored stations, large stainless steel tables covered with tools of the trade, with stacks of drawers for supplies. Many of the cast were already a work in progress. Marlene spotted her friend standing by one of the chairs, drinking mineral water. Anna Tucker was a member of the crew, and had a supporting role in the film.

She was about the same age as Marlene, and they had been friends since their early days in Hollywood. It was special when they had the opportunity to work together. When Anna saw Marlene, she waved her over. "Marlene, I'm so glad to see you."

Her friend gave her a brief hug. Anna looked fresh-faced and well rested. She had long, dark hair, and soft gray eyes. Her heart-shaped face gave her a youthful, friendly appearance, so she was often cast in supporting roles as a friend of the main character. That was the part she played in the film they were working on together.

Anna furrowed her brow. "What happened yesterday?"

"I was attacked."

"That was so scary. I saw the news footage, and all the pictures that went viral." Anna put her bottle of water on the table and plopped into the chair. "But what in the world happened? Who would want to shoot at you?"

"I have no idea," Marlene said. "It was all very alarming." She didn't have to pretend with Anna. They were friends who had shared just about anything over the years.

"I'm not sure you should be here."

"I have to be. I'm in scenes today. The filming can't happen without me." Marlene gave her friend a smile of encouragement. "Besides, I'm safe in here. There's enough security to keep an army out."

Anna laughed. "True. But still, are you okay? You must be freaked."

"That's putting it mildly." Marlene ran a hand through her hair. "But I hired a new bodyguard."

"That guy that knocked you out of the way of the bullet." Anna could be very direct.

"Yes, that's the one. He saved me. It was all so unexpected."

"I must say, he's a looker."

"That's not the point."

Anna wrinkled her nose. "It can't hurt. Did you see the photos of his ass, from when he was kneeling over you on the red carpet? The guy is *built*."

"I agree, but what's important is that he's skilled at protection."

"Well, you wouldn't have hired him if he wasn't." Anna grinned. "But he will look amazing in a designer suit."

Marlene didn't have the heart to reveal that her new bodyguard wasn't in the habit of wearing suits, designer or otherwise. "I'm glad you approve."

"So what's his name? Am I going to meet him?" It was just like Anna to turn any event into a social occasion.

"Sure, you can meet him. He's out there now. His name is Garrett Flynn."

"Mmm, sounds sexy."

"Oh, will you stop?"

Anna laughed. A makeup artist approached, distracting them from conversation. "Okay, I have to get ready. See you out there."

Marlene grabbed a bottle of water from a food tray and made her way to her station. Two artists were waiting for her. The production was a historical war movie, and it took a lot to transform her. Once her makeup was done, then her hair was styled and she was sent to costuming.

She was ready in time for her first scene, and the director gave instructions. Nicholas Hayes had been a respected actor before his career in directing. He understood how actors worked, the best ways to make them understand what he wanted. It was a pleasure to work with him, and Marlene felt that he brought out better performances. She found that she reached deeper, portrayed her role more authentically.

During the filming, Marlene spotted Garrett a few times. He wasn't sitting and enjoying the entertainment, but was milling about. No doubt that, even with the security on hand, he wasn't at ease. Heightened awareness of his surroundings and continual vigilance was probably in his DNA.

While she was performing, Marlene had to block him out. She had to forget yesterday, and that her life was in an uproar. All that mattered was the film, and her role. It meant so much, and she was a professional. Once Nicholas called for action, Marlene was the woman she played. The real world didn't exist, only the fictional creation.

Acting was Marlene's passion. Losing herself in a role was therapeutic, as it was an escape from the real world. When playing her part, she *was* the character, and the story was more real than life itself. She'd been told that was what made her good, the fact that she had the talent to become the woman she created on film. At least, for the duration of the shooting she did.

It took a bit to come down from the experience afterwards. When the director called for a break, it took a moment for Marlene to reorient to her surroundings. Garrett walked up to her, out of place in her fictional world, serving to call her back to the present. She rose to meet him. "Did you find your way around?"

"Yes, no problem. This set is probably one of the safest places you can be...provided the security company didn't botch any of the background checks, including the ones on their own staff."

Marlene threw up her hands. "Is anywhere safe to you?"

"There's no guarantee. I'm just more aware of it than most. And being alert enough to head off an attack is what I'm paid to do."

There was no way to argue with him. "Let's go over to the food station. I'm dying of thirst," Marlene said.

Many of the crew were eating and drinking, including the director. When Marlene approached, he looked up. "Nicholas, I'd like to introduce my new bodyguard, Garrett Flynn."

Garrett accepted a handshake. "It's good to meet you," Nicholas said.

"It's an honor to meet you. I'm a fan of your movies."

"I'm glad to hear it. If we have our way, this film will go down as one of my best," Nicholas said, then narrowed his eyes at Garrett. "Take care of Marlene. I don't want any repeats of yesterday."

Garrett nodded, and Nicholas went on his way. "Can we talk privately?"

Marlene selected a bottle of iced tea. "Sure, we can go to my private dressing room." She led him away from the main area to a door with *Marlene Parks* on a gold nameplate. She shrugged. "I am a star, after all."

Inside was a sitting area next to the dressing table. Marlene took a seat in a velvet chair and motioned for Garrett to sit on the loveseat. "Did you enjoy watching the performances this morning?"

"You're impressive."

"I wasn't looking for flattery. I just thought it would be a new experience for you to watch the filming."

"It's quite the production."

Marlene took a sip of her drink. Her stomach rumbled, but she wanted to hear what Garrett had to say before focusing on lunch. "Is there something you want to tell me?"

"I got some feedback. It's not much of a clue, but it's something." Garrett leaned back and crossed his ankle over the opposite thigh. His biceps flexed seductively when he gripped his knee. Marlene needed to stop doing that, looking at him that way.

"What did you find out?"

"I have an inside track to the police. Don't ask how. But I have some early information that isn't released yet." Garrett paused. "The bullet was recovered. It hit the wall on the other side of the carpeted walkway. Ballistics says the ammo was armor piercing."

"Why is that significant?"

"It's a type of bullet used to pierce body armor or shoot through cinderblock walls."

"You're losing me."

"It isn't the type of bullet a civilian would use." Garrett waited to see if she understood now. "It penetrates metal barriers and is used by the military."

"Some ex-military guy is after me?"

"It's too soon to say. Like I mentioned, it's only a clue. For all I know the dude got the ammo on the black market, or maybe he snagged some in army surplus. I'm not sure yet. But it's a start...something to go on."

Marlene shook her head. She'd lost her appetite. If the guy was trained military, she was really in trouble. That meant he was no amateur. But the important question was why. She looked at Garrett. "Why would some guy from the military want to kill me? Much of my time is spent fundraising for vets, and doing all I can to support related charities. You'd think he'd be grateful, not vindictive."

"I don't have any idea who the guy is, or why he'd want to harm you," Garrett said. "But I intend to find out. For now, consider that your security just got tighter."

Marlene had difficulty imaging how it could be any tighter.

"I've already let Travis know. He's my boss. A team will be at your home to ensure that no one gets over that wall. They'll work in shifts."

"Do you really think that's necessary?"

"Yes. I do."

Marlene assessed his body language, his expression. Garrett wasn't messing around. "I don't know if this guy is ex-military, or a wannabe. But I'm not taking any chances," he said.

Her life just had gotten a lot more complicated.

CHAPTER FIVE

Garrett noticed Marlene's reaction, and hated that she faced such a threat. Yet posting security at her home was vital. The wall was electronically protected, but an intruder could disable that long enough to get inside—especially if the guy knew military tactics.

"Come on," Garrett said, and stood up. He reached for Marlene's hand. "You need to eat."

Marlene sighed, but let him help her up. "I have a long afternoon ahead. I can't afford to dwell on the negative."

The feel of her hand in his upped Garrett's commitment another notch. Marlene was depending on him, and he didn't want her worrying. He wasn't going to let her down. She was an amazing woman, and the sooner he could handle this situation so she could get on with her life, the better.

During the performance, Marlene had been deeply focused. It was unlikely that she'd noticed Garrett looking at her as much as he was. But he could hardly avert his gaze. In her historical garb, she was just as sexy as she had been in her sweater and tights outfit the night before.

The woman looked good in everything. But it wasn't only that. Given the opportunity to observe her, Garrett had gained insight into her personality. She was a talented actress, but not only in front of the camera. When she was with the director, she took on a particular attitude. And a different one with her cook, her chauffeur, and even the head of security at the studio.

Marlene seemed able to gear her demeanor, even her choice of words, to a particular person. It was enthralling. Garrett hadn't seen anything like it before. It was a skill he didn't possess. He was a straight shooter, in his actions and his words. He didn't know how to pretend.

Yet Marlene was capable of molding to the situation. In the short time he'd known her, Garrett had seen her do it frequently. She'd be a heck of a special ops weapon. The enemy wouldn't see it coming. She could make them see anything she wanted them to believe, just as she did the audiences she played to.

The danger was that Garrett might misjudge. He could err in thinking that he'd figured her out. He'd have to guard against that. It was important to base his actions on reality, not fiction. With Marlene, it might prove to be a trick to have clarity on what that was.

When they rounded the corner, Garrett released her hand, and one of the other actors came up to them. She was a pretty woman, a little shorter than Marlene. And she had a friendly face. "Marlene," the woman said with a brilliant smile, "are you going to introduce me?"

"This is Garrett Flynn, my new bodyguard, as you know." Marlene smiled at her friend. "And Garrett, meet Anna Tucker, a great actress and my dear friend."

Garrett took Anna's hand when she offered it. He bowed in an overly dramatic fashion and lifted her hand. "Anna, it's a pleasure." That made her giggle.

"I've been anxious to meet you since I saw your pictures...you know, from the other day."

Garrett cringed. That was all he needed, to be recognized wherever he went. He'd scanned social media and wasn't pleased. But there hadn't been any shots from the front, just the back. That must have been what Anna meant. She certainly wasn't shy, but then, he wouldn't expect that an actress would be.

"I wouldn't have necessarily recognized you," Anna said. "None of the pictures showed your face clearly."

Thank God. "That's just as well." Social situations were sometimes awkward. Garrett was used to clandestine affairs, where banter about lighthearted matters wasn't a part of the scene. He probably came across as too serious to a woman like Anna.

"But then Marlene told me that she'd hired you, so I figured it out." Anna started toward the food carts. "Are you guys eating? I'll join you," she said without waiting for an answer.

"Anna and I have been friends for a long time," Marlene said. "You'll have to excuse her boldness. She says what she thinks."

"I appreciate that in a woman," Garrett said.

Marlene looked up at him. "I'll have to remember that."

The three of them sat at a small table and hot food was served. The fare was better than Garrett expected. The pasta he ordered wasn't overcooked, and the meat sauce was hearty. Marlene and Anna had salads that were meals, complete with shrimp, avocado, and sprouts. It was going to be a long day, so feeding the cast and crew well made sense.

Since everyone had to eat, the stars mingled with the lighting crew, and the director ate with a couple of assistants. The arrangement gave Garrett a chance to size up more of those who were in the studio, as some of them had been tending to business, so hadn't been as visible. He wasn't aware of any cause for alarm. He'd determined a baseline, and the activity didn't violate that. All seemed as it should be.

"They treat you well on the set," Garrett said.

"They kind of have to," Marlene said. "We're stuck here for sixteen-hour days when filming. And overtired, poorly fed people get cranky. It's not a pretty picture, trust me."

Anna munched on her salad. "So, tell me, how long will you have to guard Marlene?"

"That depends." Garrett gulped his Coke. "I'll be around until the crisis is taken care of. At this point, how long that will take is undetermined."

"So you might be staying with Marlene for quite a while, then?" For some reason, that seemed to delight Anna.

"I could be. Like I said, there is no way to know how this will unfold. It would be my hope that we nab the guy quickly. I want Marlene out of danger as soon as I can manage it."

Anna grinned as if she knew something he didn't. "Well, I'm sure having you around isn't too much to suffer through."

Garrett had to smile at that. "I will try to make the situation as livable as I can. It's not my job to interfere, just to protect."

Anna looked over at Marlene. "I had a thought about the scene we're working on. I'm going to run it by the director. If he likes it, we can practice."

"Sure, I welcome your insight. It wouldn't be the first time you had an idea that stuck." Marlene stood up. "Excuse us while we go get ready. It might be a long afternoon."

Garrett thought of missions he'd been on, waiting in the cold, without food or worse. He'd been in circumstances that had required keeping still for so long that his limbs had ached with fatigue. Hanging out on a movie set for the afternoon didn't pose much of a challenge.

As Marlene had told him, it was late before filming was finished for the day. More food was being served, and Garrett was hungry. But instead she steered him toward her dressing room. "Let me get out of this costume, then we can go to dinner. I don't want to eat with the crew. I've been here all day."

Before Garrett could argue, she disappeared into her room, leaving him to wait in the hall. It didn't take long for her to reappear, dressed as she had been that morning. "I have to go home and change first. There's a great place that serves late dinners. They cater to the theater crowd. But I can't go looking like this."

Marlene seemed to note his hesitation. "I won't be long. I can dress quickly. I'll decide what to wear on the way home, so that will save time."

Garrett waited until they were in the limo pulling out of the lot before he voiced his objection. "You have a cook. I'm fine with eating at your place."

Marlene scrunched her brow. "I need to unwind. It's been a long day. I'm craving a drink and the lobster bisque at my favorite place." She paused. "I could find someone else to invite if you don't wish to join me."

The mention of Marlene on a date irked Garrett. "There's no need for that."

"You have to eat too, so why not eat together?" She

gave him a heart-melting look. "And you wouldn't refuse a woman what little relaxation she can muster, would you?"

"I want you relaxed. It's just safer at home."

Marlene raised her brows. "Am I a prisoner?"

"That's not funny. Of course you aren't a prisoner. But staying home poses less threat than a public place does."

Marlene put her hand on his forearm, sending heat coursing through his veins. "But I have you to protect me."

Countering that argument would have done no good. Garrett knew when Marlene had made up her mind. He'd just have to see that no harm came to her. "What restaurant do you have in mind?"

"Diamonte's Grill on Franklin Avenue. It's a hub for celebrities. It's one of the places I can go without being stared at...at least not too much. Most of the clientele are in the entertainment industry, so they aren't gawkers."

Garrett scrolled on his phone, gleaning as much information as he could about the place. It had a brick storefront with a patio on the sidewalk. The French bistro had been around since the seventies. It didn't look too bad, as far as well-established, crowded eating establishments went.

Earlier, Garrett had received a text to confirm that security was in place at the mansion. He'd been contacted by the guard in charge of the first shift. That put his mind at ease. Any team that Travis sent wouldn't be easy to penetrate; Garrett considered it next to impossible.

When the limo rolled up to the gate, Garrett sent a text to let the team know they'd arrived, but they wouldn't be staying long. Marlene seemed anxious to get inside and get ready. She might be stubborn about wanting to go out, but she didn't interfere with Garrett handling his duties.

While Marlene got changed, Garrett went to his room to do the same. He passed over the suits in the closet and grabbed a suede jacket. Somebody had good taste in clothes. The jacket was tailored, so it would be passable in an upscale restaurant, yet it would easily cover his holster.

He found some nicer pants and a shirt to wear, pairing it with shoes that were presentable but good for running. Then he sat down to text Rip.

The bullet was tungsten carbide.

Rip responded in less than a minute: *Yes, that got my attention.*

I don't like it. Find out who this guy is. He's acting like ex-military. I want to know what the hell I'm dealing with here.

I'm digging. I'll have the risk assessment soon. If there is any connection to Marlene that's suspicious, I plan to find it.

If Rip said he was digging, then he was scouring for every shred of information. Garrett could only hope he'd turn up something soon that would be helpful. The bodyguard gig only went so far. Garrett preferred to go after the target, not to be on the defensive. Waiting to be attacked went against his nature.

The bistro was as upscale as it had appeared online. The guests were well dressed, and the décor was classy. The dining room was larger than Garrett expected. From the outside, it had looked smaller. He spoke to the greeter. "We need a table at the back."

The server nodded then looked at Marlene. "Good to see you again, Miss Parks." He guided them through the establishment to a table near the back wall.

As they strode past tables, Marlene garnered attention. Despite her conviction that the patrons would be other celebs, it seemed there were plenty of guests who were thrilled to catch a glimpse of her. Marlene appeared comfortable under the scrutiny, if she even noticed. Garrett hated it, and once again, wished they'd stayed home.

"Will this be satisfactory?" the greeter said.

Marlene moved to sit down. "I'm sure this is fine." The greeter assisted her with the chair, then handed menus to them. He took Marlene's coat when she slipped it off. "I'll keep this for you up front."

Garrett was satisfied that they had the most advantageous location. There was no chance that someone would sneak up from behind, and he could see anyone who came through the front door. Plus, there was an emergency exit a few steps away.

What was going to be a problem was the dress Marlene had chosen. It was black satin, and one shoulder was uncovered. The bodice accentuated her lovely shape, making Garrett imagine touching her soft breasts underneath. His lips tingled as he thought of kissing down her slender neck, then dragging his tongue along her bare collarbone and over the silky skin of her shoulder.

When Marlene looked up, Garrett studied his menu. This wasn't a date; it was business. And his obligation was solely protection. Including protecting her from his lascivious nature. He had no misconception about being the good guy. Given other circumstances, he wouldn't have hesitated. But this wasn't *other circumstances.*

The waiter came by and Marlene ordered white wine, while Garrett stuck to club soda. And he took their dinner orders. He watched Marlene smear a bit of butter over a slice of bread and set it on her dish. He remained aware of his surroundings, the movement of the waiters, diners chatting and laughing.

The lower sections of the walls were paneled in wood, with shiny gold wallpaper above. Candles lit the tables, set with silver and china on white linen. The high ceiling sparkled, and in the center was a crystal chandelier in a French-looking style, with an ornate gold base, dangling from a thick chain. The fixture widened from the top, then narrowed, and a netting of crystal beads hung over it.

Below the chandelier was a huge marble table with an elaborate floral display. "Very fancy," Garrett said.

Marlene took a sip of wine, leaving her bread untouched. "I think the filming went well today. Anna's suggestion was clever. It gave us a way to bond as friends." She put her glass down. "But anyway, enough about work."

"Is Marlene a stage name? I don't think I've met another woman with that name."

"It's my real name. My mother was a huge fan of Marlene Dietrich, so she named me after her. Do you know much about her movie career?"

"Hardly anything."

"She was in silent films in the twenties. After she got a contract with Paramount, she starred in many Hollywood films. I'm sure you've seen *Shanghai Express.*"

"A long time ago, and even then it was an old movie."

Marlene laughed. "Anyway, she was noted for her humanitarian efforts and did a lot for soldiers during World War II, appearing before troops to raise morale. She was known for her strong political convictions and wasn't afraid to say what she thought."

"You seem to know a lot about her."

"I read a couple of biographies that my mother had." Marlene sipped her wine, looking thoughtful for a moment. "In interviews, she revealed that she'd been approached by representatives of the Nazi Party to return to Germany, but she turned them down. She became an American citizen and reportedly sold more war bonds than any other star."

The waiter came by with their food, then left them to their conversation.

Garrett began to carve into his steak. "So now you're involved with charities to support vets."

"I do what I can, and it's fortunate that I have a career that allows me to do such things. I earn enough with my movies that I'm able to donate and really make a difference. Plus, I can organize fundraisers like that one the other day. Most are very successful, so funds are provided for worthy causes, and I'm proud of that."

"You should be."

Marlene tilted her head. "What about you? What got you into the bodyguard business?"

"I graduated from college before I went into the Navy. But my goal was to join the service. I was in for ten years, but in a skirmish I injured my ankle...pretty badly. It won't be the same again. I was forced to consider another career."

"Couldn't you have reposted, not gone out on deployment?"

Garrett shrugged. "I'd be a lousy paper pusher."

"Yeah, I can't see you doing that either." Marlene dipped her spoon into the bisque and lifted it to her mouth. Garrett stared as she delicately slipped the spoon past her lips...lips he'd like to kiss. "Why Stealth Security?"

Garrett scooped a bite of mashed potatoes and held it over his plate. "One of my team, Wyatt Mercer, got out before me. He went to work as a bodyguard there. He talked to Travis about me, so when I got out I gave it a try."

"And you like it?"

Since when did liking something affect one's decisions? It was duty, using one's abilities and training for good. But Garrett just said, "I can do a lot of what I was doing in the service, only as a civilian. Not missions, exactly. But I can use my skill. It's physical. That's what I'm best at."

For a few minutes, they ate in silence. Garrett marveled that he'd told her anything personal. He wasn't much of a talker, especially about himself. Marlene seemed to bring out a different side of him.

Garrett wanted to know more about her. "It's interesting that you're doing a war-themed movie."

"Yes, it's an extraordinary story about how the First World War affected the lives of a particular family and those who were close to them." Marlene pushed her plate back. "I'm honored to star in it. It's a good part for me. I'm not just a pretty face. With a role like this, viewers and critics will consider me a serious actress."

"I don't see how they couldn't." Garrett had just seen one day of filming, but he already knew it was going to be a quality movie. And he was convinced that Marlene was great in it.

Garrett felt like he was getting to know her. Marlene wasn't some remote movie star, or even just a client. She was a woman with a heart, with passions, and he admired her. Any man looking at her on the big screen would fall for her. But it was more than that.

Marlene cared. She really cared about wounded warriors, about the issues veterans had. And she did something about it, including funneling her own income to the cause and using her fame to persuade others to provide support.

Plus, she was simply gorgeous. Marlene's blond hair glowed in the candlelight, and her porcelain skin looked so soft. Garrett wanted to touch, but he didn't dare to allow himself the luxury. He was on thin ice. The woman had gotten to him, when he'd thought he was made of steel.

Behind enemy lines he could be a rock, unemotional, ruthless. Yet gazing into her soft green eyes turned his insides to Jell-O. It was time to rein in his feelings. His relationship with Marlene was strictly professional, and it was important that it stayed that way.

Plus, Garrett wasn't the guy for her, and she deserved more than a mere fling. Plus, he wasn't the type to get tied down. Some men were the marrying kind, but Garrett had always known he wasn't. His life was in peril more often than it wasn't. That was no way for a woman to live, always wondering, continually afraid her man wouldn't come home. He wouldn't ask that of Marlene. So it was best to cool things off before Garrett did something he'd regret.

CHAPTER SIX

Talking to Garrett was natural, easy. It felt as if Marlene could talk to him all night long. She was comfortable with him, not only because he was there to look out for her. He was a guy that put on no pretense. He was direct, blunt, and seemed interested in her. It was a refreshing combination.

Dating had been an arduous process for Marlene. Her life was under a microscope, allowing only a minimum of privacy. Any guy she went out with could expect to see his photo plastered across the tabloids, with lots of speculation about his relationship with her.

What the press didn't know, they made up. If not outright lies, articles were concoctions of partial truths, implications, or mere guesses. It had taken Marlene a long time to get used to being in the public eye, and really, the things that were said about her still got under her skin.

One reason Marlene had chosen this restaurant was that it had a no-photos policy. Management didn't allow the paparazzi inside, and discouraged them from loitering anywhere too close. It was one place that she could go out to eat where there was some semblance of normalcy.

Garrett was looking at the guests dining around them, and following the motions of waiters. He was on duty. This wasn't a date, as much as she wished it was. Getting to know him was a slow process. Garrett wasn't the chatty type, but he didn't hold back either. He appeared to answer questions honestly, although he didn't elaborate much.

But everyone had secrets. Marlene had learned that long ago. It was likely that Garrett had more than most, if one added up all the secrecy connected with special ops. Yet she didn't care to ask about that, knowing he wouldn't share any details. Her interest was in the man, and what made him tick.

She understood the motivation of joining the military, but taking on the role of a SEAL was a step beyond. The man's fortitude, as well as physical strength, had to be superhuman. Garrett was the whole package: physically fit and sexy as hell, handsome, smart, and the best protector a woman could ask for. Marlene's desire to know him better, to experience intimacy with such a man, was overpowering.

Garrett looked across the table at her. His blue eyes unnerved her, the way he looked at her, as if he knew...what? It was as if he knew her, understood her better than he should have, after knowing her hardly more than one day. Garrett pushed back from the table.

Marlene took the last sip of her cappuccino, her indulgence for the evening. She'd already signed the tab. A bonus was that meals with her bodyguard could be expensed—not that money was a concern. "We should probably go," she said.

Garrett gave her a nod. Then her phone dinged; it was a text. "Just a sec," Marlene said. "It's my mom. She saw the news about yesterday. I should have called her." Quickly, Marlene responded: *I'm fine. Hired a new bodyguard. No need to worry. I'll call you tomorrow and tell you everything. Love you.*

Garrett leaned forward, with his hands on his knees, prepared to get up. Marlene secured her phone in the small clutch she'd brought with her. She grasped the silk purse in one hand, then remembered her coat was up front and glanced toward the entrance.

In the next second, the sound of a rifle shot cracked like thunder, and a blinding flash of white scorched her eyes, partially blinding her. It was accompanied by the tinkling of breaking glass, and a vision of glittering crystal exploding through the air. Marlene saw tiny pieces spraying into the room like sparkling stars, and realized the chandelier had burst into thousands of flying shards.

Marlene heard a loud thud, which could only have been the heavy gold base of the fixture impacting the marble table beneath it. Garrett had his arm around her waist, and had already pulled her under the table. The tablecloth hung down over the sides, providing cover. But he didn't hesitate. With Marlene in his lap, Garrett was crouched below tabletop level, out of the line of vision to the dining room. He took a couple of powerful strides on bent legs, then was able to thrust one foot out with enough force to kick the emergency door open.

Once in the back alley, Garrett stood up. As the door closed behind them, Marlene heard shouting from the people still inside. The parking lot was across the alley and Garrett sprinted in that direction with her still in his arms. Samuel opened the door for them, and Garrett ducked inside with her on his lap. "Drive. Now!"

Faster than she would have thought possible, the limo peeled out of the lot, with tires skidding. "Don't slow down," Garrett barked. "We need to get home...out of danger." He slumped down in the seat so his head wasn't visible in the windows, and pressed Marlene's head to his chest.

Marlene's heart pounded and she couldn't get air. Garrett rubbed her arm. "Breathe, Marlene. Breathe." She gasped, drinking in oxygen, yet still suffocating. "Slow and easy." Garrett had one strong arm around her, holding her tight. "In and out. In and out."

Like a mantra, Marlene repeated the words in her head, trying to focus on breathing. Her heart was pounding so hard it made her ears throb. She was terrorized, but began to calm. Then she was angry. The attacker had returned, scaring her half to death, and she was royally pissed. Between feelings of intimidation and helplessness, Marlene raged at the injustice.

Glancing up, she could see that Garrett was on high alert. He scanned the scene out the windows, while holding her in a protective embrace. "We're almost there," he said. Marlene leaned into him, feeling his strength, imagining how vulnerable she'd be without him.

The voice of the guard at the gate was a welcome sound. Marlene was home. The place was secured, and she mentally thanked Garrett for posting guards at the perimeter. What had once seemed excessive was now vital. As soon as they were inside the garage, Samuel rolled into a space near the elevator.

Garrett released Marlene and she sat up, then slid onto the seat beside him. The driver held his phone up as if to read something under the dim garage lights. "What's this?" He had a piece of paper clutched in his hand, along with his phone.

"What is it?" Garrett said.

"You'll have to take a look." Samuel handed the

folded paper over the seat. "It's addressed to Marlene."

When Marlene reached for the note, her hand trembled. She was still shaken, and the mysterious note didn't help. She opened it, and Garrett looked over her shoulder as she read it out loud.

By now, you are aware of what I can do. You should pay attention, Marlene. Your new bodyguard is not welcome. Warn him that he should not interfere. I almost killed him yesterday. Next time, I won't miss. Heed my words, or you'll get hurt.

The message was printed in large letters, but Marlene's eyes went to the signature scrawled at the bottom, which was the initial *B*.

"He signed with his initial. That asshole wants us to know who he is." Garrett took the note and looked at Samuel, who was visibly shaken. "Where did you get this?"

"It was just in my pocket," the driver said, clearly as stunned as they were. "While I waited for you, I'd been leaning against the car, getting some air. I saw a few couples going back to their cars." He thought for a second. "One guy did brush against me, but I didn't think anything of it at the time. After that, it was quiet outside, until I heard some kind of explosion. Then you burst out the back of the restaurant."

"Goddammit." Garrett gripped the note in his fist. "The creep managed to slip the note in your pocket without you seeing him. That takes unique skill." He opened the car door. "Let's get inside."

Low lights shone in the foyer, so they didn't enter into darkness. But no one else was there. Laura had gone for the evening, and James had the day off. Marlene walked on shaky legs to the library and sank into a leather chair. Garrett typed on his phone, then said, "I let the team know there was an incident at the restaurant but we're safe. I'll give them details in a bit."

Garrett paced the carpet, still holding the note. "This guy pisses me off." He lifted the paper, then expelled a breath. "I'm trying to sort this out. It's of interest that this note was delivered in such a clandestine manner. A man who approaches like a shadow is more than likely ex-military. Or if not, a well-trained professional."

Marlene didn't know what to think of it all. Oddly enough, she thought of calling her mother, worrying over how to explain what had happened. It was alarming that there had been a random shooter at her charity event, but it painted a far worse picture that the man had returned. There was no way to tell her mother that he'd wielded a gun in a restaurant, and her life was in peril, without upsetting her horribly.

As if realizing her distraught state, Garrett stopped pacing. "I know you must be scared to death." He walked over to her. "I'll get this guy. I promise."

Then he went to the bar and poured a drink. When Garrett handed her the glass, he said, "Drink this. You'll feel better."

"It's not white wine."

"No, it's not."

Marlene cupped the glass in her hands and took a gulp. It burned on the way down, but seemed to take the edge off her anxiety. She leaned her head against the back of the chair and closed her eyes for a minute. When she opened them, Garrett was sitting on the sofa, looking at her.

"Better?"

"A little." Marlene's head wasn't pounding and she could breathe. But she was still severely rattled.

Garrett hit a button on his phone, then waited. "Travis, I hope you're still awake. There was another incident." He put the phone on the table. "You're on speakerphone. I'm here with Marlene, back at her place."

A gruff man said, "I'm awake now. What happened?"

"Some idiot shot out the chandelier, some huge French fixture, loaded with crystals. The damn thing exploded in the middle of the restaurant."

"At Diamonte's?"

"Yes, he was considerate enough to let us eat first, but I heard the rifle shot. He blew out the gold base and the force shattered the crystals. Glass sprayed over the place like fireworks."

"Is Marlene hurt?"

"Shaken up pretty bad," Garrett said. "We didn't stick around to see if the perpetrator had any bullets left. I got her the hell out of there. But I'm telling you it's the same guy."

"Has to be."

"Expect to hear from the police. See if you can delay them from contacting us. Marlene's been through enough."

Travis growled, "You're safe at home. So stay there."

"We're not going anywhere tonight. I don't like being shot at when I can't get the guy in my sights. He's a marksman, or he wouldn't have been able to hit a small target like the base of that chandelier from outside the front of a restaurant."

"You didn't see him inside."

"Nope. I was against the back wall, and no one got in the door unseen."

"Then we can assume he wasn't shooting to kill. But he was trying to make a point," Travis said.

"Yeah, well, he's on my bad side. Whatever point he's trying to make, I'm not interested. It's time to turn the tables here. He's taken his last shot at us."

"Agreed. I'll handle things from this end. We'll talk tomorrow." Travis paused. "Do what Garrett says, Marlene. I know this is all frightening, but he will keep you safe."

"Okay, thanks, Travis."

"And one more thing," Garrett said. "The shooter left a note in the chauffeur's pocket. I'll scan it and send it to you, so you can see for yourself. He signed with his initial. See if that sheds light on anything." Then he ended the call.

"I can't figure it out," Garrett said, scooping his phone from the table. "If the guy wants to kill you, then why warn you in a note?"

"It doesn't make sense."

Garrett frowned. "So what is he really after?"

Marlene sighed. "I wish I knew."

"He's taking risks. Shooting in a public place makes the likelihood of getting caught much greater." Garrett stood and walked over to the fireplace. He rested his hand on the mantel and put one foot on the stone hearth, staring at the unlit logs. "It's more than just taking risks...the dude is *showing off*."

Garrett turned to look at Marlene. "Shooting out a crystal chandelier is dramatic. It makes a big splash, says *look at me*. He's bragging."

"Why would he do that? What does he want?"

Garrett thought about that for a moment. "I keep coming back to the military...something to do with the military. It's easy to think of servicemen as fighters. But we're trained that it's smarter to run when that's an option. There's no need to prove anything. It's better to avoid conflict whenever possible. If getting away isn't realistic, the next choice is to outsmart the enemy, and to engage as a last resort. In truth, a military man is often the least anxious for combat, because he knows the consequences all too well."

"So you think he didn't shoot to kill? That he just wanted to scare us?"

"Either that," Garrett said, "or he's a coward. He won't come out in the open."

Marlene pulled a shawl from the back of her chair and wrapped it around her shoulders, shivering even though it wasn't cold.

"I don't like involving the police." Garrett sat down on the sofa again. "The restaurant will give them a list of guests, so you'll be contacted. It's another way to get to you, harass you. A public attack means your name in the news again, and police interviews."

Marlene had a thought. She'd played many types of characters, and was familiar with a variety of personalities. She had an idea. "You know, killers want their crimes in the news. They want to be known and recognized. It's an ego thing."

"That's true. He doesn't want to execute his deeds quietly. What's the glory in that?" Garrett stared at the note, as if trying to glean its full implication.

Marlene watched him, wishing the nature of their relationship was different than it was. After what she'd been through, it would make sense to go to her bedroom and hide under her covers. But she didn't want to leave. She wanted to be with Garrett. What she really wanted was for him to hold her, so she could breathe in his masculine scent and feel his strong arms around her, while he whispered in her ear that everything was going to be okay.

She wanted to run her fingertips through his silky

hair, and trace his lips with the tip of her thumb. And then she wanted him to kiss her like he meant it. Still watching Garrett study the note, Marlene resisted the urge to go to him, to sit on his lap and put her arms around his neck. Just to see how he'd react. To find out whether he felt the same way she did.

Marlene's body heated at the images she couldn't put aside. Garrett was sexy as hell in the dress pants and suede jacket. His biceps filled the sleeves, the material bulging against his rock-hard muscle, and the shirt buttoned tightly over his wide chest.

There was no doubt that Marlene had a crush on her bodyguard. Maybe it was natural. Under threat, it was probably normal to fall for the guy who rescued you. That was all. Once this was all over, her life would be back to normal and Garrett would move on. This was all temporary, so she shouldn't let the relationship get too intimate. No matter how much she wanted it right then.

Garrett looked up and their gazes locked. His expression was tender, and just for a moment, Marlene felt like he'd read her mind. He knew what she'd been thinking, what she wanted. The look in his eyes said that he wanted her too. Her heart skipped a beat.

Then it was gone. Garrett leaned back and stared up at the ceiling. When he looked back at her, his expression had changed. He looked at her with concern. "There is something nagging at my gut."

Marlene held her breath.

"There are reasons I'd be a killer's target; many enemies who would gladly take me down. But...none of my enemies are in this country. I left them behind, on one mission or another." Garrett tossed the note onto the table. "He said in the note that he almost killed me yesterday. That next time he won't miss."

The thought of Garrett getting killed because of her made Marlene feel a bit ill.

"What if he was at the charity event because of me? I have this sick feeling that the guy might not have been shooting at you at all. What if he was after me, and without realizing it, I led him to you?" Garrett took a deep breath. "Jesus, Marlene, what if I brought all this grief to your doorstep? You just happened to be in the line of fire?"

Marlene shook her head. "No, Garrett. Don't think that way."

"I have to," Garrett said. "I must consider the possibility that I drew the asshole to you, Marlene. He intends to kill me, not you."

Marlene drew the shawl tighter around her. She didn't know what to think anymore. In a twisted way, what Garrett said made sense. Fear arrowed into her heart. "Or maybe...he wants to kill both of us."

CHAPTER SEVEN

Glenn Buckner walked through the long, narrow army-navy surplus store, his chest swelling with pride. He could have picked up most items to suit his needs online, but he preferred to surround himself with memorabilia. Just like some people enjoyed bookstores for the feel and smell of books, Glenn craved the military environment.

It was where he belonged. Rack after rack was packed with shirts, pants, jackets, and nearly every item a man could need. He'd picked up more than one good pair of boots there, plus an array of ribbons and medals. Such items were often lost by their owners or donated from estate sales.

Surplus was a treasure trove of possessions. Some time back, Glenn had purchased a SEAL Trident pin, a symbol of honor and respect. He deserved both, but the armed forces hadn't seen fit to treat him properly. Yet he didn't hold a grudge. The military was his life. He lived and breathed it, even now, when not on active duty.

Glenn stepped over the shiny linoleum floor so silently that the clerk wouldn't have known he was there if he hadn't seen him. He scooped a couple of shirts off the rack, and glanced at a floor container filled with rolled-up flags. He had a US flag at home, one he displayed every day of the year in honor of those who served, risking their lives to save others. A group of men Glenn was a part of. Then there were the traitors.

One such man was Garrett Flynn, an ex-SEAL with overinflated ideas of his deeds, and false claims about his record. Oh, Glenn knew, even if Marlene Parks didn't. But she would find out. Flynn couldn't keep it secret indefinitely. In fact, Glenn would make sure he didn't.

It was his responsibility to see that Marlene wasn't duped by her new bodyguard. That was a laugh. A man who failed to protect was supposed to keep one of America's most loved stars safe. Glenn was the real hero, the man who was capable of caring for her.

And he would, as soon as he got Garrett out of the way.

He should get home now, though. The drugs were wearing off and he needed another fix. He suffered with pain, a burden he accepted, but without a little assistance he couldn't be expected to make it through the day. The service had screwed him, leaving him to fend for himself.

Well, he had done so. The drugs took the edge off, made the hours tolerable. But as soon as he was with Marlene, he wouldn't need them anymore. He'd only need her, the one woman meant for him. His purpose in life was to ensure her happiness.

Glenn just hoped she didn't die in the process.

The clerk glanced at the Marine Corps pin on Glenn's lapel, and gave him a nod. "Picking up a few more things, huh?"

The store employees rotated shifts, so Glenn hadn't spoken to this clerk before. "Can't have too many shirts." He spoke with courtesy. After all, he was a decorated hero and the masses looked up to him, as well they should.

The clerk handed the bag across the counter, and

Glenn left the store. He'd be back. It was a place that he frequented. It made him feel at home.

It was a brisk February day in West Hollywood, and a breeze ruffled the edges of Glenn's hair under his cap. The walk home wasn't far. He strode at an even pace, appearing to be a local who belonged there. Anyone observing him would see only a veteran, a man to respect. He didn't make any sudden moves, and he wasn't carrying a weapon. It wasn't needed for such an innocuous outing.

Then a tight smile stretched Glenn's lips. He remembered the night before at Diamonte's. It had been so easy to find out where the pair was going to eat. Marlene hadn't realized how simple it was to hack a cell phone. He didn't even need a mini cell tower.

It wasn't only the government or criminals with the technology to listen to calls. Glenn could even read her emails and access her photos. Even when her phone was off, he could access it wirelessly, provided he was close enough.

Too bad he couldn't have stuck around to see the results of his rifle blast, but he had no trouble imagining. When he'd blown out the base of that chandelier, the crystals must have shattered like so many stars in the sky.

Glenn kept his shoulders straight, without missing a step when he crossed the street on a green light. *I'd known they'd be there*, he thought. *Flynn thinks he's in control, but I'll show him how it is*. Turning the corner toward home, Glenn regretted that Marlene was likely shaken by the episode, which was unfortunate.

That's Flynn's fault. He's in my way, and I already warned him by nearly blowing his head off at that event. How much clearer could I have been? And now I've told Marlene that she might get hurt, unless she dumps her new bodyguard? She's been warned.

If the woman has any sense, she'll pay attention to what I say. But then she is uppity, assuming she's untouchable, thinking she's above me. She'll find out.

Glenn reached his front door and unlocked it to go inside. He lived in a small home. The neighborhood was filled with residents who were long-term homeowners. They knew their neighbors, felt secure on their quiet streets. And they welcomed Glenn, a retired Marine Corps captain, although he didn't use his real name with them.

He couldn't have some busybody looking into him. His mission was too important, and secrecy was vital. It was no one's business anyway. It was military business. Glenn was a soldier, first and foremost. That was why he trained hard and planned methodically.

Once inside he locked and bolted the door. Glenn couldn't be too cautious. A glance around assured him that no intruder had been there. He tossed the bag onto a pile of other similar ones. There it would sit, as he had more pressing matters to attend to.

Stacks of plates with dried food on them littered his coffee table. Glenn shoved them aside and spread out a map. It was time to organize. He ran his finger over the street where Marlene lived, trying to envision what she might be doing at the moment.

Glenn's head hurt, and he rubbed his temples. The medication. He headed toward the kitchen, kicking aside a stack of magazines and old newspapers, knocking them over onto the stained carpet. The narrow hall was partially blocked with a few bags of trash, and he nearly tripped over one.

After Glenn found the bottle on the counter, he downed a few pills with a gulp of metallic-tasting water. He waited, leaning against the kitchen table, his anxiety gradually lessening. But not nearly enough. Prescription meds had limited use, or maybe he'd stolen the wrong ones this time.

In any case, he had his own remedies for when he needed something stronger. Glenn plopped into a chair, scraping it on the floor. The screech irritated him. Leaning his head back, he looked up at the ceiling then closed his eyes.

Glenn felt marginally better, and a sense of relaxation flowed through his veins as he thought of Marlene. He supported her charities. She should know that. He attended when he could, although she didn't pay attention to him. But she would.

There had been one time at a crowded fundraiser that Glenn had managed to get close to her. Marlene had worn a perfume with an unforgettable fragrance. Even now, he could smell it as if he was there. She'd been so beautiful and so kind. She deserved a man like Glenn.

Her radiant smile encouraged attendees to donate for her cause, to assist retired soldiers when she asked them to. He loved how she spoke, the tone of her voice, like honey to soothe his wounds. At the bigger events, Marlene had told her personal story. She'd shared losing her own father when she had been a young girl. And then war had, sadly, taken her older brother Andrew.

Glenn seethed with hatred at Flynn, a man who claimed the title SEAL yet had failed to save a young marine, Marlene's beloved brother. The image of Garrett Flynn filled his mind, making his head ache again. *I know all about you and what you did.*

But Glenn couldn't dwell on that now. There would be plenty of time for that.

Marlene was in his mind, the memory as vivid as the moment he'd seen her. Her hand had brushed his, and Glenn had known she felt the electricity just as he had. They were meant for each other, fated to be together. And when she knew what a hero he was, the lovely star would be unable to resist him.

However, that day Marlene had brushed him off. Her treatment of him had been demeaning, and she needed to be more considerate. Glenn had been dressed in military garb, and he'd smiled at her cordially. He'd said something about his support of the fundraiser.

But Marlene had given him a cursory nod, then immediately became engaged in conversation with an injured vet who was there to give support. Hadn't Marlene realized who he was? Hadn't she known what she owed him?

But maybe she hadn't. Marlene needed to be shown. So Glenn had methodically planned out meeting her. As unlikely as an encounter would be at a well-publicized event, it had also been the perfect cover. The fundraiser at the Beverly Hilton had been mobbed with adoring fans, and Glenn had been in the audience waiting for the opportunity to gain Marlene's attention.

She'd managed to get a host of other celebrities to agree to perform at the event. Marlene was charming, and seemed capable of persuading others to do as she wished. Glenn admired her for that. Although he was one man that needed little encouragement. His sole aim was to be by her side, to take care of her, now that she'd lost her older brother.

It was Glenn's duty, and he intended to follow through. That day it might have all come to fruition. All his efforts could have paid off. Then he'd spotted Garrett Flynn, who'd had the nerve to show up at the event. Once again, the traitor was going to screw it all up.

Glenn had been enraptured with Marlene. She'd looked like an angel in her white fur coat with her blond hair flowing over her shoulders. He'd gazed into her green eyes, and she'd looked back. But Flynn, damn him, had taken notice of Glenn.

In a moment of blinding rage, Glenn had pulled his gun. If he'd thought it through, he'd have held back. He could have continued to act like he was there to see the famous stars, that he'd been a normal guy like the hundreds of others in attendance. He'd have gone unnoticed.

But Glenn couldn't be blamed. He'd had Flynn in his sights. The man was a nuisance. Always in the way. Without hesitation, like a true soldier, Glenn had gone for his gun, to shoot to kill. But Flynn had leapt over the gold rope and tackled Marlene on the red carpet.

Flynn's stupid move had nearly gotten *her* killed. If the bullet had gone awry, his aim had been off just a hair, Glenn might have hit Marlene when aiming at Flynn. That would have been a misfortune.

The scene had unraveled in the blink of an eye. With Marlene's body pressed to Flynn's, it had been too risky, and that moment's hesitation had cost Glenn the opportunity. He was an experienced marksman and could have hit Flynn right in the back. There had been one big problem with that. He'd been using tungsten bullets; they penetrated armor. He hadn't been willing to chance the bullet going right through Flynn and injuring Marlene.

Glenn hadn't stuck around to see what happened in the aftermath of the gunshot. He'd disappeared into the crowd and gotten the hell out of there. His bravery knew no limit, and in the emergency situation, he hadn't been concerned about his own safety. But if anything had happened to Glenn, then who would look after Marlene? Who would she have to turn to?

It certainly wasn't Flynn, and she'd realize that soon enough. But the man was going to be a problem. After the attempted shooting, the ex-SEAL had hung around. From what Glenn could see, he wasn't going anywhere soon. And he'd found out that the man had been hired as her bodyguard. What a joke that was.

So he'd warned her by leaving a note with her chauffeur. Exploding the chandelier had just been to get her attention. And to demonstrate that Glenn meant business. The message he'd sent had been clear: get rid of the bodyguard. He hoped Marlene didn't ignore the implication.

Glenn was deadly serious about his mission. His purpose was now compounded. Now that Flynn was associated with her, it was up to Glenn to get him out of the picture. He'd kill him with no regrets; that would be justice at work. But if there was a way to do it without undue personal risk, getting himself killed in the process, then it was all the better. Glenn needed to be around, so Marlene would be able to rely on him.

It was quiet in his house. The air smelled of old food and beer. It was very much like the mess hall atmosphere that he'd grown accustomed to. But Glenn didn't have the luxury of seeing to his own needs. He ate what was available, and used his precious time for other activities besides cleaning up like some old woman.

Glenn got up from the table and went back to the living room. It looked like a war room, except for one framed picture of Marlene that had been taken at a fundraiser—she'd been gracious enough to autograph the photos for attendees. His living room was where he strategized his battles, planning the details of beating the enemy. On a high circular table Glenn had a diagram spread out. He studied it carefully. Each key location was marked: Marlene's home, the studio, her favorite restaurants, and so on.

There wasn't much she did that Glenn didn't know about. He'd been keeping track of her for months. And he'd been so close. Then it had all fizzled when Flynn had interceded. But Glenn would take care of that. There was no way that Marlene would be loyal to her incompetent bodyguard. It wasn't right.

Marlene belonged with Glenn. That was how it should be. She'd understand. Glenn would make her understand. He'd do whatever it took for her to see the truth. His blood boiled over at the thought of her with Garrett Flynn. Rage surged, but he pressed the emotion back, down where it belonged.

Glenn didn't have anything to fear. He would overcome, because he was smart, and he was a capable soldier. No man could overpower him. It was only a matter of time until he won out. He was an expert with firearms, and wouldn't hesitate to use force if necessary. He had a steel gun locker with plenty of guns and ammo. He practiced often, but wisely, did so at a range out of the area.

Marlene had been offered a chance to cooperate. If she didn't, then Glenn would see that her bodyguard had drawn his last breath. Because he *would* get to

Marlene; he *would* have her. His pulse sped up; he could feel his heart beating too hard in his chest, and his breathing was shallow.

He could not allow her to be with another man, one less worthy. It was demeaning, a life he couldn't bear to allow her to endure. It was beneath her. And if Marlene didn't see it his way...then he might be *forced* to kill her too.

CHAPTER EIGHT

Despite the traumatic experience at Diamonte's, Marlene convinced Garrett to take her to the studio the next morning. "I'm not letting some psychopath intimidate me." Garrett just shook his head, but didn't refuse. She would have gone anyway.

Fear was ever present. Both times the shooter had appeared without warning, and likely would again. It was no way to live, but for now, there was no choice. Marlene had to be brave and not give in to the terror. Last night, the guy had aimed at a chandelier; next time, she might not be so lucky.

The stakes were higher now, because Garrett was as much of a target as she was. Marlene was distressed that she might be the source of disaster. In an effort to get to her, the maniac wouldn't hesitate to shoot her bodyguard.

That was what it meant to be a bodyguard under these conditions, but she didn't have to like it. Garrett suspected that he'd been the target in the first place, that he'd attracted danger to Marlene, targeted toward him.

Either way, they were in it together until the crisis was over, however it ended. Garrett wasn't about to leave, even though Marlene had told him he could. She'd hire another bodyguard, increase her security. But he wouldn't hear of it, and flatly refused to go.

In truth, Marlene was relieved. She felt more

secure with him around, as secure as possible, considering the death threat hanging over her head. Also, she didn't want to separate from Garrett yet. There was no future in any relationship. There wasn't really any relationship, other than their professional one.

But Marlene wanted to get to know him better, and preferred having him in her life for now. Later...well, she'd deal with that when she had to.

When they walked out to the car, Marlene saw that Garrett had a barely noticeable limp. He hadn't complained of it, but then, he wouldn't have. Once in the back seat of the limo, she said, "What's wrong with your leg? I noticed you're limping."

Garrett lifted his right leg and flexed his foot. "It's my ankle. I told you I injured it." He seemed very blasé about the whole thing. "Last night didn't do it any good. Kicking the emergency door open aggravated the injury. Those self-closing doors aren't meant to swing open easily."

"So you were unable to stay in the service after your ankle injury?"

"I would have been on a desk job...so no I wasn't able to stay in." Garrett leaned against the seat. "Deployment was out after that. The ankle isn't going to fully heal; it won't be the same. To be a SEAL requires physical integrity. There's no room for failure on a mission, no margin for error."

Garrett's expression darkened, but she decided not to press for more. She assumed it was difficult for an ex-Navy guy to acclimate to civilian life. It must have been a disappointment to sustain an injury that forced him out of the service.

"How did you injure it?"

A sardonic look came over Garrett's features.

"Let's just say that jumping out of helicopters can stress the joints." He rolled his shoulder. "There's a bone fragment in there. High-impact activity— running, jumping...kicking heavy doors open—can aggravate it."

"But it doesn't deter you from your bodyguard duties?"

Garrett looked over, his blue eyes melting her. "You didn't have any complaints last night, did you?"

"No, I didn't." Marlene smiled. "You have a habit of saving my life."

Once they got to the studio, Garrett went inside with her but didn't stay. He had told her earlier that he needed to go to the office. "I can't do everything by phone, and I need to get some stuff at my place."

"I'll be filming all day."

"The studio is the safest place for you." Garrett wore a cotton shirt and jeans under a blazer, making him drool-worthy. His hair was combed but looked so touchable.

Marlene's eyes lingered on his kissable lips. "I'll be okay."

"Security here is good, but I had one of the guys from the team assigned to you today." Garrett nodded toward the far wall, where a buff guy stood at attention. Marlene had seen him at her place, as part of the new security crew.

"That's Wyatt Mercer. I trust him. He's the teammate I told you about that recommended me to Stealth. If anything at all concerns you, don't hesitate to let him know. And I'll be back before you're done today. Don't leave until I get here."

"I wouldn't dream of it."

Garrett barely cracked a smile. "Okay, then. Behave." Then he was gone.

When Marlene entered the dressing area, Anna strode toward her. "There you are. I couldn't reach you this morning. I was worried."

It would only make Anna feel bad if she thought their texts had been intercepted. Garrett was going to get her a secure phone, so there was no reason to make a big deal about it. "Sorry, I was a bit rattled."

"You must have been." Anna's eyes were wide. "You texted that Garrett was taking you to dinner at Diamonte's. Then this morning it's all over the news."

"The chandelier?" Marlene hadn't bothered watching the news, or turning on her computer either, knowing it would only upset her.

"Yes, the *chandelier*." Anna frowned. "The thing blew up. I heard it was shot from the ceiling by a rifle."

"Yeah, that's what I heard too."

"But you were there. Did you see it? Did it happen before you left?"

Marlene sighed. "I'm afraid so. It was shocking. One minute I was about to stand up to go, and the next Garrett has me on the floor, under the table."

"Danger seems to follow you too closely," Anna said. "I'm worried."

Marlene squeezed her friend's arm. "Don't be. I have the best security that money can buy. Garrett won't let anything happen to me." She paused. "If he can help it."

"You should stay home until this blows over."

"You know I can't do that," Marlene said. "This movie is too important. I can't let everyone down."

Anna shook her head. "Well, if anything happens to you..."

"I'll do all I can to stay safe. Garrett is consulting with his team today. He'll figure this out. I know he will." Marlene spoke with more confidence than she felt. She trusted Garrett, but still—being terrorized by a guy handy with guns was enough to make her seriously doubt her personal safety.

They went to makeup to get ready, but surely Anna was still concerned. Marlene was too, but the best thing to do was to focus on work. After getting ready for the first scene, she went out to consult with the director. Nicholas Hayes looked particularly handsome in his wool slacks and sweater. It was no mystery why he was so popular with women.

He was a talented director, and Marlene was grateful to work with him. The emotional depth of the filming had escalated. They were creating key scenes that showed the impact war had on the characters. It affected Marlene, and she found it more difficult to pull herself out of the scene once the cameras were off.

The film was on a topic dear to her heart, and Marlene poured herself into the role. It was mentally draining, but she was determined to do it right. The part offered a chance to demonstrate her acting skill, as well as make a statement about the devastation of war.

During a break, Marlene took the opportunity to call her mother. She used a secure phone on premises instead of her cell. The last thing she wanted was for an unwelcome stranger to tap into her call. The man might be trying to kill her, but he didn't need to know about her personal life.

She closed the door to the private room, glad to know that Wyatt Mercer was just on the other side. If Garrett had faith that he'd protect her, then so did she. He wasn't much of a conversationalist, but then, protection wasn't a social event.

Settling into an overstuffed chair, Marlene dialed. It was later in Boston, but hopefully her mother would be available to talk. Fond memories of her family warmed her heart. Her mother Cynthia had married her childhood sweetheart, Dean Parks. Had tragedy not occurred, they'd probably still be together.

It was sad to think about. When her father was only in his mid-twenties he'd been killed in the line of duty. Even as a child, Marlene was acutely aware of how devastated her mother had been. And her own childhood loss had been nearly too heavy a burden to bear.

Losing her father when she'd been so young had its effect. Marlene didn't think she was capable of moving past the loss entirely. Her father had meant so much to her. A father's love couldn't be replaced, and it was a loss she felt deeply.

Dean Parks had been her mother's true love, so she hadn't remarried for quite a while. Marlene had wondered if she would, but then she married an attorney in Boston. Unfortunately, he had passed away several years ago from a sudden heart attack.

As if fate hadn't doled out enough heartache, her brother Andrew had then been killed in Iraq. Time hadn't healed that wound, but then, it had been just over a year. Marlene had adored her brother, and his death had hit her hard. He would have been twenty-eight now, just a year older than she was.

She was close to her mother, and it was just the two of them now. The phone rang a few times before Cynthia picked up. "Marlene, I'm so relieved to hear from you."

"I'm so sorry to worry you, Mom. Everything has been happening so fast. I should have called sooner."

"That's okay, honey. I feel better hearing your voice. Are you okay?"

"Yes, I haven't been hurt, although it is frightening."

"I can only imagine," her mother said. "Have they figured out yet who shot at you?"

"Not yet. The police are working on it, and I have a new bodyguard team, too. It's only a matter of time."

"I saw the pictures. It looked like some guy shielded you with his body. He's a hero, as far as I'm concerned."

Marlene thought so too. "Yes, well, he's my bodyguard now, and you'll be pleased to know that he was a SEAL."

"You can't ask for a better-trained man."

Marlene dreaded telling her mother that there had been another attack. But it would be worse if she saw it in the news, if she hadn't already. As calmly as possible, she told her mother what had happened at the restaurant. There was no way to make it seem unimportant, but she made an effort not to sound overly alarmed.

"That is bad. This has to stop." In a softer voice, her mother said, "I've lost Andrew...I can't lose you too."

For a moment, neither spoke. Marlene's heart ached. Then her mother took a breath. "What are the police doing about all of this?"

"I'm sure they're doing all they can." Although Marlene wasn't sure at all. Even though she was a big star, it didn't mean her case was their sole interest. But she did hope that it got proper attention. The media was all over this story. The police would be under pressure to get it resolved.

"I need to get back on the set," Marlene said. "I

promise to keep you informed. And don't worry too much. I'm in good hands."

"I'm so glad you called, honey. I'm on my way out too. I love you so much."

"I love you too, Mom." At the moment, Marlene was relieved that her mother lived so far away. She was out of harm's way. And she had so many friends in Boston. After Andrew had died, Marlene had tried to get her mother to move to California so they could live closer. But that hadn't happened, which was for the best. Marlene's lifestyle was a challenge, so her mother was better off removed from the drama.

Garrett hadn't wanted to leave Marlene, but he had business to attend to. He took a cab to downtown Los Angeles, since public transit would have taken too long. It was important to get back as soon as possible, although she was in capable hands while he was away.

Even then Garrett wouldn't have left her side unless he'd had to. There was no time to waste in getting a grip on this situation before another incident occurred. He entered the office building and took the elevator to the fifth floor.

Tessa greeted him. She was attractive and well dressed. Her tone was all business. "Travis is waiting for you. Go right in."

Garrett hardly slowed as he passed her. Tessa Pate had been with Stealth since she'd graduated college, not long after the company had been founded. It took a lot to impress her boss, but Travis had assured Garrett the woman had more training than met the eye. That could only mean that she could handle herself in the field if needed, because her typing skills wouldn't have gleaned such admiration from the SEALs she worked with—a team she was dedicated to.

Travis sat behind his desk studying some reports. When Garrett strode in and sat in the chair across from him, he looked up. "So what's next, Flynn? I have to say you've got one determined asshole after you."

"Tell me about it. Plus he's a show-off. I mean, shooting out a chandelier? That's like flaunting the fact that he's a firearms fanatic. He's waving a flag, saying, 'Look what I can do.'"

Travis leaned back in his chair. He was one tough-looking guy; even Garrett thought so. Mid-forties, he was built hard as a rock, with broad shoulders and a barrel chest. Sporting a neatly trimmed beard, short-cropped hair, and a silver earring in his left ear, he looked menacing. But only to the wrong sort.

To his team, he was as loyal and caring as they came. Garrett had gotten to know him since he'd been hired, and he thought a lot of him. After eighteen years of service, Travis had come home when his wife had twins. It seemed that for the first seven years of marriage, she'd been unable to conceive, and they'd considered adopting. Then she'd gotten pregnant.

Garrett glanced at the photo at the far end of the wide desk. It was of Travis's wife Melanie with the twins. The girls were ten years old now, and as pretty as their mother. Travis adored his family and made no secret of it. "How are the girls?"

"Very good. They're into gymnastics now. It's always some new thing." Travis leaned on the desk. "Go ahead and hustle down to Rip's office. He has some stuff you've been waiting for."

Garrett left his boss and walked down the long hallway. Rip had a reputation for thoroughness. Not much got past him. It was his job to analyze and evaluate the risk associated with a client the company was assigned to protect. Then he'd determine appropriate ways to eliminate or control the hazard. But what he did was so much more than that.

At a company like Stealth Security, the norm wasn't nearly good enough. Celebrities and other important persons hired the team when the usual routes failed. So it was expected they'd go above and beyond. Garrett entered the room, taking stock of his teammate.

Rip didn't work in the field now, or not very often. Thus, he dressed as he pleased, flaunting his rebel personality. He wore his dark hair tied back in a ponytail and a silver chain around his neck. A leather jacket had been carelessly tossed into a nearby chair. The dark shadow on his jaw gave away that he'd been working nonstop, as was his habit.

"Flynn. Sit. You'll want to take a look at this."

"Let me see what you've got." Garrett took his time going over the documents. Photos and aerial views were included. First was the estate threat assessment. The focus was on the details, because if the little things were right, the big ones tended to fall into line by default. Rip didn't do some half-assed job, brushing it off in a couple of hours. He dug down to the level required.

Garrett studied the report. It addressed issues such as perimeter control, high-speed avenues of approach, observation points, and alarm systems. And that was only the beginning. As he read, he narrated, not really expecting a reply. "And with the team on site, her home is fairly secure."

To minimize risk, anyone with access to Marlene had been vetted. The motto was: trust but verify. It was good to see that her staff checked out. Then there were all those she worked with, and the list went on. There were even details about her mother, and background about her brother Andrew.

Garrett shifted uncomfortably in his seat. Guilt carved into his gut, razor sharp. But this was not the time to dwell on what had happened to Andrew Parks.

Social media was a problem. The two incidents, one right after the other, had things in an uproar. Rip had taken steps to suppress what he could, such things as public use of photographs, including those of Garrett's backside on the red carpet. But there was only so much he could do.

"What about connections? Is there anyone who would want to harm her?"

Rip rolled his chair back from the desk and furrowed his brow. "There have been stalkers, death threats. Marlene Parks is a celebrity, so that's to be expected. But there doesn't seem to be a connection to what's happening now. Not that I could find...yet."

Garrett slapped the thick binder onto the desk. "There has to be something."

"Too bad we didn't get the gun along with the bullet. Then we could track this guy down," Rip said. "Any idiot walking the streets with tungsten bullets in his gun is a menace."

"And he's trigger happy."

"He wants to show you what he's got."

"I'm not impressed with some guy wielding a gun at a woman. That's the lowest..."

"Yeah, I agree." Rip drummed his fingers on the desk. "My next step is to look into the fundraisers. All the charity functions that Marlene organizes, and personally attends, put her at risk. It's an avenue to get to her, and one that's not as easily screened as her domestic staff. I'm looking into those connections...see what I can find."

"She's a high-profile personality. Yet even after being attacked, she refuses to temporarily stay home." Garrett frowned. "I don't like it."

"Have you been to see Coop?"

Garrett shook his head. Cooper Brennan, Coop to the team, was ex-Navy like the rest of them. He was the computer specialist, and most likely a pro hacker, although he hadn't openly admitted it. But the data he got his hands on couldn't be explained any other way.

"I stopped here first."

"He's got a secure phone for you to take to Marlene. Only one way that guy knew where you were dining last night. He hacked into her phone, probably into a text she sent. I know he didn't get into your phone," Rip said. "So that's how Coop figures he knew...unless you told him." He gave Garrett a fake smile.

"Right. I thought I'd make friends so I invited the creep to dinner." Garrett let out a long breath. "Okay, I'll head down the hall to see if Coop's got anything solid for me. Otherwise, get back to me on those connections. It's damn little to go on, only knowing the guy's first initial, and a description that fits half the men in the city." *Except for those ice-blue eyes.*

Coop was a computer geek turned Navy SEAL, now ex-SEAL. He was a genius when it came to the techie stuff that baffled Garrett. And he'd been no slouch out in the field, from what Garrett had heard. But he didn't have a lot to go on just yet. Although he knew more than Garrett could have imagined, from Marlene's computer and phone, as well as those close to her. There was no privacy anymore. Secrets were a thing of the past.

Except for the dark secret that haunted Garrett's every waking hour. At some point, he was going to have to tell Marlene what had happened in that battle. And he would have to confess his failure. But not yet. She had enough going on, and more than enough pressure to deal with. Unburdening his soul would have to wait.

CHAPTER NINE

For the next few days, Marlene was immersed in filming. It would be easy for viewers to think it was all mocked up, that when acting the scenes she was playing a role; it wasn't real. But it wasn't that straightforward. Her method of bringing the story to life was to get into character, become the character for that brief period. In doing so, she felt every heartbreak and joy that the woman she portrayed did.

The movie was filled with the love of friends and family, along with a romantic interest, but it wasn't a lighthearted story. The war scenes and reactions to the personal losses that resulted from battle were difficult to play. The emotion paralleled Marlene's own experiences. Thus, she could create the character's feelings realistically, but not without it taking an emotional toll on her.

During breaks, it cheered her to see Garrett. His familiar presence was reassuring. Just noticing him watch all that transpired, Marlene didn't feel quite so alone. He appeared stoic, standing there without smiling or chatting with the others. Yet he exuded warmth that wrapped her in a sense of security.

Marlene looked forward to dinner with him in the evenings. After the one meal out, she acquiesced to staying home in the interest of safety. Laura cooked gourmet meals, so the food was as good as anyplace they'd go. Dining alone was intimate, and that couldn't be avoided. Nor did she want to.

Garrett did little to encourage her, but Marlene was falling for him. She cautioned herself that it was a reaction to being alone too much. And maybe it was. The public was given the impression that, as a movie star, she led a charmed life.

And in many respects, Marlene supposed that was true. But men were a challenge. Too often a man wanted to be with her for her fame or fortune—even those that had plenty of both already. It had been a crushing blow, after opening her heart a few times, when Marlene had realized that she was little more than a possession.

It boosted a man's ego to have her on his arm, show her off, and to be seen in the entertainment magazines with her. Speculation did much for careers, pushing a star into the public eye. It was easy to perceive more than was there, to conjure romance where none may exist.

Too many times, articles claimed she was seeing a man in secrecy, that she was engaged, and even that she had marriage plans. All were falsehoods, and were hurtful. Marlene strove to ignore most of it, in order to fend off the effect of such publicity.

That wouldn't have been so bad if there had been love involved. But each relationship turned out to be one-sided. While Marlene wanted to get to know a man she dated, it was demeaning to realize that not one of them actually knew her or cared to. Rarely did they know anything about her that truly mattered.

And Marlene began to think that anyone outside her circle of friends, any man she might really connect with, would be too intimidated to call her or ask for a date. So her fame was a double-edged sword. She didn't want a love affair based on superficialities, but she scared away any authentic relationship before it got started.

Garrett was in a category all his own. He was in her employ, and she wasn't dating him. The usual stigmas didn't apply. There were no social pressures or expectations. So as the days went by, a relationship of sorts developed.

Marlene was able to talk about personal issues without having to put on a show. After all, Garrett was with her due to her most pressing issue, the precarious situation that had been thrust upon her. And from all the background checks and security assessments, she was certain he knew a lot about her.

Although she could hide her emotional pain from her fans, she couldn't keep it from Garrett. Whether by training or instinct, he was a perceptive man. When he looked at her, Marlene sensed that he saw beyond what she showed to the rest of the world.

Having Garrett with her did much to alleviate the loneliness, but she dared not depend on him overly much. His presence in her life was temporary, yet she already dreaded him leaving. It was foolish, really. But feelings of the heart weren't easily subdued.

On Saturday, the studio shut down and Marlene had the day off. She didn't want to stay at home, and preferred to do something enjoyable, like going on a date. But with Garrett along that would be awkward.

Since she didn't have to be on the set early, Marlene took the luxury of sleeping in. After eating a leisurely breakfast, she found Garrett in the study scrolling through his phone. His hair was slightly messed up, as if he'd raked his hand through it. He wore jeans that hugged his lean thighs, and a cotton shirt with tight sleeves that strained against his biceps.

One glance at his strong jaw with a bit of scruff on it sent heat spreading low in her belly. Marlene's imagination began to run wild, so she looked away.

"Good morning," Garrett said. "I thought I'd let you eat in peace. I got up early and jogged on your treadmill. That's quite a workout room you have. I've been making use of it."

The way Garrett spoke, he might have been a friend, not a hired protector. It was nice when threats weren't hovering, and his guard was down. He was a man, like any other—even if he was a force to be reckoned with, and sexy as hell. Home was the safest place to be, he'd told her, so it was likely the one environment where he could relax some.

Marlene sat on the edge of the sofa, across from him. "It's my day off. I don't want to be cooped up all day. I want to go out, and do something. But..."

Garrett raised his brows.

"Danger aside, I could make a call, go on a date, I suppose." Marlene hesitated. "But it would mean that you'd tag along."

Garrett frowned.

"I didn't mean it exactly like it sounded." Marlene fidgeted with the hem of her top. "The thing is that I'm not really dating anyone. It's frustrating, really."

"Not having a boyfriend?"

"Not so much that. I'm used to it. I hire escorts for events when I need to." Marlene sighed. "But just for once, I'd like to go out to the movies like a normal person. I star in movies, but I can't watch them. Except in private theaters, and that's not the same thing."

"Why can't you go out?"

Garrett really didn't get it. Even following her around day after day, it hadn't really sunk in. He hadn't lived like she had, under a microscope with eyes on her every time she went out. "Whatever I do is media-worthy. Anytime I go out in public, I'm recognized. I'm seen everywhere I go."

"You don't have to be."

Marlene laughed. "Yeah, right."

"No, I mean it." Garrett leaned forward with his elbows on his knees. "Clandestine missions are my specialty." His eyes lit up. "You're an actress. We'll do our own version."

"How will we do that?"

"I'll show you." Garrett stood up and reached for her hand. Pulling her up, he said, "If you want to go the movies, then we'll go."

"I can't believe you aren't cautioning me about danger and risk and..."

"No need. There's only danger if you're seen." Garrett grinned. "Stick with me. This will be an adventure."

Garrett was right about that. Every day with him was an adventure, and Marlene had no doubt this would be too. She followed him to her closet, and he walked into it like he owned it. After scanning the rows of dresses and racks of shoes, he said, "Is this all you have?"

Marlene laughed. There he was standing in the middle of a fortune's worth of dresses and designer shoes, acting as though she had nothing to wear. "What was it you had in mind?"

"Don't you have any clothes you wear just to hang around the house? I mean, other than cashmere sweaters and ballet slippers?"

"Hmm, maybe something like this?" Marlene slid open a drawer and pulled out a pair of ratty beige pants and a faded cotton shirt. "My gardening clothes." She shrugged. "It's a hobby."

"That's more like it," Garrett said. "Now you need something to wear over it."

Marlene fished through some shirts hanging on a rod, and found her gardener's jacket. She lifted it up. "It's even color-coordinated...beige."

"You're catching on."

Next Garrett shuffled through her casual shoes and picked out some hiking boots that she'd actually worn enough for them to look used. Then he selected a hat that would shield her eyes from a casual observer. "No makeup," he said. "It's better to look au naturel. Twist your hair up under the hat, and bring sunglasses."

Garrett headed back toward the hallway. "I'll go change. Meet me in the kitchen."

Marlene dressed as instructed, hardly recognizing herself. Then she went to the kitchen and chatted with Laura until Garrett emerged. He wore slacks and a shirt that were baggy enough to cover his muscular build—or sort of, anyway. Over one arm, he had a winter coat, and he held a pair of sunglasses. The ball cap he wore low on his forehead made it more difficult to see his face.

Laura was busy cleaning up from breakfast. She was too professional to question their antics. But Garrett let her in on a secret. "We're playing a game," he said. "As you can see, we're in disguise."

Laura smiled, but didn't comment.

"You can have the rest of the day off," Garrett said, and the cook glanced at Marlene to see if she offered any objection. "We just need to leave with you. When you pull out, we'll be hiding behind the back seat with a blanket over us."

"The gate guard won't see you. He just waves me

through," Laura said.

"I thought so." Garrett gave her a warm smile. "So, are you just about ready?"

Laura finished up, then they went to her car and took their positions. There was no problem getting away without being seen. "Drive to the mall and go up a crowded aisle in the parking lot. Then you can stop and let us out."

It wasn't far, and when Laura stopped, they slipped out of the back seat. It was a busy area and no one seemed to pay attention to a blandly dressed couple walking toward the mall entrance.

Garrett pulled his phone out. "I'll let the team know we're fine. We're not hiding from them."

Marlene had left her phone at the mansion. It was the new secure one, but she didn't need it as long as she was with Garrett. It had been a clever ploy. Anyone watching her home would have seen the cook leave, just like she did every day. And would assume that Marlene was still at home.

It was a bit like being a young girl again, and sneaking out to see a boyfriend. There was a certain thrill involved that made Marlene feel more alive.

Garrett stopped beside an outdoor planter. "So, what do you want to see?"

Marlene marveled at his appearance. "You look like a janitor," she said. "And I notice that you're walking differently, with your shoulders kind of slumped."

"It's part of going unnoticed. It's best not to act or move like you normally do. You'd be surprised how many people can be recognized by how they walk." Garrett smiled. "Try it. Pretend you aren't a movie star. You're a regular girl, kind of average, nervous about being on a date with a good-looking guy like me."

Marlene giggled. "You had to add that last part in, didn't you?" She took on the role with ease, and walked along the length of the planter then back. "This is kind of fun. I haven't been cast as a plain Jane before. I rather like it."

"I'll see what's showing." Garrett scrolled on his phone and listed off movie choices.

After some deliberation, they decided on an old Marlene Dietrich film. "That's the thing about LA. It's so big, you can get any type of food, see any movies you want...well, most people can."

"Today, you can too." Garrett took her hand. "We're supposed to look like a couple."

His big hand wrapped around hers, and Marlene's heart beat in a staccato rhythm. She took some shallow breaths to calm down, but it was useless. She was on a date with Garrett. It was a pretend date, but it felt as real as a real date. "How are we going to get there?"

"The bus."

"The bus?"

"Sure. You're not a snob, are you? The bus will get us there in time, and it's better than a cab. Even your most ardent fan wouldn't dream of seeing you on a bus. That's part of our cover. People see what they expect to see. And they don't see what's not believable."

"I'm learning a lot."

Garrett squeezed her hand. "It's not so hard, once you understand how things work."

They made it to the theater in time to see the previews. Marlene was so excited. She was sitting in a dark theater, crowded with people. The padding of the seat was a bit worn, and the interior of the place could use some renovation. She loved it.

Garrett bought her popcorn, Coke, and Milk Duds to go with it. "They still sell these in regular theaters?"

"Sure, what's a movie without Milk Duds?" Garrett whispered in her ear. "You can take off the sunglasses now."

The lights were low, and they'd sat in a crowded area midway back. The audience focused on the previews flashing in front of them. Marlene blushed when she saw her face ten feet high on the big screen, followed by a few scenes from her upcoming movie.

Garrett put his arm around her, but had no reaction to her picture as it loomed large for the audience. He was just another guy at the movies with his girl. Marlene took her clue from him, and didn't say anything—although she sank deeper into the squeaky seat.

Then the main feature started. It was a 1936 romantic drama called *Desire*. A devious French jewel thief, played by Marlene Dietrich, sped off to Spain with stolen pearls, then dropped them into the pocket of Tom Bradley, an American vacationing in Europe—played by Gary Cooper.

It wasn't the only time Marlene had seen the movie, but it was one of her favorites. She ate handfuls of popcorn and sipped her drink. Out of the corner of her eye, she saw Garrett munching on the candy. It was the first time, in longer than she could remember, that she was on a date that had no particular cachet or sophistication. And it was the most fun that she could recall.

The mood was just right. The movie was romantic, as well as delightfully humorous. Garrett's thigh pressed against hers, evaporating any resistance to his charms. Her only regret was that they couldn't make out in the dark theater. But it wasn't truly a date. And Garrett wasn't her boyfriend.

Marlene knew from memory what Garrett's buff physique looked like, dressed in his usual jeans and shirt. So she had no trouble imagining, even though the too-large clothes covered him up. He was just as luscious in his nondescript outfit as he was in his macho casual wear. And he would be even better without any clothes at all. Or so she envisioned.

When the movie ended, they put their sunglasses back on and went out to enjoy the afternoon. Garrett was game for doing silly stuff like playing pinball machines, browsing in a bookstore, and even sitting on a bench, talking about mundane subjects.

Marlene managed to escape her life for one day, and had such a good time. She was glad that Garrett could be her friend, even if that was all he could be. When it began to get dark, they ducked into a local pub. It was crowded enough to get lost in, yet small enough to be off the radar. They sat near the back, with Marlene facing the wall, out of anyone's direct line of vision.

Garrett ordered his usual club soda, and Marlene had a glass of wine. The fare was very average, but the ribs and coleslaw tasted delicious. She wiped at her face with a napkin. It occurred to her that she didn't go out without makeup on, or she hadn't before. Yet she hadn't given it a thought all day. Now she probably had barbecue sauce on her face, as well.

"I must look a fright. I'm surprised you aren't embarrassed to be out with me," Marlene said. "Maybe that's why we're dressed like this, so no one will see you with me." She laughed.

Garrett looked at her, making her heart skip a beat. "You look beautiful." He stared at her. "You are beautiful...inside and out." As if regretting that he'd voiced his thoughts, he glanced down at his plate. "We should go back, before it gets too late."

"I want you to know what today meant to me." Marlene looked into his blue eyes, wanting to touch his handsome face. "I had a really great time."

Garrett hesitated. "I did too." Then he pulled out his phone and told Samuel where to pick them up. They waited inside until the limo pulled up out front. Then Marlene slid into the back seat, with Garrett right behind her.

On the way back, Marlene rested her hand on Garrett's thigh, and he didn't object. She needed the closeness, dreading being alone again, knowing the magic would end once the car pulled into the garage. She didn't look over at Garrett, just enjoyed the moment of intimacy.

When they were inside, Marlene shed the gardening jacket and kicked off the hiking boots. She'd left the hat in the car. Garrett tossed the ball cap on a table, then walked over to her. They stood in front of the fireplace, where a fire burned low. The flickering light was romantic.

Marlene tried to brush aside her feelings, and suppress her craving to be in Garrett's arms. It wasn't really fair. She couldn't be expected to spend an entire day with him and keep her distance. Passion surged inside her, and she barely held back from wrapping her arms around his neck.

Then Garrett reached out and plucked the clip from her hair, letting it fall over her shoulders, making her feel naked, while still fully clothed. He brushed a strand of her hair away from her cheek, and she tingled all over. Marlene looked into his eyes, filled with longing. She trembled like a schoolgirl, and knew in that instant that she couldn't be responsible for her next actions.

Garrett cupped her face in his hand and gazed into her eyes. He whispered, "You are so beautiful." Marlene's pulse raced, and she thought her heart might pound right out of her chest.

In the stillness of the room, Garrett bent toward her and touched his soft lips to hers. She heard a low moan, and realized it was her own voice. When she parted her lips, Garrett dipped his tongue inside her mouth, and deepened the kiss as if he wanted to devour her.

Marlene trembled and her knees gave way. Just in time, Garrett wrapped his arm around her and pulled her against him. He kissed her long and hard, barely taking a breath, and she dug her hands into his hair. All she wanted to do was feel him, touch him all over, have him. To kiss without end.

Garrett tasted so good, sexy and male. He smelled of cologne mingled with sunshine and buttered popcorn. He stroked her back and dug his other hand into her hair, holding her close. He could kiss like no man she'd known. He kissed sweetly yet with such ferocious need. Marlene folded into him, wanting more.

She gasped when Garrett pulled back from the kiss. He wrapped his arms around her, and held her silently. Marlene could feel the beat of his heart, and the heat of his arousal pressed against her. She closed her eyes, savoring the moment, afraid of what was next.

Then Garrett pulled back. He took her hands, and her heart sank. "Marlene..."

What could she say? What possible reason could she offer for giving in, for encouraging Garrett?

Garrett traced his thumb over her lips, then along her jaw. Marlene shuddered with pleasure. "I shouldn't have..." The blue of his eyes was dark, like a turbulent ocean. "You are an amazing woman, and I won't deny that I want you. But you come first...your safety...your future." He looked torn up about it.

Marlene wished she'd met him at a different time, under other circumstances. She knew it was against the rules to have a romantic relationship with her bodyguard. But she really didn't care. Yet Garrett did matter to her, and such an act might put him in a bad light.

"I can't protect you if I let emotion get in the way." Garrett put a little more distance between them. "It's my duty to see that you're safe, and I won't let my own needs or desire interfere." He looked at her again, as if she might say something to make it otherwise. "I'm your bodyguard...I can't be more than that."

Garrett turned and left the room, leaving Marlene alone. Tears filled her eyes and rolled down her cheeks. She should have known better. It wouldn't work out; she had known that from the start. It had all been playacting. The escape to normality had been merely pretend. And now it was over.

CHAPTER TEN

Garrett was a liar. He hadn't given Marlene the real reason he'd left her standing by the fireplace, the truth about why he couldn't allow intimacy between them. He went to his room and locked the door. Then he stripped off his clothes and took a long, cold shower.

The icy spray pricked his skin like tiny needles, until Garrett was freezing. The discomfort was less than he deserved. If only he'd been able to save her brother, but he hadn't. There was no way to wipe away what had been done. Even though he would have given his life to save Andrew's, he hadn't had that option.

His attraction to Marlene was pushing him to the limit. Garrett wanted her, lusted to hold her in his arms and caress her. He'd been smitten long before the day he'd met her. He knew more about her than she was aware of. Andrew had spoken of her, sharing his short lifetime of memories of family, many of his younger sister.

Garrett had felt close to Marlene before she'd known he existed. He'd gone to Hollywood to see her. His purpose had been to make sure she was okay, as he was all too aware of her personal loss. But maybe all along he'd wanted to get to know her better. He just hadn't thought that far ahead.

Then fate interceded and thrust them together. Garrett didn't regret that for a moment, although he wished the circumstances were different. Marlene depended on him now, and he wasn't about to let her down.

Garrett thought of the day they'd spent together, a day he would long cherish. Marlene had been more herself than before. She hadn't needed to put on an act, had shed any role other than the authentic one. During the hours they'd spent together, Garrett had seen the real woman.

And he liked what he saw. Away from all the pressure, safe in a brief window of time, Marlene had experienced joy. Garrett had seen it in her eyes, and he'd felt it. He preferred seeing her happy, and vowed to do all he could to ensure her future happiness.

But that didn't include him as part of her life. It didn't matter that he craved her more than the air he breathed. Nor did it matter that she'd been so willing, that she'd opened her arms to him. There was the matter of Garrett as her hired protector, and the fact that getting emotionally involved was off-limits. But that hadn't been his strongest motivation for calling it off.

Garrett turned the water off, quickly dried, then wrapped a towel around his waist. He stretched out on the bed and stared at the ceiling. The vivid memory of Andrew dying in his arms, of the message he'd trusted Garrett to relay, darkened his thoughts. Guilt riddled him.

The sweet thrill of kissing Marlene promised so much more. Warmth spread through his body, and his arousal surged. But it was not to be. As luscious as she was, and as much as Garrett dreamed of feeling her pressed against him, it wasn't possible.

Any intimacy between them was doomed. And it was Garrett's fault. That very evening, Marlene had melted against him, wanting him as much as he wanted her. She was all Garrett could hope for, everything he wanted in a woman. But she would find out about his failure.

And he was obligated to tell her at the first opportunity. Then Marlene would be repulsed. Her hot kisses would turn ice cold. She wouldn't want anything to do with him. She wouldn't want him near her, and even more certainly, she wouldn't want him as her lover. She'd lost Andrew, and when she learned of Garrett's role, it would be over between them.

It was worse than Garrett had anticipated. In the days that he'd been with Marlene, he'd fallen in love with her—or maybe he had been for a long time, and being close had just confirmed it. Destiny could be cruel. After putting duty first for so long, sacrificing with no regrets, Garrett had expected to live out his days without the happiness that a woman of his own could bring.

Then, in an impossible situation, Marlene had appeared. But Garrett couldn't have her. When she discovered his secret, it would be over. So he'd best not let her hope that there could be more between them. It would only break her heart, as it would surely break his.

After a torturous night, Garrett rose before dawn and went to the fitness room for a hard workout. He managed to get showered and dressed before breakfast. More than likely he'd upset Marlene by his actions, and he needed to be in the dining room to reassure her.

Garrett couldn't allow emotion to destroy the trust he'd built. Marlene needed to know she could rely on him, that the kiss hadn't changed his commitment to her. He had no clear idea about how to convey that, but hoped his presence would be enough.

He'd reconciled his own feelings, and intended to resume his professional role in her life. Until the crisis ended, his duty to Marlene was paramount. When the situation was over, and she was safe, Garrett would leave. But until then, he couldn't release her from his care.

Marlene came to breakfast in white jeans and a cream sweater, looking good enough to eat. If she'd had trouble sleeping, it wasn't apparent. She wore makeup, and had her hair tied back in a velvet ribbon. Garrett's resolve to keep his distance nearly evaporated the instant he saw her.

Garrett tried to read her expression. But he was unable to tell if she was annoyed with him, hurt, or just pissed. The woman was exasperating. She played so many different roles that it was next to impossible to see through them. How was he supposed to tell if she was acting a certain way for effect, or if what he perceived was her honest emotion?

"Good morning," Marlene said, and sat across from him. She held a stack of envelopes in her hand. "I didn't look through the mail yesterday." She put the pile beside her plate.

"About last night..." Garrett had started talking before he had a clue what to say to make things okay.

Marlene looked into his eyes. He didn't sense any anger, although she had every right to be upset with him. Nor did he see any aloofness. If she planned to give him the cold shoulder, it wasn't obvious. "Before you say anything...I understand." She took a breath. "You were right. We got carried away."

Garrett was silent.

"It was a wonderful day, and I want to remember it that way." Marlene paused. "Can we do that?"

"Yes. We can."

Then Marlene turned to the pile of letters and began to flip through them. Garrett was relieved. She could have made things much more difficult. But then, he should have known. That wasn't Marlene's style. She wasn't like that.

The letters skidded over the glass tabletop as she thumbed through them. Then Marlene froze.

Garrett glanced at her mail to see what had her attention. A plain white envelope had a return address written in script. It was the initial B, with no further designation. Marlene's hand trembled when she picked it up.

"Let me." Garrett put the cloth napkin over his fingers and reached for the letter. He didn't think the sender would have left fingerprints, but just in case. He slit the top open with a knife and dumped the contents onto the table.

Marlene gasped. Several photographs tumbled out together, all of a similar nature. Each was a picture of her bed, the one she'd just slept in. But the images were horrifying. With the napkin, Garrett shuffled through them. They were different views of her bed, after it had been violently slashed with a knife, the satin comforter ripped apart with stuffing strewn across the sheets.

The worst part was the blood. Bright red blood was smeared over her pillow and pooled on her sheets, images of horror. Marlene gripped the edge of the table, and stared at the pictures. "That's my bedroom."

"Pictures of it, anyway," Garrett said. "The guy couldn't possibly get into your bedroom. Not a chance. As real as they look, they're absolutely fake."

"It's...terrifying."

"It's meant to be." Garrett turned the pictures over. She didn't need to stare at them.

Marlene looked at him with wide eyes. "Why would he do that?"

"I'm no psychiatrist," Garrett said, "but choosing the bed has to be significant. It's sexual, in the most horrifying, gory way."

"It's disgusting. All the blood. It's a message. He intends to kill me."

Rage reared its head, but Garrett kept his cool. He'd deal with this guy, and make sure the creep regretted his actions. But he didn't want to alarm Marlene any more than she was. "My question is how he got the photos of your bed."

Marlene rubbed her temple. "Those look like pictures that were taken last year. It was for an article about the rich and famous. There were photos of the homes of celebrities, you know, to see how they live. A photographer took hundreds of pictures here."

"That has to be it. He just scanned them off the magazine pages. Then added his own personal touches." Garrett noticed a folded note that had been under the pictures. He opened it and turned it so Marlene could read it too. It said: *It's time to break up your little romance - B*

"Another threat," Marlene said, and looked at Garrett. "He wants you out of the way."

"That's not going to happen." Garrett pushed back from the table, then scooped the note and photos into the linen napkin. "We'll get these to the police."

"I'm glad it's Sunday. I don't think I could face going to the studio after seeing those pictures." Marlene shuddered. "It's creepy. This guy is freaking me out."

"He has to resort to cowardly tactics," Garrett said, royally pissed at a guy who would terrorize a woman in such a fashion. "The guy can't get to you. He has to go through me, and he knows it. If he thinks he can scare me off, he's wrong."

"Well, he's scaring me." Marlene clasped her hands in her lap. "Jesus, what next?"

Garrett managed to get her calmed down, and convinced her to eat breakfast. "We can't let him get to us. That's what he wants. If we react to his displays of insanity, we'll play right into his hand."

The staff had the day off, so Garrett bused the dishes into the kitchen, while Marlene finished her coffee. He had to give her credit: she was holding up pretty well.

He'd just set the plates on the counter when his phone vibrated. It was a text from Rip: I know who your shooter is. Come to my office. And bring Marlene. She'll want to hear this too.

Garrett relayed the message to Marlene. "I'll get my coat," she said. "Samuel is off today. I didn't know I'd be going anywhere."

"I'll have one of the team drive us. That's a good idea anyway, in case we run into trouble."

It didn't take long to get to Stealth, since it was Sunday morning and traffic was lighter than normal. From the underground garage, Garrett used his key card to take the elevator up to the company's floor. Marlene was unusually quiet.

When they entered, the place was silent. It was a day off, so only Rip was there. Garrett guided Marlene down the hallway to his office. His teammate looked about the same: ponytail, scruff on the jaw, silver chain around his neck. But he'd changed shirts. This time it was a white t-shirt.

"Don't you ever go home?" Garrett said.

Rip looked up. "You should be glad I don't."

"Marlene, this is Ripley McConnel, the team's security analyst...and superhero."

Rip chuckled, then stood up and shook hands with Marlene. "Good to meet you. Just call me Rip. Only Garrett gets away with using my given name.

"It's nice to meet you, Rip." Marlene sat in the chair next to Garrett. "I understand that you know who's after me?"

Rip's expression was serious. He straightened a stack of folders on his desk, as if deciding where to start.

"How did you find him?" Garrett said.

"I know *who* he is," Rip said. "I didn't say I *found* him."

Garrett was disappointed, but any information about the attacker would be useful.

"One of Stealth's specialties is cyber threats. And we have real-time monitoring."

Garrett knew that Rip was prefacing with that for Marlene's benefit.

"You'll have to translate all that into layman's terms," Marlene said. "I'm afraid that technology isn't my thing."

Rip leaned back in his chair and swiveled side to side. "Let's just say that we hacked the hacker." He looked smug, and it sounded like he had reason to be.

"When he tapped into Marlene's phone?"

"No, even better." Rip's thin lips stretched into a smile. "Humans are not infallible. And our man's blunder cost him his anonymity. The guy got sloppy. He used a method called phishing, which is simply a tactic to gain sensitive information by masquerading as a trusted entity. In this case, his interest was in

Marlene. We have our client database locked down. But this guy is smart, if careless, and with lesser security he might have succeeded."

Garrett was anxious to hear the rest.

"I spotted the attempt and Coop dug into it, traced the free email address."

Marlene leaned forward. "You can do that? Find out who's using a free email?"

"Coop, our computer expert, has all sorts of geeky abilities. He ran it all down for me. I'll summarize for you," Rip said. "We traced the email back to the IP address, then to the location of the device, including the computer name."

"And it led to our guy?" Garrett was impressed.

"Not immediately. He was being cagy by using a public computer." Rip narrowed his eyes. "Remember I mentioned his blunder? Well, he'd used that computer before—lots of times, in fact."

"He obviously didn't think ahead," Marlene said.

"He's cocky, thinks he can't be nabbed." Rip continued, "I'll cut to the chase. We cross-referenced other transmissions, names, and so on. We have some pretty sophisticated software." He grinned. "And we hit the jackpot."

"Don't leave me in suspense," Garrett said.

"All information trails lead back to a man named Glenn Buckner. I did a full background on him, and I know his life story, or most of it."

"I'm all ears," Garrett said.

Marlene just listened.

"I'll give you the highlights, because I don't think you care where he went to grade school or his mother's maiden name." Rip recited the information he'd committed to memory. "Buckner is a military wannabe. He has a history of violence and drug addiction, so no branch of the service would take him. He applied, but didn't get far. He has a quick temper and apparently takes things too personally. He's been under psychiatric care at different times, but I didn't need to pry those records loose to find out that he's a psychopath."

"I could have told you that," Marlene said.

"It seems the guy went to work for a PMC—private military contractor," Rip said, looking at Marlene. "Their records are accessible, if you know the right people. Buckner is handy with computers, so the company hired him as a technician. He was overseas in some small corner of the world, working the desk for them."

Rip rocked in his chair as he spoke. "But he couldn't control his temper...beat the shit out of a coworker and got fired. He'd falsified his records to make it past the screening process for new hires. But afterwards, the truth came out.

"The contractor's records show that they uncovered his history after he got in trouble with them. They wanted to make sure he didn't pose any further risk once they'd relieved him of his duties. They learned that he'd exhibited a particular pattern of behavior beginning in his youth. Let's just say that the man is textbook crazy." Rip paused to let that sink in.

"The dude's been diagnosed, but I'll skip the technical words for what's wrong with him. He has an overinflated ego, delusions that defy all logic...but are reality in his world. He claims to have been a soldier, even brags about it, when documentation shows that he was *rejected*." Rip took a breath. "Which might have been a tipping point for him."

"I need to know where Buckner is, then, so I can

put a stop to this," Garrett said.

"That's the thing. He's good at falsifying his background, has used more than one alias. That's what we're working on now, tracking him down. I'm sure he's using a false name, staying off the grid."

Garrett let out a breath. "Well, he can't be far." He told Rip about the disturbing photos and the threatening note that had arrived in the mail.

"He's likely getting desperate," Rip said.

"Then let's hope he makes another mistake," Garrett said. "I need to take this guy out before he decides to get brave. He seems to be staying in the shadows, but if something pushes him over the edge...who knows."

Garrett and Marlene left Rip to get back to work. He gave no indication of taking the day off. Once they were on the way home, Marlene looked over at Garrett. "Do you think we'll be able to find him before anything...happens?"

"We'll find him," Garrett said. "And when we do, I'll handle him, for good." He looked into her green eyes, wanting more than anything to keep her away from danger. There was no way in hell he was going to allow this crazy asshole to hurt Marlene.

CHAPTER ELEVEN

The next week Marlene went back to filming, as she refused to let the trauma of her personal life affect her career. She saw Anna and pulled her aside to tell her the latest about the shooter. It was better to update her friend in person than over the phone, although it still seemed every bit as alarming.

Anna listened without interrupting, but Marlene could tell from her expression how amazed she was. Insight into the mental instability of the guy who'd been pursuing her was enough to share. Marlene skipped telling her about the awful pictures, not knowing quite how to convey it without terrorizing Anna. She didn't need to know about that. Maybe after it was all over, she'd tell her.

"So it's progress," Marlene said. "At least I know who the guy is. But until he's stopped, I'm at risk. It will end—soon, I hope. Garrett is with me, and his team is working on finding the creep."

Anna rubbed her hand over her eyes. "Oh my God, Marlene. Knowing how crazy this guy is doesn't make me feel better at all. Garrett better not take his eyes off you for a second."

"He doesn't leave me by myself. I'm protected at all times." Marlene spoke the words, but doubt crept in. A man as insane as Glenn Buckner posed great danger. She didn't need Garrett to tell her that. He might attack and they wouldn't see it coming, so there were no guarantees.

Anna stared at her. "Why you? What does this guy want?"

"I've thought about that...a lot. I just don't know. There must be some connection, a reason he picked me. But I haven't a clue."

"Maybe he's just a nut case. Most stalkers are. He latched on to you after seeing your pictures, or watching your movies. That's what happens when you're a big star."

"That could be..."

"You don't think so, do you?"

Marlene shook her head. "It's the whole deal about him being an ex-military imposter. It's connected to the service in some way. From what Rip said, the guy lives in a world of delusion. I think that he *believes* that he was a soldier. And he's handy with firearms. He's shot at me twice."

"But you're a spokesperson for the support of veterans. Look at all your charity work. This guy has it all wrong."

"I didn't say it was rational," Marlene said, "just that he's a military reject. Wouldn't you think he'd be vindictive, that he'd want retribution for the injustice—at least, what he perceives as an injustice."

"It makes sense that he'd hold a grudge against Garrett then, because he was a SEAL. Maybe he hates military guys. That could be it. I can see him feeling that way, not that I'm into psychoanalyzing."

"Even Garrett thought of that a while ago. But that doesn't explain how I'm involved. As you said, what does he want with me?"

Anna shivered. "All I can say is the guy gives me the creeps."

"Yeah, same here."

Before going to makeup, Marlene texted her mother to let her know that she was fine. She didn't mention the upsetting photos, or even that she had more information about her attacker. There was no reason to add to her mother's concern about her. Instead she wrote: *Garrett and his team are working hard to get this situation handled. Please don't worry. Love you.*

During filming, Marlene wrestled with internal conflict about the movie. The stress of having a crazy guy trying to kill her, along with her bodyguard, was a definite distraction. She had trouble blocking images of the disturbing photos from her mind. She was playing the role of a woman who had suffered great personal loss due to war. Yet at any moment, Marlene's life could senselessly come to an end at the hand of a maniac.

But wasn't war just as senseless? Marlene had to suppress her true feelings and pretend. She had to stay in character, portray a woman who was heroic. The character supported the war effort, and despite personal losses, was convinced it was all worthwhile.

A seed of resentment crept into Marlene's consciousness, and she sought to deny it. She had to pretend that she felt as her character did, and put aside her true feelings. But was the result authentic? Was it reality? Women and family members of those killed in war must feel as she did...abandoned. It was difficult not to resent it, and to cling to the patriotism that was expected.

In the scenes, Marlene pretended that she felt what the script called for, but she began to struggle with the emotion of it. She couldn't let her personal feelings show, so the way she played the role had become increasingly false to her. And it was so like her real life, always pretending. Even with Garrett, the man she cared for more than she was willing to admit, she had to fake it. Marlene had to pretend she felt otherwise. And it struck her that maybe her entire life was no more than pretense.

The week went by without further incident, but Garrett was on his guard. He was prepared for an attack, knowing that Buckner wasn't about to quit.

Marlene focused on work, and that was good. It kept her from dwelling on any potential doom. Then at the end of the week, she had a fundraiser to attend.

It was on Friday night, and her event manager Alan had been organizing for months. Garrett learned that such occasions required extensive preparation. There was going to be quite a turnout, and Stealth Security had obtained the attendee list, in order to go over it in advance. Backgrounds were done on every guest, no matter their status.

Garrett dreaded the evening for another reason entirely. Marlene had insisted that he wear an Armani suit. So she'd arranged for a tailor to make any adjustments, including allowing room for his covert vest to fit discreetly under the dress shirt. "The press will be there," she'd said. "You'll be next to me, and need to look the part. I'm sorry, but this is my life. You're a part of it now, whether you like it or not. Appearance is very important."

Garrett could have lived with wearing a designer suit, but it was the press he didn't like. He was inclined to stick to the fringes and stay out of sight. The thought of having his face plastered all over the media disgusted him. But he had no choice. It was vital that he stay by Marlene's side, especially at a public event. So he'd just have to suck it up.

The event was in one of the large meeting rooms at the Montage in Beverly Hills. Cocktails and socializing were on the agenda, followed by several presentations. Then there would be a formal dinner, and Garrett didn't even want to think about how many thousands of dollars per plate it cost.

That wasn't his concern. Security was his only interest. Plus, the money went to a good cause, so he was all for it. The organization used the funds for the physical, mental, and financial support of former soldiers. They also had programs for the family members, such as those that had become the full-time supporters or caregivers.

The limo had been waxed and shined until it glowed. Samuel drove them to the hotel, then stayed with the car. Marlene was expected early, since she was the main sponsor. Raymond had already arrived with her event security team, and he greeted them, assuring Marlene that he'd staffed up for the evening. She didn't need to be concerned about any repeat of the disaster at the last event.

In addition to Marlene's security team, the hotel had its own security. And Stealth had a special ops crew hovering. It felt more like a presidential event than a local fundraiser. Still there might be a vulnerability that could be exploited. Garrett had been in too many situations that had nearly unraveled after being thought secure.

Marlene spoke with Alan about a few details of the event, assuring all was in order, then greeted a couple of volunteers she seemed to know well. The guests began to filter in. They drank cocktails and talked in groups. Garrett hadn't seen so many wealthy people in one place before.

Without knowing their names, he could determine their income level. It wasn't only the expensive clothes, it was their demeanor. Their success in life was reflected in their confidence, how they carried themselves and dealt with those around them.

Garrett wasn't the only bodyguard in attendance. Billionaires, corporate execs, sport figures, and others in the entertainment field required their own security. So it was a very crowded affair. Although he tried to stay in the background, Garrett was acutely aware of his surroundings, taking stock of each person and their movements.

He found no reason for alarm, but didn't relax his vigilance. After the cocktail social was over, guests were shown to their seats. Garrett was at a table in front with Marlene, since she was a key speaker. He angled his chair so he could see out into the room. The area had high ceilings with gold chandeliers, and rows of balconies above. They were occupied by security, and Garrett spotted a couple of his team looking down on the proceedings.

After she was announced, Marlene went to the podium. She wore a black satin cocktail dress with a lace overlay. Her long hair was in a fancy upsweep, adorned with diamond-studded pins. And she wore a diamond choker. To say she was stunning would have been an understatement.

Garrett watched her glide to the front of the room, graciously accepting the applause. Without apparent effort, she seemed to own the room, and he was proud of her. Marlene could captivate an audience with just a smile, and when she spoke, every guest was under her spell.

A movie-sized screen hung on the wall behind the podium, and slides changed to provide a visual for points she made during her presentation. Marlene spoke from the heart, and Garrett was appropriately moved.

Marlene addressed the issue of how the funds were administered, and made a point that the charity kept costs low, so the greatest share of each dollar went directly toward the needs of the veterans. The room was silent as she shared her personal story.

Without a plea for pity, Marlene revealed to the crowd that she'd lost her older brother in Iraq, and her father to war before that. She understood the losses of war from a personal perspective. And she told her story to garner greater support for the cause.

At the end, the audience erupted with applause. The lights went up and Marlene opened her arms, as if to embrace the crowd. "Thank you for all you do," she said. "Thank you for caring."

Then Marlene went back to her seat beside Garrett, and he smiled. She beamed at him, her eyes filled with tears. It was nearly too much. She'd spoken of Andrew, even told a couple of anecdotes about growing up together. She exhibited so much pride, such love. Her words had ripped Garrett apart.

The speech had affected another man, though not quite in the same way. Glenn Buckner hung back in the dark, out of sight. Clandestine missions were a talent, and he knew how to go unnoticed. It was important that Flynn not catch sight of him. It had been unfortunate that the bodyguard had gotten a good look at him before, and he couldn't risk being recognized.

His training as a soldier had been thorough. He knew background checks would be done on the guests and the organizers—maybe even the volunteers. Marlene had held other events at this venue over the months, so Glenn had made sure he was employed by the hotel restaurant. But only as part of the temporary crew, for events such as this one.

Of course, once the food service began, he'd disappear. He had no intention of waiting tables. But it didn't matter. This would all be over soon, and Glenn wouldn't need to impersonate a waiter. That had been a new development anyway.

Before Flynn had interceded, things had been fine. Glenn had worked as a volunteer for the veterans' charities. He'd blended in, and no one had taken particular notice of him. It gave him a chance to be with Marlene, but he knew that would no longer be possible. There was too great a risk that Garrett would spot him.

Glenn had heard Marlene tell her story many times, and each time he'd been affected by it. It wasn't right that she'd lost her brother to battle, especially when it could have been avoided. Flynn had fucked it up, just like he was doing now.

If Flynn hadn't meddled, it was likely that Marlene would have already been in Glenn's arms. Her sad tale would have a happy ending once she was with him, and realized the true hero he was. Glenn would be her protector, and she would see the wisdom in that arrangement.

Glenn was mesmerized by Marlene's beauty. She looked especially lovely tonight. She'd captured the attention of her audience, Glenn in particular. He was drawn to her, and knew that she'd feel the same about him once he told her the truth.

The sight of Flynn at the table next to her, watching them smile at each other, pissed him off.

She's not yours, asshole. Glenn's goal loomed large in his mind. It was up to him to save Marlene from her traitorous bodyguard. So it was time to get Flynn out of the way...permanently.

CHAPTER TWELVE

Marlene sat at the table next to Garrett, smiling graciously at the nearby guests, most of whom she knew well. They congratulated her on the presentation, and voiced support for the cause. The look on Garrett's face was one of pride, and that made her feel good.

The room buzzed with activity and the noise of clinking glassware. Now that the lights were up, a team of servers refilled drinks. It was a festive occasion, and the purpose of the dinner made it more so. But an odd feeling crept over Marlene, for no reason that she could explain.

Without being obvious, Marlene scanned the dining room, but found no cause for her untoward feeling. It was probably her imagination, as she couldn't quite forget the last charity event and how disastrously it had turned out. This time Garrett was already beside her, and she was certain he remained alert to the room's activity.

Yet Marlene shuddered when an eerie feeling came over her, as if someone's eyes were on her. She tried to brush it off. This was not the same situation, as the event was indoors, with the number of security likely rivaling the number of guests. No attacker could get to her, and besides, she was just freaking out with no cause.

Garrett leaned toward her. "Are you okay?"

Marlene nodded. "Of course. I'm fine. I was

distracted for a moment, that's all." She was glad that Garrett was beside her, as it gave her more confidence. Often the bodyguard was expected to stand and observe. Yet in a close setting like this one, that would seem odd.

It was better to stay seated and out of the way of the waiters. Marlene had noticed the security guards above on the balconies. Not a soul could enter the room without one of them seeing. It was like being in battle, always watching for the enemy, preparing to defend.

War was on her mind too much. It was a result of filming the movie. After living and breathing war scenes, day after day, the shadows of that desperation clung to her long after she'd left the set. Marlene sipped her wine and engaged in polite conversation. It was okay for her to relax now that the event was winding down.

Out of the corner of her eye, Marlene saw Garrett watching the room. He did so discreetly, but she knew him. The way he held his body, and how he looked onto the proceedings, affirmed that he remained alert. Social event or not, he was on duty, and she knew that he didn't take his role lightly.

The meals were served and the food was delicious, although Marlene wasn't very hungry. It was probably the stress of organizing the function. Her nerves were a bit frazzled, but she was pleased with the results of the evening.

Garrett didn't settle into eating his dinner either. Marlene saw him take bites without taking his eyes off the crowd. It would have seemed like a date, except for the fact that neither of them was really enjoying the occasion.

Yet to anyone who looked at them, Garrett appeared

to be Marlene's escort. He'd dressed the part, and the suit looked pretty damn good. She decided that he should wear them more often, even though she knew he wouldn't agree. When conversation lagged, she was acutely aware of him beside her.

Garrett's suit pants fit in a way that showed off his muscular thighs, and the tailored jacket fit snugly across his shoulders and biceps. Marlene hadn't seen an Armani suit look quite so sexy before. She wanted to put her hand on his thigh, and imagined the hard muscle beneath his pants. But she didn't do so, despite the urge.

Others might guess that Garrett was her man of the moment, but she had no right to make that appear true. All anyone witnessed were two people sitting together for a formal meal. No one had any inkling of what went through her mind—except maybe Garrett.

A couple of times when he looked over at Marlene, she wondered if he knew. Feeling momentarily caught with sexy thoughts, her cheeks warmed. Garrett had agreed to go back to the way things had been between them, and not make a big deal of their one intimate moment. Yet Marlene couldn't forget his hot kiss, and she wanted more.

By the time dessert was served, the noise level had died down, and Marlene heard the music playing through the speakers. Maybe she'd host a dance as a fundraiser. That would be fun, plus more entertaining for all. She'd ask Alan about it.

At the end of the evening, guests began to filter out, some of them coming over to say goodbye to Marlene. But her responsibilities weren't over yet. The paparazzi waited in the lobby for photographs of her as she exited. They were welcome in the hotel, and their coverage would result in good press for the fundraiser.

In the enormous marble lobby, at the foot of a sweeping staircase, Marlene took her position to address the media. Garrett stood beside her, unwilling to leave her in the hands of the mob. And she spotted Raymond and his team tending to crowd control.

Cameras flashed, nearly blinding Marlene, but she made no objection. Calmly, she answered the questions called out to her, and kept a smile on her face. She could feel Garrett tense beside her, and hoped nothing was amiss. He was probably just uncomfortable in the face of so many cameras.

After an acceptable period, Raymond began ushering the press away, and Garrett escorted Marlene to the limo with the aid of one of his team. Once inside, the doors locked and the limo pulled away. She breathed a sigh of relief. "That went well, don't you think?"

Garrett looked over at her in the dim lighting of the back seat, but didn't comment.

"I know you're going to say that I'd be safer at home, that I shouldn't take chances by being in crowds." Marlene waited for him to agree.

"I didn't say that." Garrett leaned against the seat and let out a breath. "You were great out there. It takes courage to be in the public eye like you are."

That surprised her.

"I mean it," Garrett said. "It's not something I'd want to do, but you handle yourself well. I'm not sure I could put up with a gaggle of photographers flashing bulbs in my eyes and firing inane questions at me."

Marlene laughed. "It comes with the territory."

All the excitement should have exhausted her, but

instead Marlene felt energized. On the way home, she was quiet. It was nice just to be next to Garrett, to feel his masculine presence. She didn't need to talk, and he made no effort to.

Once safely at home and inside, Marlene scrolled through her phone. Standing in the foyer under the bright light, she kicked off her high heels and checked for messages. Then she smiled; she couldn't help it. Already, the photos had hit social media, and there were several shots of her with Garrett.

He wasn't going to like that. There was speculation on the nature of their relationship. No one would know that Garrett was merely her bodyguard, especially with him standing beside her in the designer suit. He did look impossibly handsome, and the pictures made her tingle with desire. Her fans would be drooling over him.

The comments had a predictable pattern to them. *Who is Marlene's new heartthrob? Will he star in her next movie? How long has she been seeing him, and is it serious?* She was used to such intrusions on her privacy, but Garrett wasn't.

"What are you looking at?"

Marlene handed the phone to him, and Garrett thumbed through a few of the posts. His jaw tensed, and he frowned. "This isn't good."

Marlene gave him a wide-eyed expression. "Why...do you have a girlfriend that I don't know about?"

"If only that's all it was," Garrett said. "I'd have told you if I had a girlfriend."

That was an admission of sorts. If they had no relationship, Garrett wouldn't feel the need to tell her about his girlfriend situation, whatever it was.

"I've spent a good chunk of my life hiding in the

shadows. I don't need my face plastered all over." Garrett handed back the phone. "At least they don't have a name to go with it."

"They'll get it." Marlene knew how doggedly the press pursued the tiniest tidbit of gossip. "But don't let it worry you. My press agent will kill the rumors quickly."

"It's not rumors that..." Garrett sighed. "Forget about it." He paused. "I should leave you, so you can get some rest."

"No...please...don't go just yet." Marlene smiled. "I'm wide awake." She motioned to him. "We can look at the view. It's one of the reasons I chose this house."

Garrett followed her to a comfortably furnished room, with glass doors out to the terrace. "I guess we can stay inside, since it's so chilly. But isn't it lovely?" Marlene settled into a soft chair and pulled her feet underneath her.

Garrett sat in the chair next to hers and gazed out to the horizon. The sky was an inky blue, but not fully dark. City lights sparkled brightly, and stretched wide across the vista before her. Marlene sensed the nighttime activity below; the city didn't seem to sleep. No matter the time of day, she looked out onto a sea of lights.

Without consciously making an effort, barriers that had kept them apart seemed to crumble as the days went by. Marlene supposed that was bound to happen, since they spent so much time together.

She was glad about it. Garrett had become a part of her life, and she didn't want to envision him leaving. It would happen. She knew that, but she didn't want to think about it. He was with her now, and it felt so right.

Marlene lightly fingered the arm of the chair, and

Garrett's eyes followed her movements. She wanted him to reach out, to take her hand. Yet she knew he wouldn't. The electricity between them was palpable, and she closed her eyes for a moment.

When she opened them, Garrett was looking at her. He still wore the jacket, and she barely resisted the urge to remove it, followed by the shirt. Her fingers twitched as she thought of touching his warm skin under the clothing. How amazing he would feel.

Garrett's blue eyes pierced into her. He had a gruff edge to him that turned her on more. His silky hair had been trimmed, but was still stylishly long, and Marlene craved running her hands through it. Then she realized that Garrett had to be feeling the desire too, the passion that flamed between them.

When Garrett looked at her with a lust-filled expression, Marlene felt weak. She wanted him so badly. She'd settle for one more kiss. Even just that. She eased out of the chair and knelt before him. With her hands on his knees, she looked up at him.

Garrett was strong, silent. Marlene knew he wouldn't make the first move. He'd already made it clear that he couldn't cross the line. Yet that didn't seem to matter. She moved her palms along his thighs and felt him shudder. Her gaze drifted to the bulge between his legs, and seeing his arousal sent heat searing through her belly.

Marlene slipped her palms inside his jacket and flattened them against his shirt. He still wore the vest underneath, and she would have loved to peel it off, so she could kiss his bare chest. Then Garrett cupped her cheek, and their gazes locked.

When he leaned closer, Marlene held her breath. She could feel his heat, smell his musky cologne. Given any shred of encouragement, she would have ripped his clothes off. His mouth was a fraction from hers, and she looked deep into his eyes.

Then Marlene touched her lips to his, and her pulse raced. Her mind blanked. If there was any reason they shouldn't be together, she didn't know what it was. Kissing, first sweetly then deeper, Marlene unraveled. When Garrett pulled back, she whispered, "I know...don't say it."

Marlene braced herself for rejection, but instead, Garrett dug his hand in her hair roughly. He covered her mouth with his, ravenous for her, making her moan with desire. He wasn't gentle about it. She'd started it, and Garrett didn't seem inclined to end it.

With consuming passion, Garrett kissed her long and hard. And when one kiss ended, another began. Marlene wrapped her arms around his neck and drank in his sexy kisses. She wanted so much more, and didn't know how it could possibly end between them. She couldn't get enough of his taste, of his feel. And it seemed he felt the same about her.

Neither made a move to the bedroom, but instead kissed until they were both breathless. Marlene wanted him as she hadn't wanted any man before him. He was singular in his sexuality, in the way he possessed her, pressing hard against her lips.

Kissing was more than she'd had with any man before. Marlene felt close to Garrett, as if they merged into one. He didn't admonish her, just kissed her endlessly as if he might not stop. And she didn't want him too. The touch of his lips was what she craved, and as long as he'd give her delicious kisses, she'd be deliriously happy.

CHAPTER THIRTEEN

Garrett couldn't forget those kisses. That night he'd nearly given in. Marlene had been a temptress, and his earlier resolve had melted at the feel of her hot lips. He wanted her badly, and his self-control had weakened. He'd fallen for her, but that was an admission he couldn't make.

He'd kept kissing, drinking in her sweetness, unwilling to take it further—despite his physical reaction. Even in the heat of passion, he couldn't put aside reality. He'd only hurt her later, when she learned the truth. Marlene wanted him, but that was because she didn't really know him.

Yet the kisses lured Garrett, and he wished circumstances were different. Marlene must have felt it too, or she had reasons of her own for slowing things down. The heat of her lips hadn't cooled, but she'd pulled back and looked into his eyes.

His heart had fallen. It wasn't to be. It couldn't be. But Marlene hadn't left him. She'd sat on his lap and rested her head on his shoulder, with her arms around his neck. And there they'd sat, peacefully looking out into the darkness for hours. It had been so special, an intimacy that Garrett wouldn't soon forget.

Marlene had been as hot for him as he had been for her. But she hadn't pressed, and he was grateful for that—even though releasing her from his embrace had nearly killed him. Garrett had felt an unfamiliar emotion.

In the past, not having a long-term relationship hadn't stopped him from enjoying a woman's company. Garrett had been used to taking, to controlling the situation. With Marlene, he was out of his depth. Just holding her in his arms and spending quiet moments together was more satisfying than he could have imagined.

It was new for him, and he didn't know quite how to deal with it. What concerned Garrett was where it would lead. There was no future for them. And he couldn't see a way around that. He couldn't change who he was, and soon enough she'd know his secrets.

When Garrett thought of what her reaction would be, his gut twisted. He'd lose the woman who meant the most to him. But then, he hadn't really had her anyway. Marlene wasn't his, so it would be best not to take liberties with her. She wasn't like any other woman, and much to his surprise, Garrett realized he couldn't sleep with her purely for carnal pleasure. It had to mean more. *She* meant more.

Later in the evening, Marlene had fallen asleep in his arms. Garrett would have sat in the chair all night, just to hold her, to feel her breathing against his chest. But then she'd stirred and lifted her eyes to meet his. His heart had skipped a beat, and it had taken all his will not to resume kissing her senseless.

Marlene had quietly slipped off his lap then touched her fingertips to his cheek. Garrett had grabbed her wrist and pressed his lips to her palm. She hesitated, then without a word, she'd gone off to bed...alone.

The following week, Marlene's cast and crew went on

location. Scenes of the movie about the First World War had been filmed at several locations, even before Garrett had met Marlene. Recently, the indoor scenes had been filmed on the studio lot. But a couple of key scenes required a more military setting.

The production didn't have to go far to find the environment they needed. Southern California was home to the entertainment industry for a reason. And it wasn't only because of the sunny climate. There were many diverse locations for filming. Fort MacArthur Museum offered what the producers of Marlene's film were looking for.

The Army installation was south of Hollywood, but not unreasonably far. The location included spectacular ocean views and historic military structures. Garrett learned that it was a great place to shoot war scenes, as it had everything from underground bunkers to grassy fields.

Since the location was beyond the boundaries of Marlene's regular routine, Garrett arranged for his friend Wyatt to work security with him. After dealing with protection concerns, they checked out the museum. The place wasn't limited to being typecast as a military facility. They scouted around, and learned that the location had been the setting for such things as a baseball field, a Caribbean island, and even a high-security prison.

But for war films, it was ideal. The military vehicle collection was extensive, and the facility provided genuine period uniforms, non-firing weapons, tents, and other props. Garrett and Wyatt took the opportunity to examine the mobile antiaircraft gun that was going to be used in one of the scenes.

As their first order of business, Garrett and Wyatt had scoped out security. The production company had brought their own security crew, experts in safety at the studio and on location. So during the shooting, the crew would be well protected. And Marlene's risk was further reduced by having Garrett and his teammate nearby.

While Marlene acted in her scenes, Garrett kept a sharp eye on the situation. When the cameras were rolling, he watched while chatting with Wyatt. They'd been on numerous missions together as SEALs, and Garrett trusted him. It was no place to talk about their experiences, but it was good to have a buddy around.

A long day of filming made traveling to Beverly Hills each night unfeasible. For the convenience of the cast and crew, the production company had secured rooms at the Crowne Plaza. At the end of the day, Marlene rode to the hotel in an armored car, with Wyatt in the front beside the driver, and Garrett next to her in the back seat.

Marlene seemed to hold up to the rigorous schedule fairly well. Extended hours of filming weren't new to her, and she didn't complain. Garrett wished he could have put his arm around her and let her rest against his shoulder. But that was pure fantasy.

Filming on location hadn't been kept secret, so word had gotten out. The first night when they pulled up to the hotel, a small group of fans and photographers greeted them. Garrett had no choice but to hustle Marlene inside, shielding her with his body as best he could. Wyatt walked on the other side of her, using his body as an additional barrier.

Cameras flashed in a rapid-fire sequence. Garrett kept his head down, with a hand blocking his face to avoid being photographed. Once they were inside the elevator and the door closed, they were free from the onslaught. Marlene looked over and gave Garrett a tiny smile.

"What?"

"I saw you hiding your face," Marlene said. "Camera shy?"

Garrett wasn't amused. "Are we trying to make the cover of the tabloids...or doing our best to keep you alive?"

Wyatt looked on without comment.

When the elevator opened at their floor, Garrett located the suite. Marlene would have the main room, with Garrett and Wyatt adjacent to her. The connecting door would be left unlocked. Her privacy wouldn't be violated. But if she needed them, they'd have quick access.

Their luggage had been delivered earlier. After freshening up, they ate dinner in the main dining room. The food was welcome, though conversation was minimal. It had been a long day, so Marlene didn't linger. She returned to her room to rest for the evening, in preparation for an early start.

Garrett stretched out on the twin bed, and went over the highlights of the day with Wyatt. Neither of them was aware of any weaknesses in security, but they went over the details anyway. After his teammate dosed off, Garrett stared at the ceiling.

He thought of Marlene just next door, and wondered if she was sleeping. Maybe she was tossing and turning like he was. He hoped not, since she had many days of filming ahead of her. Staying at a nice hotel would have been like a romantic getaway, yet it was anything but that.

Garrett was tense, since the environment was untested. There might be something he hadn't thought of, although he didn't know what that could be. As far as he knew, security was tight, as much as it could be on location. If he'd had any cause for alarm, he would have called Travis and requested more backup. But he didn't see any reason to do that.

Marlene was safe, although he'd feel better if she was in his arms. In a hotel suite, with an unlocked door between them, Garrett could have gone to her. So it was an advantage that Wyatt shared the room with him, as that made his transgression much less likely.

Since the day he'd met Marlene, his will to avoid intimacy had gradually weakened. Garrett loved her, and he wanted to hold her in his arms. She wanted it too; he could tell. And that made it all the more unendurable. Yet he couldn't let personal need cloud his judgment or take precedence over his duty to protect her.

During the week of filming, Garrett's confidence grew. Although guarding Marlene outdoors was more of a challenge, there had been no incidents. When he called Travis, he reported that the situation looked good. He expected to return to Beverly Hills the following evening, and resume the usual routine. Yet even as he assured his boss that all was well, he had a sense that all might not be right.

Garrett had been around long enough to know that things were just too quiet. While Marlene had been on location, absorbed in the film, it was unlikely that her pursuer had been idle. Buckner had been busy, but doing what?

That was what set Garrett's nerves on edge. He almost wished for an attack. At least the enemy would be out in the open, with his moves visible. Then there would be a chance of grabbing him, taking him down. He'd gotten away with too much already. But while off in movie land, there was little that Garrett could do.

He voiced his misgivings to Wyatt. "I was thinking the same thing. That's the sort of thing that spooks me most, when the enemy goes quiet. The dude has not vanished. The question is: what's his next move?"

Garrett didn't have to wait long to find out. After a day of shooting, they returned to the hotel. When his phone vibrated, he thought it was Travis checking on their expected arrival time in Hollywood. He probably needed Wyatt for another job.

But it wasn't his boss. Garrett stared at the text on his screen, and was royally pissed. "Shit," he said, "look at this." Wyatt took the phone and read the message out loud: "*I warned you. You can't have her. Marlene is mine. I'm done waiting. Your time is up, Flynn.*"

Wyatt said, "Buckner?"

"Damn straight. The question is..."

Wyatt already knew. "How did the guy send you a text? That's a secure phone."

"It *was* a secure phone. Not anymore." Garrett didn't like any man getting past security he'd set up. It was damned annoying. But that wasn't all.

Wyatt's phone rang, and he answered. "Hey, Davis, what's up?"

Garrett knew the name. Hunter Davis was supervising the crew at Marlene's mansion. He didn't like the sound of this.

"Say that again... Okay. I'll tell Garrett. He won't be pleased." Wyatt ended the call. "More bad news."

"What now?"

"It seems the security system at Marlene's house went down."

"What does that mean, exactly?"

"It means the dude hacked into the electronics and took it over. The system was instantly useless— actually, worse, because your friend Buckner had control."

Garrett didn't question how Wyatt knew it had been Buckner. Who the hell else would it have been?

"What's the status?"

Wyatt tossed his phone on the bed. "Travis was all over that one. He sent a crew out to install a security system that Stealth Security helped develop."

"It should take Buckner a while to figure that one out," Garrett said. "Although if the system got the stamp of approval from Travis, I'm guessing he won't be able to override it."

"Yeah, I'm pretty sure you don't have to worry about any security system Travis installs. I've seen how he works. He creates failsafe systems. Buckner has just made it harder for himself."

"Let's hope so." Garrett was still stuck on the fact that security had been breached, not once but twice. Not a good sign. He looked at Wyatt. "I don't get it, though. Marlene's security system cost a chunk of change. It was state of the art." He let out a long sigh. "Yet Buckner got right through it. How in the hell did he do that?"

Wyatt offered no reply.

"Next you'll be telling me that the asshole took out our team." Garrett's blood boiled. He didn't like what was happening. It was too dangerous. What else did Buckner have in his arsenal?

Garrett decided that with the new security system in place, the safest place for Marlene was still at her mansion. The perimeter was guarded by a well-trained crew, hired by Travis. He dared Buckner to get past them. And if he did, then Garrett would squeeze the life out of him with his bare hands.

It wasn't a pleasant task, but Garrett had to tell Marlene what was going on. He waited until the next evening, when they were in the car headed home. Wyatt had gone ahead with some of the crew, to report in for his next assignment. When they got on the freeway, Marlene leaned her head against the seat to rest for a bit. When she opened her eyes later, Garrett seized the opportunity.

"I don't want to alarm you, but you need to know what your attacker has been up to." Garrett filled her in on the highlights of Buckner's recent breaches of their security, without belaboring the point. She didn't need to know how riled up he was, as that would make her worry more.

"You mean, while I was off filming and thinking everything was okay, this creepy guy gained control of my home security?" Marlene looked as incredulous as Garrett felt. "So he could have gone into my home and...done *anything*."

"I wouldn't say that. You're forgetting that the wall around your residence wasn't only electronically protected, but guarded by my team. I'd like to see Glenn Buckner face off with a bunch of special ops guys." Garrett rather liked that scenario.

"That's true. Just the whole idea that he got past security makes my skin crawl." Marlene shuddered. "He's like a...snake."

"He's a hacker, and a good one from what I can tell. But he'll screw up. Guys like that always do. And we'll get him. He hasn't outsmarted us yet, although he's tried."

"But he got into your phone too. Who knows what else he is capable of?"

Garrett put his hand over Marlene's. "Don't give him too much credit. So far he's trying to scare me away, but he's not sticking his neck out too far. The dude has to know who he's up against."

"But Garrett...he *is* dangerous. His actions show that." Marlene frowned. "Your life is in peril...because of *me*. It's not... I couldn't live with myself if something happened to you."

Garrett squeezed her hand. "My life has been at risk more times than I can count. This guy's antics don't faze me. There isn't a chance in hell I'm moving aside and letting this monster have his way."

Marlene didn't argue, but he could tell that she was still concerned. "It's my life; it's my choice. I haven't been one to cower in the face of danger, and I'm not about to start now. I'll protect you from this asshole...discussion over."

After a few seconds, Marlene smiled. "Still as bossy as ever, aren't you?"

"Some things don't change."

It would be good to be home. He'd had enough of Buckner's shenanigans. Garrett needed to talk to Rip, and put the pressure on to find the guy. But if Rip had the goods on the attacker, he would have called. Now he wouldn't call, since Wyatt had reported the phone security issue.

So Garrett needed to get back and see what was going on. But when the car rolled past the gate and up the driveway at Marlene's place, something was off. The crew guarding her place had rotated shifts every day, but it wasn't the same crew.

Garrett noticed new guys at the wall. He knew them from Stealth, or had seen them. But they hadn't worked this job before. Alarm bells went off. When the car pulled into the garage, Garrett got out and spoke to Hunter Davis, who was in charge.

"What's with the change of team?" Garrett wasn't sure he wanted to hear the answer. Things hadn't been going so well in the last few hours.

Hunter shrugged. "Yeah, the guys apologize for that."

"For what?"

"They ordered pizza, and it was delivered to the gate. It seems they all got food poisoning, and I have to say, they're pretty damn sick. I was the only one who didn't get violently ill," Hunter said. "I wasn't hungry."

"Goddammit. He might have killed them. If he'd put a bit more of the poison in the food..."

Hunter furrowed his brow. "They ordered from a local place, but I guess with security breached and all..."

"What happened?" Marlene said.

"It looks like Buckner intercepted a takeout call. He hacked the network; probably all the phones, too. And he just happened to have some poison on hand for the right occasion." Garrett dug his hand through his hair. "How in the hell is he doing this?"

Garrett was rattled, but he had to stay focused. The perpetrator was too close. Hell, he probably lived in the damn neighborhood. The dude had gotten away with too much; he posed a serious threat. And he had to be stopped soon. Marlene's own home was no longer safe. Maybe nowhere was safe.

CHAPTER FOURTEEN

Marlene was shaken. She didn't like what had happened one bit. When they went inside, she went to the living room and collapsed on the sofa. Garrett assured her that she was safe. But it was difficult to feel secure when the bad guy was able to find cracks in the armor.

"The new security system was installed before we returned. It has Stealth's approval, which gives me confidence. No matter what that other setup cost, it hadn't been updated frequently enough. Given enough time, crooks eventually figure out how to get past systems. Technology has to be continually modified in order to keep up," Garrett said.

Marlene wrapped her arms around her waist. "I feel violated." Tears formed in her eyes. "And if this guy nearly killed your crew, then he could kill you just as easily."

"It was food poisoning. Once they flush out the toxins, the guys will be okay." Garrett sat across from her and leaned forward. "You are the one I care about. And the unpredictable situation poses a threat."

Marlene waited, knowing what was coming.

"You shouldn't be as visible as you are. I know...I've said it before. But you'd be better off staying out of sight until I get my hands on this guy. I can hide you in a safe house where no one can get their hands on you."

"I can't do that." Marlene sighed. "My career is my life. This movie means a lot to me. The subject matter is—"

"Just a few days," Garrett said. "The team is all over this. We'll find Buckner. Then you can resume your normal routine."

Marlene shook her head. "The cast depends on me. I can't sacrifice the film because of a personal matter."

"It's your life we're talking about."

"I get that. I do." Marlene rubbed her hands over her face. "But it's not my style to hide. Too much is at stake." She wasn't sure that she was getting through to Garrett. "Would you run from danger? Let a psycho ruin all you've worked for?"

Garrett looked at her, unflinching.

"You aren't answering because you know you wouldn't run. There's not a chance you'd let anyone intimidate you."

"Of course not, but we're not talking about me."

"It doesn't make a difference whether it's you or me running away, it's still cowering in the face of danger." Marlene looked into his eyes, trying to read him. Garrett wasn't backing down. "I refuse to give in to his threats." She paused. "That's why I have you...and Stealth. I have faith that you won't let anything bad happen to me."

Garrett let out a deep sigh. "You are so infuriating. How can I protect you if you won't listen?"

"I listen," Marlene said, "but I just happen to disagree. As you said earlier: it's your life, so it's your choice. It's the same for me."

"I can't keep you hostage. All I can do is recommend what I think is best."

"And I appreciate that. I'm aware that I'm taking a risk. But some risks are worth taking."

Marlene could tell that Garrett still didn't like it, but he didn't continue to argue. She was exhausted from a long week and the strain of the situation. "I'm going to get some sleep," she said, and left Garrett to wrestle with how to keep her from harm.

She went to her bedroom and locked the door behind her, needing privacy. A lot had changed. Not much of her life was the same as it had been just a few short weeks before. After a warm shower, she settled into bed, knowing that sleep wouldn't come easily.

What Marlene really wanted was for Garrett to hold her. She'd give anything to be in his arms, and to be assured that it was all going to be okay. By continuing to be her bodyguard, he put his life on the line every day. Yet she was glad he was around, near enough to reach out to.

In some ways, it seemed as though Marlene's life was falling apart. She had some maniac trying to kill her, or, just as bad, trying to kill Garrett. There was no corner where she felt truly safe. It appeared the man who pursued her was capable of more than anyone had anticipated. She wasn't sure where that would lead.

Plus, Marlene had fallen hard for Garrett. He had a way of kissing that made her want him unbearably. Yet she'd exhibited more restraint than she'd thought possible. That night she'd sat on his lap, gazing out at the stars, his heart had softened.

She'd known it, but still held back. In the back of her mind, a familiar thought nagged at her. She'd vowed that she wouldn't have a serious relationship with a military man. But he wasn't in the military anymore. Yet did that make any difference? Garrett's job was fraught with danger, and he could get killed— if not today, then some other day.

Could Marlene live that way—always wondering, worrying? She might open her heart only to have her worst fear realized. It was something that she wasn't certain she could deal with. So she wavered, and her life hung in the balance. It was Garrett's commitment to shield her from harm that prevented *him* from making the move. But she hadn't tried to talk him out of it.

As if all that wasn't enough, Marlene had issues with her part in the movie. Filming in the midst of a military setting had magnified her inner torment. She abhorred war and the horrors left in its wake. Even during filming, she'd harbored doubts about her portrayal of the character. The urge to escape from the sense of emotional loss was strong.

Marlene thought of her brother Andrew, how young and virile he'd been. He had been so proud to be a marine, and hadn't balked, no matter what had been asked of him. And it had cost him his life. She loved him, and wouldn't stop loving him. The burden of the loss was heavy in her heart, making her wonder if his sacrifice had been worth it. Yet she kept that to herself, voicing only her support. But the doubts ate away at her.

Not that far away, Glenn Buckner sat in his dark apartment, gloating over his recent wins in the battle for Marlene. He'd shown Flynn who was really in control. The traitor would get the idea, if he hadn't already. There was no way to beat a competent soldier like Glenn.

He'd taken pains to hone his skills. A situation didn't always require brute force, although if it came to that, Glenn was top notch with his guns. In the modern world, no matter the battle site, it was technology that often made the difference.

When he'd been a boy, others had teased him, and called him a geek or a nerd. But that didn't bother Glenn anymore. He knew they'd only been jealous. It was to his credit that he was talented in that way. It had come naturally, then he'd seen the value and perfected his ability.

Hacking into the outdated security system hadn't been much of a problem. It surprised him how much companies charged for inferior equipment. He could design something better. Shaking his head, Glenn let out a huff. He scoffed at such incompetence.

The phones had proved to be more difficult to get into. Stealth Security had installed software to make sure no intruder accessed them, yet it was patterned after the type the military used. Most barriers could be overcome, given enough time and motivation. And since Glenn had familiarity with the military's security software, it hadn't been that much of a challenge. Of course, they'd just replace the phone security with something harder to crack.

That was beside the point. The issue was that Glenn had succeeded in demonstrating that he could get what he wanted, proving that he wouldn't fail in his mission.

The vulnerability of Stealth's crew had been the icing on the cake. They hadn't seen it coming. Glenn laughed, the shrill sound echoing against the walls of the room. The fortress that Flynn had created around Marlene wasn't impenetrable after all.

Earlier that day, while Marlene's excuse for a bodyguard had still considered she was safe, Glenn had taken a long ride on his motorcycle. His crotch rocket was solid black, and it was mean looking. Over time, he'd tested it out, and it was fast. The bike was one luxury Glenn allowed himself. It had been a purchase worth saving up for.

While cruising down the streets, he'd been planning and plotting. The quiet ride had taken him through his neighborhood, into Hollywood, then along Mulholland Drive.

It was a route he'd taken many times, so often that he knew the roads like the back of his hand. He could take the curves without blinking. It was good to get out, and to have time to go over the details of his strategy, while the powerful engine hummed underneath him.

Today had been the start of Flynn's downfall. It wouldn't be long before he'd be out of the picture. Left to the leisure of his thoughts, Glenn had no shortage of ideas, but not all were usable. With self-satisfaction, he remembered the Molotov cocktail scene he'd painstakingly worked out.

Glenn's thin lips stretched into something that was almost a smile. But he didn't give in to such frivolities as humor. However, if anything were to give him pleasure, it would be seeing the look on Flynn's face. He could envision it now, real enough to touch.

Racing past on his bike, Glenn had thrown a Molotov cocktail at the ex-SEAL. It was a device of his own making, and he'd done it expertly. The device had burst into flames, catching the bodyguard's clothes on fire. The flaming liquid had doused him well, and the man rolled on the ground to stop the flaming liquid from burning him worse than it had. The added gunpowder had increased the explosive nature of the mixture, resulting in serious harm.

Glenn allowed himself to laugh. He couldn't help it. The scenario was mere folly, a figment of his imagination. Although, it would be a thrill to pull it off, it would be too big of a risk. The throwing range would be an issue, as he'd need to get too close to the target.

The scene played out in Glenn's thoughts, but not in reality. He knew the difference between truth and illusion. He wouldn't forget the enemy using Molotov cocktails in battle. He'd been in the kill zone and had nearly been injured in the skirmish. The enemy, numbering in the hundreds, had thrown the fire bombs, and had even exploded tanks.

That had been a battle to witness. And Glenn had played his part, heroic, strong, invincible. In comparison, setting Flynn's clothes on fire would be child's play. But it wasn't worth bothering with, no matter the delight Glenn would get in watching the horror transpire.

There were better ways, more clever plans. And that was what Glenn worked on, in excruciating detail. His mission was of the utmost importance, and Marlene's future was at stake. He wouldn't fail her.

The following week, Garrett made sure that Marlene got to the studio safely. Daily, he changed the limo's route, and altered the departure time. He had coerced her into wearing a bulletproof vest until she was safely inside the studio.

He kept in touch with Stealth, waiting for updates. Buckner had some pretty slick tricks, and they needed to get a step ahead of him. A secure phone had been delivered to Garrett, and his computer transmissions were encrypted using new code.

But he was uneasy. The one thing Garrett needed was Buckner's location. That was taking some work. Then midweek, Travis called with news. "Come on in," he'd said. "I prefer to tell you in person."

So with Marlene secure on the set, immersed in filming, Garrett took a trip to Stealth. He entered the concrete building and took the elevator up, to find Tessa smiling at her desk. She looked younger than thirty, but she was wise beyond her years. He'd heard a few stories, and knew that in a pinch, she was a woman to have on your side.

"Hey, Tessa."

"Garrett, good to see you. You're looking...healthy."

Garrett laughed. "Nice to hear. Is Travis available?"

"He's on a call. You might want to stop by Cooper's office first, if you have any business with him."

"Will do." Garrett strolled down the hall and bumped into Wyatt. "I thought you were on assignment."

Wyatt shrugged. "It was just a weekend deal, escorting a music bigwig around a bit. He needed some extra protection. Anything new with you?"

"That's what I'm here to find out. Travis called, so he's got something for me."

"I'll let you get to it, then," Wyatt said. "If you need me...I'm here."

Garrett knew the truth of that statement. They'd been on enough missions together that Wyatt's loyalty was not in doubt. "That works both ways," he said, then proceeded to Cooper's office.

The room had lots of equipment, including multiple computers, and some electronic stuff that Garrett couldn't put a name to. But he didn't need to. That was what Cooper was there for. He'd served in a similar capacity when on deployment. The former SEAL had fought with his team, as well as providing technical backup, as only he could.

Garrett looked around at his friend's tools of the trade. "Hey, Coop. You must have been a child prodigy."

"You could say that. I was taking apart the kid's computer my parents got me before I hit grade school." Cooper waved toward a chair. "Take a seat. Make yourself comfortable."

Cooper Brennan was a self-taught computer tech. He'd been building his own machines since high school. And with the Navy's training, he'd become a technical genius. He kept his dark hair short, military style, and dressed neatly—not at all the image of a tech guy. He looked more like a high school heartthrob turned Navy SEAL. Garrett was sure that when he cast his steel-blue eyes on a woman, she didn't turn him away. Although he hadn't found anyone special enough to call his own just yet.

"So this Glenn Buckner is handy with electronics. He's no stranger to computers or networks."

"You would know," Garrett said. "The dude seems able to penetrate security a little too easily for comfort."

Coop smiled. "He has made inroads, but I wouldn't be too concerned. I'm familiar with the security system that Marlene had originally installed. It's a good one, and normally very sound. It took skill to override it, expertise that not many have."

"That doesn't inspire confidence."

"The Stealth system is in place now," Coop said. "I don't see the guy messing with that."

"And the phones?"

"We had security software in there, similar to what the military uses." Coop frowned. "This guy seems to know a lot about the military, considering he didn't make it into the ranks."

"He fancies himself as a soldier."

"Well, he takes it a step further," Coop said. "He's been studying. It took a lot of persistence to crack that security software. He must have a lot of time on his hands. And he's motivated."

"Again, that doesn't make me rest easy."

"The phones are locked down tight now." Coop rocked in his office chair. "The guy was able to get his hands on military coding...somehow. But he won't crack our stuff. Guaranteed."

"What's next, though?" Garrett furrowed his brow. "I need to get my hands on this guy. You're working with Rip to track him down, right?"

"I feel like we're getting close, but it's hard to say. Buckner is a slippery one. He may be mentally unstable, but there's not a thing wrong with his intelligence. He's good at faking backgrounds, cracking codes, hacking into systems. Just when we think we've got him, he morphs into some other identity."

Garrett shook his head. "Just great."

The intercom buzzed, and Travis said, "Are you with Garrett?"

"We were just wrapping up."

"Send him to my office, then."

Coop inclined his head toward the door. "You got the word. I think you'll want to hear what they have to say."

"You already know about it?"

"Yep, I worked with Rip and then did a bit of hack... I mean computer work." Coop grinned. "Let's say it's interesting."

Garrett left, anxious to hear the news. Rip was sitting across the desk from the boss, and they both looked up when he entered. "There you are," Travis said. "Sit down. I'll let Rip tell you."

"Tell me what?" Garrett plopped into the other chair, next to Rip.

"I came across information that gave me pause,"

Rip said. "Then Coop did some of his fancy footwork and we learned something quite relevant about our friend Buckner."

Garrett was riveted. Whatever they'd learned, he needed to know. "I can't wait."

Rip paused, as if considering how to say it. He glanced at Travis, then took a breath. "Remember when I told you Glenn Buckner had worked for a private military contractor?"

"Yeah, and they booted him out."

"Yes, well before that, he shipped out with them. They worked with a Marine platoon, gave them backup on the desk. You know, ran the computers, managed communications...that type of stuff."

Garrett rubbed the back of his neck. "Why is that important?"

"Not all that long ago, Buckner was in Iraq." Rip waited, but when that didn't seem to register with Garrett, he continued. "The PMC that Buckner worked for provided backup to a Marine platoon in Iraq...at the same time that you were in Iraq."

Garrett shuffled the facts in his mind: the battle in Iraq, and Buckner working alongside the Marines.

Rip sat up straighter. "Glenn Buckner was in Iraq, as a civilian employee, at the same damn time you were there. And the company he worked with functioned as technical support for Andrew Parks' unit."

Garrett scrambled to put the pieces together. "So Buckner was there the day Andrew...was killed." It began to make sense. "Buckner probably knew Andrew, and there's no doubt he knew that he didn't survive that battle."

Travis spoke up. "The Marines fought that battle with you and your team. It was a joint effort."

"I wouldn't be surprised if he knew you too, or knew of you," Rip said. "Even though you looked a lot different then, with the longer hair and beard, it doesn't mean he wouldn't recognize you."

For a moment, Garrett didn't say more. As he'd thought all along, this whole fiasco was connected to him. Buckner had known Garrett before that first day at Marlene's event. Had the psycho been following him? Had Garrett unwittingly led him to Marlene?

Garrett felt sick in his gut. This had disaster written all over it.

"What does Buckner want with Marlene? That's what I'd like to know," Travis said.

"That's impossible to say without getting inside the dude's head," Rip said. "Suffice it to say that he lives in a world of delusion...where I'm sure he's the hero."

Travis, Rip, and the rest of the team knew about what had happened in Iraq. Teammates didn't keep secrets from each other. Doing so could be deadly. Garrett hadn't concealed his guilt from them, so they all knew about that battle. But Marlene sure as hell didn't.

Garrett stood up. "This really sucks."

"We're working flat out to nail this guy. We'll find him," Rip said.

"You better do it soon." Garrett headed for the door. "I'm running out of time."

CHAPTER FIFTEEN

*M*arlene saw her brother's face. Light brown hair, innocent green eyes, a bit of scruff on his jaw. She reached out her hand... Andrew. He was in his twenties, still so young, with so much to live for. Her loyal, loving brother. She missed him so much, and reached out to hug him.

But he was gone. Vanished—leaving grief in her heart and her life. Her friend growing up, her older brother, was gone. Marlene couldn't make sense of it. She had to find him, save him. But she couldn't.

She struggled, tried to run, but her legs wouldn't move. She had to get to him in time...or she'd lose him forever. Guns going off. Fire and smoke everywhere. Screams and panic.

Then Marlene was in the hands of a madman. A man she didn't know. He was calm, so normal that it made the hair stand up on the back of her neck. Something was wrong. He shouldn't be there. She had to get away. But she couldn't.

The more she pulled back, the closer he was. His shrill laugh struck terror in her heart. She couldn't get away...couldn't get to Andrew. Suffocating, Marlene looked at the maniac threatening to kill her. She couldn't breathe, couldn't move.

His eyes locked with hers. Vacant eyes...icy...blue. She gazed into his eyes, seeing into his soul. Then he reached for her, and she gasped.

Marlene's eyes flew open. Sweat soaked her sheets.

She sat up, breathing hard, her pulse racing. It had been a dream, only a dream. Her heart pounded in her chest. It had been an awful nightmare. Grief consumed her. She'd seen Andrew, but it hadn't been real. He was gone. And he wouldn't be back. She'd lost him forever.

The images were vivid in her mind, and Marlene was unable to shake off the terror. She was so alone, and lost. The gaping hole in her chest left her in agony. "Andrew..." She closed her eyes, but didn't want to remember.

Marlene opened her eyes and threw back the covers. She slid from her bed, feeling the thick carpet between her toes. She was in her bedroom, in her own home. There was no one there to terrorize her, no one that could harm her.

She wrapped her arms around her waist and shivered. Those cold blue eyes. She couldn't forget them. She couldn't banish them from her mind. It was the way Garrett had described her shooter, and she'd seen him in her dream. The man had seemed too real, as his eyes bored into hers.

Marlene shuddered and went to look out the window. She gazed at the gardens in back, and tried to think of normal things. She worked to keep her breathing steady, even. Yet the fear didn't easily subside. A creepy feeling that the man was behind her, and could grab her, made her skin crawl.

Garrett was next door, in his own room. All she had to do was push the red button by her bed and he'd be there in a flash. But it had only been a dream. She knew that. The intercom was within reach, and she could talk to Garrett. If she shared her fears, it would all be better. He'd come into her room and assure her that she was safe.

But it wouldn't make it all go away. And Marlene would feel foolish. She wasn't a child, and couldn't call out in the night to be held when a nightmare disturbed her sleep. Instead, she took a deep breath, then another. The images in her mind began to fade, but the terror didn't.

It was a workday, and Marlene needed to shower. Although it was early, she could go down for coffee and get her bearings. She doubted that she'd so easily recover. The dream was over, but the nightmare of her life wasn't. The worst part was wondering when the next attack would come.

Marlene had done her best to disguise the stress building inside her. When on the set, she poured herself into the role, able to block out all but the scene. And with Garrett, she worked to hide the depth of her distress. He was already overprotective, and if he knew the effect that the current circumstances had on her, he'd order her to abandon her regular activities.

He'd already cautioned her about the dangers of continuing to be visible, but Marlene knew that hiding would be worse than facing the threat. Death loomed, because a man who knew how to use firearms could strike without warning.

Marlene went to the shower. She stepped out of her nightgown and onto the tile floor. If only there was someone she could talk to, and share how she truly felt. But she'd avoided calling her mother recently, sticking to short texts with a positive message.

I'm fine. I miss you, Mom. I'll call you when I get a break. Marlene had avoided confiding her worst fears, as she didn't want to alarm her mother. And she hadn't phoned her mother, for fear that if she talked about what was going on, she might break down.

The hot water poured down, drenching her hair and flowing over Marlene's shoulders. It was good, a symbol of warmth and security—yet reminders of what she didn't have. Her life was anything but secure. As each day went by, the situation worsened.

Garrett had implied such, as he'd mentioned that the enemy had too much time to plan. He avoided going into detail with her, and Marlene knew he didn't want her to worry. But how could she not? It all seemed to be closing in on her: the ever-present threat, the importance of her role in the movie...and her sexy bodyguard.

Garrett was so near, tempting her mercilessly. Not that he knew. She was good at not showing her feelings. It was just one more role she played. Yet she thought of Garrett as her knight in shining armor. He'd appeared in her life at just the right moment, as if by magic.

And he'd stuck by her, despite the reasons that he should have left. Garrett was honorable, and swoon-worthy besides. But Marlene wouldn't allow herself to give in. He was ex-military, and there was a reason she'd sworn off heroes. They were brave by nature, and danger was inherent in their career. That meant inevitable loss. Marlene would lose her heart to Garrett, and then life would take him from her. She knew it, and her past had proven it. She'd lost her father and her brother.

Tears formed in her eyes, but she vowed not to cry. No more. Her heart was already broken, and now Garrett had worked his way into her life. She had no tears left. Losing one more man that she cared about would be her undoing. She couldn't let that happen.

Marlene got out of the shower and dried off. She put on a robe and looked in the mirror, seeing too much sadness in her eyes. Then she put her fingertips to her lips, remembering Garrett's hot kisses. She had no business encouraging him, no matter how much she craved more. What could she have been thinking?

When Marlene went to the breakfast nook, she found Garrett leaning back in a chair scrolling through his phone. "Good morning, bodyguard." She grinned at him. "You're up early."

"It's a necessity. I'm sure you'd leave without me if I wasn't ready in time."

"You're quick with the jokes this early in the morning." Marlene poured a cup of coffee and sat across from him. She nodded toward his phone. "Anything new? You went to Stealth and I didn't get a chance to ask what you learned."

Marlene knew him well. Garrett couldn't hide his concern from her, but he didn't seem willing to share much. "They're still looking for Buckner."

Garrett's hair was wet from a shower, and Marlene wanted to dig her fingers into his damp locks. His strong jaw was free of scruff. Her eyes went to his kissable lips, then drifted over the buff chest stretching and filling out his shirt.

His expression was stern, making him impossibly sexy. A vision of Garrett, passion unleashed, flashed through Marlene's mind. When he moved, his biceps flexed under his sleeves, making her drool. If she wanted any man to throw her on the bed and take her, Garrett was that man.

Marlene waited, but Garrett didn't offer any more details about his visit to his team. Yet she had the sense that his commitment to her safety had been fueled by whatever he'd learned. She could see it in his eyes, read it in his expression.

As much as she considered herself independent and self-reliant, Marlene responded to his alpha ways. She needed his care and protection. It was a relief not to have to deal with the situation alone. Since Garrett was obviously finished updating her on the status of the threat, she changed the subject.

"It's been an intense week," Marlene said, and sipped her coffee. "The plot has reached a peak, and emotions are tense."

Garrett's eyes didn't leave hers. "I've been observing."

"It's challenging, beyond any role I've played before." Marlene thought of how to relay what it all meant to her. "It's an opportunity for me, and that's why I've worked so hard."

Garrett's eyes softened, and she sensed that he understood.

"This role is a big deal," Marlene said. "It could seal my career, and result in offers for new types of roles. With such a quality film, a respected director and cast, I stand a chance of winning an award."

"You deserve it."

Marlene smiled. "I do deserve it, mostly. I mean, I've worked for years to get to this point. And it's not easy. You've only been around for a few weeks, but you must see what it really takes in this business."

"Probably, but not like you do. I haven't been around filmmaking before," Garrett said. "But I see how much you put into it, the toll it takes on you."

Marlene widened her eyes. "You do? I thought I hid that pretty well. Do I complain too much?"

"You don't let it show, and I wouldn't describe you

as a complainer." Garrett's lips stretched into a smile that touched her heart. "But you don't fool me as much as you'd like to think you do."

"Is that so?"

Garrett put his hand on her arm, and Marlene warmed to his touch. "It's true. So you don't have to fake it with me. You can be yourself. On stage, and in the public eye, I understand the pretense. But not with me."

It was as though Garrett could see right into her heart, and knew more than she'd voiced. Marlene felt vulnerable, and she glanced away before things went too far. "We'd better get going." She pushed back from the table without looking at him again. She dared not.

At the studio, Marlene waved Anna into her private dressing room. She wanted to talk with her before they went into makeup. Her friend wore tights and a short top. "Did you work out this morning?"

"Yep, just came from the gym, an early aerobics class." Anna's hair was in a ponytail, and it swung over her shoulder as she plopped into a chair. "So how's it going with Garrett?"

Marlene sank into the velvet love seat. "Is that all you think about?"

"I have to live vicariously through you," Anna said. "All of my dates recently have been a bore."

"Really, you were on dates? How come I don't know about any of these guys?"

Anna wrinkled her nose. "There was nothing to tell. Anyway, you have enough on your mind." She tucked her legs up underneath her. "So tell all. Has Garrett made a move?"

Marlene laughed. "He's my bodyguard, you know. He's not supposed to get intimate with a client."

"And you're sure he always does what he's supposed to do? Besides, he's a hunk. I would think you'd make the first move."

"Anna...your imagination is running away with you. I admit Garrett is...desirable. But you know me. I've told you when I hook up, it won't be with a military type. They thrive on danger. And in the past few weeks, I've had enough danger to last a lifetime."

Anna pouted. "You're no fun."

"I wanted to talk to you about something else." Marlene thought about how to phrase it. "I'm having some issues with my role. The last few days I've had trouble getting into it. If Nicholas hadn't coached me on how to approach it, I'd have floundered."

"I did notice that you seemed to be struggling more, but that happens. Sometimes you just have to work through it."

"It's more than that," Marlene said. "I guess on some level, I feel like a fraud. I'm trying not to make it personal, or about my life. The film has a broader scope. But I can't brush aside the feeling that it doesn't explore what it's like to be left behind when a loved one dies."

"I can see your point."

"It's as though the reality of war is being romanticized." Marlene pinched the bridge of her nose. "I'm not sure if it's the script, or just me."

"The movie is meant to explore the realities of war, so it's not only about the soldiers," Anna said. "The script is rich with family scenes and romance. It's supposed to show their experiences. Your role is especially important, and what you do reflects on my character. I guess you could say as your character's best friend, I need to stay aligned with how you're portraying the emotions."

"But you can't do that properly if I've strayed from the path," Marlene said.

"Talk to Nicholas off set. Maybe he will know, or will make some changes." Anna shifted in the chair. "So far, he's been very true to the script. But that doesn't mean he won't listen to you."

"I have to try to convince him that there are issues. This film means a lot to me, and this role is important; yours is too. We need to be in sync on the message we convey." Marlene stood up. "I'll talk to him on break. I hope I can make him understand."

Later on the set, Marlene did her best not to let her internal conflict affect her performance. But she anticipated the break so she could talk to the director. If she could get his agreement to make the changes she had in mind, it might make all the difference.

When the camera wasn't on her, Marlene caught sight of Garrett. He stood off to the side, alert and ready for action. He didn't seem to let the filming lure him into complacency. But then, his service career had likely trained him to stay alert. His patience impressed her, as so many other things about him had.

Unfortunately, Marlene wouldn't be able to spend the break with her bodyguard. She pointed at Nicholas Hayes, and Garrett nodded. He understood that she needed to meet with her director.

"Nicholas, can we talk in your office for a few minutes? I have something important to go over with you."

The director broke free of the other cast members who were chatting with him. "Of course. It will be more private in there." He strode down the hall, and

Marlene followed him.

She had gone over the points she wanted to make, but hadn't settled on her approach. Any way she viewed the argument, it seemed like she was criticizing the film. That wasn't it. But she did care about how it turned out, and hoped that Nicholas wouldn't be defensive.

The director sat at his desk and motioned for her to take a seat. "What is it, Marlene?"

"It's about my role." Marlene launched into her feelings about the film, and her misgivings about her role. She presented the highlights of what she felt was wrong with the script, and the changes she wanted him to consider. Once she began pouring out her feelings, she couldn't stop. But when she looked across at Nicholas, she questioned whether he understood or not.

"I see your perspective, Marlene. And I appreciate you sharing it with me." Nicholas frowned. "Unfortunately, I disagree with you. This film is on track, and the script is brilliant. Your portrayal has been just what I'm looking for."

"I've reached deep, Nicholas, but I'm not finding the emotion. Something is wrong."

"Then you'll have to dig deeper," Nicholas said. "I have no inclination to change the course of the film. I think you can do this. I'll work with you out there. But I'm not altering the character or the script."

Marlene sagged with failure. She had to pull this off. It meant so much. "Will you at least speak to the producer and relay my suggestions? Maybe he will see things differently."

Nicholas sighed. "I'll do that, solely because I respect you. I will talk to Mason, merely to relay what you've said. But realize that I'm not going to recommend the changes."

Mason Henslow had produced many blockbusters, and knew his business. It would be difficult to argue if he really thought the film should continue without any changes. Marlene would have liked to speak with him personally. But that wasn't possible. It made more sense for the director to meet with him. Plus, she was aware that his schedule was tight, so even the meeting with Nicholas wouldn't happen immediately.

"I appreciate you listening, and conveying my concerns." Marlene stood up. "I won't take more of your time." She paused. "I'll do my best out there, no matter what."

"That's what I expect of you." Nicholas pushed his chair back. "We'll get through this, and be all the better for it. Think of it as growth as an actor."

Marlene went back to the set, and noticed Garrett watching her. But she didn't have a chance to talk to him about her meeting, since she had to get back to work. Of course, he'd noticed her disappointment. Marlene thought she was so good at keeping her feelings buried. But with Garrett, that didn't seem to work as well.

The cast resumed positions, and Nicholas walked up to one of the actors to give some direction. Marlene stewed about her lack of success in convincing the director. She still felt that the way she portrayed the lead wasn't true to life.

Anna came over and leaned close. "Any luck?"

Marlene said in a low voice, "It doesn't look like it. I got him to agree to discuss it with Mason. But that's the most he'll do."

"So he wasn't willing to try any changes?"

Marlene shook her head. "He thinks I'm off base. Swears that the film is fine."

EMILY JANE TRENT

One of the cast members called to Anna, and she went to take her place for the scene. Marlene strolled around the perimeter to stand close to her male costar. In the recent filming he'd been off to war in the story, so they hadn't shot any scenes together. A few of those were coming up.

Marlene had been thrilled to get a dramatic role in the historical war film. Now she questioned the wisdom of accepting. Maybe it wasn't right for her. She had too many bad memories. The director seemed to think that she could play the role. But could she?

What Marlene hadn't told Nicholas was that she felt sick in her gut. She felt downright unpatriotic, and couldn't seem to do anything about it. She harbored guilt for her secret feelings. Yet they were her true feelings.

In truth, Marlene saw no reason for the senselessness of war, or a need for all the violence. She was tired of it all. Since she'd been so involved in fundraisers for the cause, she had received voluminous communications on the subject. It seemed she wasn't alone in her purpose to mitigate the suffering left in the wake of battle, or to make life better for the soldiers who came home.

But Marlene had been dishonest, and had trouble living with that. She'd continued to organize events, help where she could, and to act in a movie portraying the disaster of war. But she was tired of it all. She thought if one more email with a plea for assistance showed up in her inbox, she'd scream.

It didn't stop. Whether in the news or social media, the onslaught of heartbreak and need pulled at her heartstrings. If she heard one more story about a loved one who had died in battle, or about the

172

destruction of war, she wouldn't be able to take it.

Yet Marlene was filming a movie on that very topic. Every day, she was faced with her own doubts and traitorous thoughts. As the star, she wasn't about to speak up, or make her true feelings known. But it was wearing her down, all of it.

The way things were going, Marlene would crack under the pressure, fold in the face of the lies. And what were the lies? That was what she'd tried so desperately to make Nicholas see. It all hinged on what war left in its wake, how lives were affected, and families were changed forever. It was all fine to glorify the heroes, and they deserved it, without question. But what about those left behind?

Deep in her heart, Marlene felt that her role should convey that part of life. It had to show the true emotions or else it would be a false portrayal. She was an actress, and put herself into each role. But this time she hadn't fully been able to do so.

Although she'd reached for the emotions, they hadn't come. If only the director had agreed to make some changes. As it was, Marlene was left to figure out how to play the role convincingly. And she wasn't certain that she could pull it off.

The actors were called for the next scene. Marlene smiled at her costar and stepped onto stage. It was time to get back to the movie. She needed to give everything she had to the role. But all she felt was overwhelming emotional pain—the hurt that hadn't diminished—from the loss of her own family members.

CHAPTER SIXTEEN

Garrett stood off to the side watching Marlene perform. He'd seen the look on her face after meeting with the director, and didn't like what he saw. Something was off, but he couldn't tell what it was. And he wasn't sure that she'd confide in him.

The scene was ramping up, pulling Garrett into the drama. Then Marlene was in another man's arms, her costar's embrace. It was only a movie, yet it looked real. He hadn't stopped to consider how he'd feel seeing the woman he cared about kissing another man.

It was pretend, but it sure didn't look like it. Garrett's blood heated. He wanted Marlene, and felt the urge to rip her away from the other guy. He didn't want to watch, but couldn't avert his eyes. His heart ached as the cameras rolled.

Then someone yelled "cut" and the man released Marlene. She smiled at him and turned to speak to the director. Garrett stared at her, and Marlene glanced over. Their gazes locked briefly, and heat flooded Garrett's veins. He wanted to sweep her into his arms and carry her away.

It wasn't over yet, as the scene had to be redone several times. Garrett thought it had been fine the first time, but the director was looking for chemistry between the characters. Hell, he'd give him chemistry. But he had to hold back, and endure watching. It just seemed too damn real.

And with Marlene it was so difficult to tell. She played roles on stage and in life. Sometimes Garrett didn't know what was true. She was like quicksilver. Just when Garrett thought he had a grip, Marlene slipped right through his hands.

Yet Garrett observed some of what she tried so carefully to hide. Marlene might think he didn't notice, wasn't that observant, but he was. The sadness was there; he could see it in her eyes. As hard as she tried to hide her pain from the world, she didn't quite succeed.

The losses that Marlene had suffered, as well as her loneliness, were evident to Garrett. It was a challenge to tell what was real from what was mere pretence. He wondered sometimes if Marlene even knew. If only she'd let down that emotional wall, but she'd had to be thick-skinned for too long.

Garrett wished to save her from that, but had no ready way to do so. Yet how could he expect her to be open with him when he continued to deceive her? Although she'd asked, Garrett had avoided telling her what he'd learned at Stealth.

There was no way that Garrett could tell her what he'd found out about her pursuer. Maybe it was wrong of him, but he couldn't add more stress. Marlene's life was stressful enough. The situation was tense. To hear about Buckner's familiarity with Andrew just wouldn't be good.

Garrett couldn't tell her about his part in it all. He wanted to, and he'd planned to from the start. But the timing hadn't been right, and it certainly wasn't now either. He would have divulged his secret, unburdened his conscience, and moved forward from there.

But Marlene needed to focus. She was in the midst

of an emotionally charged film, stressing over her role. That much he knew without her mentioning it. So she needed to focus on filming and let Garrett worry about the rest. She needed to trust him to deal with the threat, and she surely wouldn't if she knew the truth.

Garrett couldn't deny that he had another reason for holding back. He wanted to see things through, save Marlene from harm. If she severed the relationship, even their professional one, he'd be obligated to turn away. His conscience wouldn't let him. Until he knew that she was safe, Garrett would stay close.

And in his heart, Garrett didn't want to leave for a very personal reason. He cared about Marlene, and although they couldn't be together, it still drove a knife in his gut to think about what he kept from her. As sure as he breathed, Marlene wouldn't want anything to do with him once she knew his discreditable secret.

When filming was over, Marlene had the weekend off. Garrett guided her to the exit, but not to her limo. He opened the door to a luxury SUV and shuffled her inside. Garrett tapped the window separating the driver's compartment and the vehicle began to move.

Marlene sat in the plush seat. "What are we doing?"

"It's a surprise," Garrett said. "You wouldn't let me hide you in a safe house, so this is second best. We're in a bulletproof SUV—that's tracker free, I might add. I had the vehicle checked. It wouldn't do to have anyone follow us."

"But where are we going?"

"I've arranged for a weekend away in Bel Air." Garrett was getting a kick out of her reaction. "Let's just say that a certain billionaire, a hedge fund manager who is grateful to Stealth, offered his place for the weekend."

"So we can just take off and party all weekend? What about my stalker, shooter, or whatever he is?"

"Couldn't be better." Garrett grinned at her. "This home has the Stealth seal of approval. The billionaire, who prefers not to be named, has this place locked down tighter than Fort Knox. The walls of the building go deep into the ground to make them earthquake proof. And the bedroom is its own panic room. Once the doors shut, not a soul can get in."

Marlene's mouth was open and her eyes were big.

Garrett crossed his ankle over the opposite knee, feeling pretty relaxed. "Need I go on?"

"I think you've made your point." Marlene wrinkled her nose. "How did you know whether I had plans or not?"

"Did you have plans for the weekend?"

"Only to be with you, it seems. But you could have *asked*."

"This is much more fun. Besides, if I'd asked, you could have said no."

"And this way I have no choice?"

"Exactly," Garrett said. "But I don't think you'll complain too much when you see this place. It has pools, a theater, a gourmet kitchen, and much more."

"So we're cooking?"

"I didn't say that. I made sure the cook left provisions for us. All we have to do is heat and eat," Garrett said. "I prefer not to have any service staff around. If you're recognized, that could be trouble."

Marlene shook her head. "What about Samuel?"

"What about him? I sent him home. Anyone watching will see the limo go to your place, as usual. The back seat is blacked out, so no one can tell whether you're in the car or not." Garrett was rather pleased with himself. "All weekend, anyone stalking you can stare at your mansion, wondering when you'll emerge."

Marlene raised an eyebrow. "How long have you been planning this?"

"It was fairly spur of the moment. I heard about the availability and didn't hesitate. The owner is out of the country. I'm not at liberty to share the details of our employment with him. But let's just say that he wishes to show his appreciation for the safety of his wife and children."

Marlene appeared to relax. It had to be good to know she'd be out of harm's way for an entire weekend. "You see, if you'd let me take you to a safe house, you wouldn't have to worry about the maniac pursuing you."

Marlene tilted her head. "Um, don't get carried away. The answer on that is still no. I'm not hiding. I have a movie to finish, remember?"

"How could I forget? Well, a weekend away will do you a world of good." Garrett was in control now, which was just how he liked it.

They could see out the windows, although no one could see in. The SUV rolled up a long hill, winding along the driveway. Then it went into a tunnel that took them to the garage. The grounds were secured with motion detectors, and guards were stationed out of sight, in case they were needed.

Garrett opened the door for Marlene and they walked through a breezeway to a steel-reinforced elevator. It opened onto the main floor, and when they stepped out, even Garrett was impressed. He'd seen photos of the place, but they didn't compare to the real thing.

Marlene walked around, then went over to look out the windows. The architecture was modern, and the home had a geometric design structure. The stark white walls contrasted with the blue furniture and the chrome tables. The exterior walls were windows that started at the floor and disappeared into the ceiling. Low music played in the background, a nice touch.

"I had James pack some of your things, so they are in the master suite."

"That was thoughtful of you." Marlene kicked off her shoes and walked barefoot over the polished wood floor, looking sexy as hell. "Is there any wine around here?"

"There's an entire cellar full of it, and you can have anything you want." Garrett observed her reaction, glad that he'd come up with this plan. Marlene glided toward him, appearing calm. Hiding out was a good stress reliever.

Garrett saw past Marlene's regal posture, her movie star personality, and caught a glimpse of the real woman. He liked what he saw. "Right this way," he said, and she took his arm.

Once they had the wine and glasses in hand, they found a comfortable sitting room with plush sofas. There was another wall of windows, and a white stone fireplace set at an angle. Garrett found the music controls and changed to something jazzier.

Then Garrett settled in a chair across from her. He opened the bottle of wine, and poured some for each of them. "I didn't think you ever drank."

"I don't, but I'll make an exception. I'm not anticipating having to wrestle an intruder to the ground." Garrett lifted his glass, then clinked it against Marlene's. "Here's to staying out of sight."

"I must say I approve. This is a great way to throw off my attacker."

"Buckner can look forward to a long, boring weekend," Garrett said, and took a sip of wine. The silky liquid slid down his throat, and he took another sip. "This is delicious."

"I thought you'd like it." Marlene had found some snacks in the kitchen, so they had cheese and nuts with their wine. "A girl could get spoiled this way."

Garrett laughed. "You *are* spoiled." He wished to spoil her even more.

While they drank and nibbled, Garrett enjoyed looking at Marlene. She was so beautiful, and he was content to look. She gazed back, her expression inviting, and his body responded. He hadn't brought her away to seduce her, only to care for her.

If Marlene kept looking at him that way, he might give in to the urge to hold her. And that would lead to more, guaranteed. So Garrett shifted the focus. "So what happened when you talked to Nicholas? What was that all about?"

Marlene glanced away. "What do you mean?"

Garrett looked into her lovely green eyes. "I saw your face. What did he say to you?"

"You would notice. It's not anything you need to hear about."

Marlene was strong, independent, and she was used to handling problems on her own. But she didn't have to, not as long as Garrett was there.

"You can share it with me," Garrett said. "I won't think you're weak. You've had to face a lot in life, yet you continue on. That's all anyone can ask." He paused. "It's all right to lean on someone. You don't have to do it all alone."

Marlene looked into his eyes, and hope flickered in her expression. "It's too much. You wouldn't understand."

Garrett held her gaze. "Try me."

Marlene hesitated, leaving him unsure if she'd tell him. Then she took a breath and set her glass on the table. "You say I'm strong, and I feel like you have me on some sort of pedestal. But I'm not as pure as you believe," Marlene said.

Garrett couldn't imagine what she was keeping from him. But whatever it was, it couldn't rival the secrets he had. "I don't expect you to be perfect," he said. "I'm certainly not."

"I feel tremendous guilt," Marlene said. "I support charities, and I'm in a movie playing an emotionally wounded lover...left behind when her husband dies. But I have serious doubts about the nature of my role, thoughts I don't share."

Garrett's heart wrenched at watching her agonize, when he couldn't do a thing about it.

"I feel even worse with you as a central part of my life. You're the last person I should share this with."

"Why is that?"

"Because you're a hero, a soldier—your life is the military. You're all that I admire, just like my own father and brother. But..." Marlene's eyes met his. "I've lost my way. I'm torn. I don't see the sense in it all anymore."

Garrett was reminded of all that he'd seen, all that he'd done. It was more than she needed to hear, and most of it he couldn't share anyway. But he did understand the strange sadness he saw in her eyes. He felt it too, deep in his heart.

"I'm horrified by the losses, and this movie I'm in

drives that point home for me." The pleading look in Marlene's eyes got to him. "I'm conflicted, and unable to find the right emotion for my character."

Garrett thought of the men he'd killed in battle. Many were fathers, brothers, husbands. But they had been the enemy. That was war; that was the cost.

A tear rolled down Marlene's cheek. "I'm sorry. I really am. I shouldn't feel this way. But it all seems so pointless." She rubbed the tears away. "I know the necessity for war. We have to protect our country. But there's a flip side, one that has personally affected me. Battles leave orphans and widows in its wake...sisters without brothers."

Garrett felt her pain. "Like you?"

"Yes, like me, and so many others." Marlene looked into his eyes.

Tears rolled down her cheeks, and Garrett opened his arms to her. "Come here, sweetheart." She came to him and folded into his embrace. He wasn't sure what to say, so all he could do was hold her. Her sobs came steadily until his shirt was soaked, and still he held her.

When Marlene calmed, they didn't discuss it further. Garrett poured her another glass of wine, limiting himself to one. Despite what he'd said, he didn't intend to be open to attack, even one that had a low probability of occurring. He was glad Marlene had shared her feelings; it was good to be trusted.

Garrett wanted to make her happy, even though he was the wrong guy to do it. Yet he sensed that something between them had changed. Marlene had opened up to him, dropped her tough-girl façade. She had a heart; she was a good person. He felt close to her.

As Garrett comforted her, barriers melted away. There had been safety in the forbidden nature of their relationship. But with his strong arms around her, and tenderness in his eyes, Marlene found it impossible to resist him.

Garrett was her protector, her hero, and he'd stolen her heart, despite her best efforts to make sure that didn't happen. Alone in the quiet fortress on top of a hill, out of harm's way, Marlene was temporarily away from the harshness of life.

Marlene leaned against his rock-hard body and breathed in his masculine scent. Garrett was the only real thing, an anchor in a treacherous sea. He was controlling, yet caring—everything she wanted. Nothing else seemed to matter except their connection, the vibrant feeling that existed with him near.

When Garrett dug his hand in her hair, Marlene's breath caught. She looked up into his eyes, the intensity of his gaze making her weak. His sky-blue eyes filled with lust, a hunger that she longed to satisfy. It flashed through her mind that having sex would put him in a bad light.

It violated his rules of employment. But Garrett didn't seem concerned. Instead, he took charge. Marlene trusted him; any barrier between them had crumbled. She could reach out for him and he wouldn't refuse her.

The lure of feeling his warm skin, touching his soft lips, consumed her. Marlene wasn't asking for forever, just for one night—a night alone with Garrett to show him how she felt. No one had to know what they shared. Marlene would cherish the intimate moments with him, remember them long after. That would have to be enough.

Garrett touched his lips to hers, and electricity shot through her. Marlene trembled and a whimper escaped her lips. She dragged her fingernails over his scalp, through his silky hair, thrilling to the sensation. Then Garrett pressed deeper into the kiss, parting her lips with his tongue and delving into her mouth.

His tongue lashed against hers, and she moaned softly. Garrett tasted so good, all man with a hint of red wine. He kissed her with abandon, unleashing her desire. Marlene let her hands roam over his solid form, feeling the muscle underneath his clothes.

She wanted more; she wanted it all. Garrett was sexual in a way that unraveled her. His control and confidence weakened any resistance she clung to. To be taken by him was like a dream come true.

Garrett kissed her lips, her forehead, her cheeks, and her eyelids. He adored her with his mouth, his hot breath grazing her skin and making her tingle with excitement. He licked around the curve of her ear, then nibbled on the lobe, driving her crazy.

Heat flooded her belly, and she tensed in the most delicious way. Garrett's hands roved over her body, loving each curve, knowing her intimately. Then he reached under her shirt to cup her breasts. "So lovely." His words escaped in one breath just before he kissed her again, harder this time.

Marlene drank in his kisses, craving more. She put her hands on his strong shoulders, holding him close, as he pressed his mouth to hers. Then she couldn't wait anymore, and he seemed to know. Garrett scooped her into his arms and carried her to the bedroom.

She nuzzled her face against his neck, kissing the

tender skin there. The room was lit in a blue cast, illuminating a bed on a polished wood platform. She glimpsed toward the foot of the bed to see an aquarium that filled the entire wall. A soft blue glow backlit the exotic fish, swimming behind the glass.

Garrett lowered her until her bare feet touched the carpet. He held her face in his palms and looked into her eyes. "I want you," he whispered. His gaze pierced into her, and Marlene's skin tingled.

In a raspy voice, Marlene said, "Don't make me wait any longer."

Fire blazed in Garrett's eyes, and he traced her lips with his thumb. "I'm yours, sweetheart." He grabbed the hem of her shirt and pulled it off over her head. Then he leaned down and stroked his tongue over the mounds of her breasts.

Marlene shuddered and tipped her head back. Then he undid her lacy bra and it slid to the floor, leaving her exposed. Garrett cupped her breasts and took one nipple in his mouth, while he fingered the other with his thumb. The feel of his wet mouth on her made her come unglued.

Garrett licked across her nipples, then kissed her lips. Marlene reached under his shirt and put her palms against his hard chest. Her nipples peaked harder, and warmth filled her. Garrett removed the shirt and she stared at his sculpted form. Then she stroked her palms down his chest and over the ridges of his abdomen.

Their lips met, passion exploding with a fury. Garrett shed the rest of his clothes without releasing her from the kiss. Then he peeled off her pants and underwear. He stilled for a moment as his gaze roamed over her naked form, a caress of its own.

"You're gorgeous." Garrett's eyes glistened with

need, and his arousal was evident.

Marlene looked at him in all his masculine glory, awestruck with his form. Garrett was solid muscle, as if carved from stone. Taut skin stretched over the dips and valleys of the striations, and a trail of hair went from his low belly downward.

The sight of him hard and ready for her made her breathless. Marlene reached out and wrapped her hand around his erection. He was so hot, and his skin was like velvet over steel. Garrett groaned when she stroked him, squeezing and unwilling to let him go.

Garrett spoke in a guttural voice, and she loved the sound of it. "You're going to have to stop that, sweetheart, or I won't last."

Then he put his hands on her waist and lifted her to the bed. Marlene sat on the edge and Garrett parted her thighs. He knelt in front of her and kissed her sex, then licked her as if she was a goddess. She thrust her fingers into his hair, and Garrett flicked his tongue over her most sensitive spot.

Marlene cried out. It had been too long, and she wanted him so badly. "Yes, sweetheart, I want your pleasure." Then he swirled his tongue just so, and sucked alternately, until she released against his hot lips. Waves of pleasure coursed through her, and when they subsided, she fell back against the mattress.

Garrett hovered over her, his hands on the bed beside her head, and kissed her sweetly. The taste of her cream on his lips was a turn-on, and she wanted more. Marlene wrapped her legs around his waist to pull him closer. With his arms around her, Garrett lifted her fully onto the bed, with her head on a pillow.

Then he reached into a side drawer and retrieved a condom. His sexy smile warmed her heart. "Full-service accommodations," he said, then rolled the sleeve over his thick erection. Straddling her, Garrett kissed her deeply, and she reached between them to feel his heat.

Marlene gazed into his handsome face, watching his eyes fill with emotion as he dipped into her. "Oh, God," she gasped. "You feel so good." She arched her back to take him deeper.

Garrett dipped inside, filling her and igniting her need. She clenched over him, holding on, wanting his pleasure as much as her own. With a shove, Garrett went deep, and Marlene's breath was ragged as he stroked her. She wanted the moment to last and last, yet craved the pinnacle of sensation.

The slow, sexy loving exploded into wild abandon. Garrett thrust hard, still looking into her eyes. And Marlene reached behind to cup his round, firm ass and let her hands drift over the backs of his muscular thighs. When she raked her fingernails down his back, he grabbed her wrists.

Holding her hands over her head, Garrett ravished her with kisses, his hot mouth on her jaw and then her neck. She panted harder, moaning at his touch. Then she tightened under him and felt him swell inside her. The gleam in his eyes told her all she needed to know.

Garrett's body stiffened then stilled. Marlene felt him pulse once inside her, and she whined shrilly as her orgasm surged. Then Garrett moved again, with hard, fast thrusts, releasing into her with a deep, feral groan. The scent of sex drugged her, and calm satisfaction engulfed her. Marlene wrapped her legs around Garrett's thighs. Entwined that way, they clung to each other, still breathing hard. And Marlene closed her eyes, floating in pleasure.

CHAPTER SEVENTEEN

Garrett must have drifted to sleep. He woke up with Marlene in his arms. She had one leg draped over his thigh and her face was buried against his neck. She stirred, and he wanted her again. They'd made love through the night, but he'd been unable to get enough of her.

Her lovely feminine scent filled his nostrils, and Garrett squeezed her tighter. He watched the colorful, exotic fish glide through the water and around the coral, mesmerized by their slow rhythm. He stroked Marlene's back and she looked up into his eyes.

Garrett brushed her hair away from her face. "I wasn't comfortable watching you kiss your costar," he said.

Marlene smiled. "Mmm, you were jealous?"

"Very jealous." Garrett kissed the top of her head and held her close.

Marlene turned onto her stomach and put her palm on his cheek. "You have no one to be jealous of."

Grasping her shoulders, Garrett tossed her to the mattress. He held her arms to her sides and kissed down her neck and over her breasts. Her arousal surged, her eyes lustful. He made love to her, long and slow. She excited him as no woman had before.

Marlene was the woman for him. He knew he couldn't have her, yet he couldn't turn away. He was fucked. There was no way to tell her that she'd misjudged him without crushing her. It was better if she didn't find out, as it would be the last straw.

That was the trouble with the past: Garrett was unable to change it. He wished that he could, just like he'd planned to tell Marlene everything. He wanted to overcome any barriers between them, and make her his woman. But he wasn't sure he had any right to.

What he needed to do was catch the man who threatened her and take him out of action. Once Buckner was out of her life, then Garrett would move on. As much as he cared for her—hell, he loved her—Garrett wasn't right for her.

Marlene's happiness mattered most. Once Garrett ensured that she was safe, he'd let her go. But he'd always have this weekend, and the memory of her in his arms. He wouldn't forget the feel of her against him, or the sexy sounds she made when pleasure consumed her.

The fairytale weekend had come to an end. Marlene had experienced joy that she was certain would escape her. But it hadn't. And Garrett had wanted it as much as she had. The way he held her, whispered to her, and made love without inhibition revealed the truth.

But Garrett was a soldier, and she'd already had too much grief connected with the military. And her life wouldn't suit him anyway. Stardom was far afield of clandestine activity. Garrett preferred the shadows, not bright lights. She wouldn't ask that of him. She couldn't, because it wasn't fair.

Why was she even considering that, anyway? Garrett cared for her, and she was crazy about him. Marlene loved him with all her heart, but the only outcome would be heartbreak—if she let it continue.

She didn't need to tell him that they had no future together, because he already knew.

But that didn't mean they couldn't steal a few hours of heaven, so they had. In Garrett's arms, Marlene had felt that she was where she belonged. She pretended it would last, that she could wake each morning to the warmth of his touch. Yet the special weekend was over without any commitment. Garrett hadn't asked for any, and she was grateful for that.

The magic was over, and now Marlene was back in her dressing room alone. She needed to mentally prepare for her scenes, but she was shaken by what had happened between them. Garrett had gotten too close; the wall she'd so carefully erected around her heart had tumbled down. She was vulnerable now, and didn't like it.

Garrett had touched her deeply, and Marlene couldn't easily put aside her emotions. It scared her, and she was more than a little confused. She trusted him, wanted him too much, but she knew it could only lead to disappointment.

Yet Marlene's world had changed; she feared she was in over her head. Pent-up emotion had flooded forth when she'd opened her arms and her bed to Garrett. But it didn't end there. All the torment she'd tried to put aside resurfaced, and the hurtful memories threatened to swallow her up.

Only they hadn't quite done so. The well of repressed emotion had surged, yet she'd survived it. Marlene had been so afraid of it, just as she'd feared being in Garrett's arms. In allowing herself to fully feel, the impact of both had hit her.

Marlene wanted to play her role in the movie with skill. She wanted to show why it all mattered, and make the losses count. She realized with some surprise that her love for Garrett had shattered her defenses, but renewed her verve for life. At last, she knew that she could play the part authentically. She could feel the emotions of her character.

That was what had been missing, and the knowledge empowered Marlene. She felt strong, and knew she could give the performance of her career. Her portrayal of the character had been unfeeling, not caring enough, because she hadn't been able to deal with the emotion.

Tears of joy filled her eyes. *Those left behind are heroes too.* Marlene felt it deep in her soul. She stood up and walked toward the door. She was ready. Loss was a part of life that couldn't be avoided, but it was the triumph of the human spirit that gave her inspiration.

On set later, Marlene glanced over at Garrett before the director called for action. He nodded, giving her a vote of encouragement. He didn't know that she'd figured it out; no one else did either. Her performance would tell all.

The cameras rolled and Marlene was lost in the scene. She was her character, living and breathing. Time had no meaning, only the moment. The exhilaration of acting surged through her. She had been in too much emotional pain before to play the part realistically.

Marlene had been unable to take her character's perspective, but now she could. She'd pushed through the fear of loss, broken through emotionally, and could let go. Immersed in the film, she lived the scene, more real than life for those brief moments.

When it ended, Marlene looked up, coming back to

the present. The director's expression was one of approval. He lifted his hands and said, "Wonderful, Marlene." Then Anna rushed up to give her a big hug. "You were awesome."

When Marlene gazed around at the other cast and crew, she saw tears in their eyes. They'd been moved by her performance, and her heart swelled with pride. It was the role of her career, and she'd nailed it.

There was no call to reshoot, or request for changes. Marlene had accomplished what she'd wanted. The director called for break, and she went over to Garrett. He beamed at her, and she laughed with relief. It was over. She'd done it.

At the end of the day, Samuel drove them back to her home in Beverly Hills. As much as she'd like to, Marlene couldn't hide out forever. It was time to face things again. Garrett assured her that Buckner hadn't given up. He could make his next move at any time.

No doubt Marlene's disappearance over the weekend had only aggravated him, and if anything fueled his vendetta against her. She still didn't know what the guy wanted. Maybe she was making too much out of it and he was merely a stalker. She'd had many, although not as threatening.

But Buckner wasn't a stalker. Garrett had assured her of that. His lack of acceptance into the military might have ignited a need for revenge, yet that didn't explain Marlene's involvement. Her part in the situation remained a mystery to her. She just didn't see the connection, and Garrett seemed unusually quiet about the whole thing. Likely he didn't know any more than she did.

After her recent success, Marlene didn't want to

talk about Buckner, so she didn't bring it up. Garrett had taken every precaution to keep her safe. They waited impatiently for Stealth to do what they were good at, and find the guy. Marlene didn't want to let it ruin her evening.

James greeted them when they arrived. He saw to his duties then took his leave. "Will there be anything else before I go?"

"No, James. I'm going to stay in this evening, and I won't be entertaining. I'll see you tomorrow." Marlene didn't consider enjoying her bodyguard's company the same as entertaining a guest. So her butler was off duty, since she wouldn't need him.

Laura was different, as Marlene needed her cook. She was hungrier than usual, and assumed that Garrett was too. "I'll speak to the cook about dinner," she said to Garrett.

"I'll check in with the team, get a status on everything."

Marlene followed the fragrant aromas to the kitchen. "Mmm, Laura, what are you cooking? It smells so good."

The cook looked up from her stirring, and wiped a hand on her apron. "It's a dish I know you like to serve guests, my special recipe for beef tenderloin with chimichurri."

Laura had told her that the combination was a specialty of Argentina. Marlene loved the tangy condiment with the grilled meat. It was good for entertaining, and she'd asked the cook to make heartier meals while Garrett was staying with her. "I might be able to live on soup and salad, but my bodyguard will need some real food," she'd said.

The cook had been pleased. Since she liked to cook, it was good to have someone around with a healthy appetite. Although she did well with the healthy but light meals Marlene required. The ten-foot-high screens in the theaters made Marlene look at least ten pounds heavier, so she had to compensate.

"I'll take the wine into the living room. When dinner is ready, just let us know."

Laura smiled and resumed her work. The wine had been opened so it could breathe, and Marlene carried the bottle out to the other room. She poured a glass, but since Garrett wasn't around, she decided to change. In her walk-in closet, she set the glass on the center island.

She shed the clothes she'd worn all day, and looked for something more casual. She chose a knit top and pants, then slipped her bare feet into a pair of ballet slippers. They were comfortable, plus she'd noticed that Garrett seemed to like them.

In the corner, her gardening clothes were neatly folded. It made her smile to remember her date with Garrett, a day at the movies incognito. She'd have to ask him to do it again sometime. But then, she shouldn't look too far ahead. He could be gone anytime.

Garrett's bodyguard duties would end when the threat was resolved. That was unfortunate, as she'd really miss him. It seemed unfair that returning her life to normal meant that Garrett wouldn't be a part of it. She was unsure of the nature of the relationship anyway.

The weekend seemed like another world. And neither of them had spoken of it, so Marlene wasn't sure what to think. She picked up her wine glass and went into the other room to find Garrett. He was sipping Coke and starring into the fireplace.

Garrett had changed clothes too, and wore a simple T-shirt with jeans. Yet he looked desirable in whatever he wore. The denim hugged his thighs, making her itch to touch. And the cotton shirt fit over his muscles just barely. It hadn't been that long, and Marlene remembered how he felt pressed close to her.

"Is everything okay?" she said, then sat in a chair next to Garrett.

"As far as I can tell. The guys will let me know if they notice anything suspicious." Garrett swigged his drink.

Marlene enjoyed being at home, and it had been a comfortable respite from the world. Now she wondered if she'd ever feel truly safe there again. The unpredictability of the situation was hard to take. While she sat and sipped her wine, a madman was plotting her death.

And Garrett didn't say that she was safe. He had to know that she was worried, but there were no guarantees. He was doing all he could, and that meant a lot. But it was better that he didn't give her unsubstantiated assurances. Instead, he picked a different topic to discuss. "You were great out there today," he said. "I mean it."

"I want you to know how much you helped me," Marlene said.

Garrett balanced his Coke on his thigh. "You were up there alone, as far as I could tell."

"Yes, but over the weekend you said something that made all the difference." Marlene wanted him to know that she viewed things more clearly now. "That morning when we sat by the pool, and talked..."

Garrett nodded. "Yes, we talked about a lot of things."

Marlene remembered it clearly. One thing about Garrett was that he viewed life in straightforward terms. For him, issues were reduced to simplicity. It was refreshing.

"I was on stage today, and I balked, just for a moment. Then I remembered what you'd said: 'We protect those we love.' And it all came together for me." Marlene didn't say more, but she knew Garrett understood. "So, thank you."

The look in Garrett's eyes was that of a fierce protector, leaving no doubt that he'd do all he could to ensure no harm came to her. It was immensely reassuring. "I'm glad you're here with me," she said. "I wouldn't want to be alone, especially now."

Their gazes locked, and Marlene wondered if he'd open his arms to her. But he shouldn't; it wasn't right. She'd indulged her fantasy, and had a few stolen days alone with him. She shouldn't be greedy.

Then Laura entered, and the mood shifted. "Whenever you'd like to eat, I'm ready to serve." They followed her out and sat in the dining room.

The food was delicious, and during the meal, they talked about whatever came to mind. But Marlene didn't broach the subject of their relationship, and Garrett didn't bring it up either. She was disappointed, even though she had no right to be. Yet she knew it was better that way.

By the end of the week, the filming was nearly complete. Nicholas was pleased, and invited the cast to a private party at his home. Garrett was relieved to hear that there would be no photographers allowed. There were wild rumors within entertainment circles that he might star in her next movie. Photos of him by Marlene's side had gone viral. Her publicity agent had officially referred to him as her bodyguard. But it seemed the public preferred a juicier tale, and refused to be dissuaded.

The party was informal, so Marlene wore a simple cocktail dress and pearl earrings. She convinced Garrett to wear a blazer and slacks. He looked handsome and sophisticated. She rather liked having him by her side. Attending events with hired escorts just wasn't the same at all.

Nicholas lived with his wife Althea in a stunning penthouse, suited to such a celebrity. Some of the walls, as well as the floors and bookcases, were rich, dark wood, contrasting with the lush, cream-colored area rugs. The décor was grand and a bit eccentric. A few priceless pieces of Andy Warhol art hung in special recesses, and the kitchen was done in a 1950s style.

The event was catered, and he'd hired a band to play out on the terrace. Nicholas greeted them upon arrival. "I'm so glad you could make it. The bar is over there. Please enjoy."

Garrett had a club soda and Marlene accepted a glass of champagne. Then they circulated. The cast knew her bodyguard, since he'd been around the set so much, so conversation flowed. Garrett seemed mostly at ease, although she noticed he remained aware of their surroundings. Marlene, on the other hand, threw caution to the wind and just had a good time.

Anna spotted them early and raced over to say hello. She grinned at Marlene, then gave her a big hug. "Isn't this just so much fun? This house is amazing."

"It really is," Marlene said. "Nicholas has good taste. Did you meet his wife? She's a lovely woman. She used to be in theater in New York."

"I chatted with her for a while. She's led an interesting life." Anna looked up at Garrett and beamed. "Good to see you here. Great party, isn't it?"

"It's very gracious of Nicholas to invite everyone."

"Oh, he loves it. I've heard he's had some unforgettable parties. I hope to be invited again." Anna smiled. "That is, if I behave myself."

Garrett smiled. "Looks like I have two women to look out for tonight."

Anna giggled. "Well, I have to tell you, Garrett...you are good for Marlene—even though she won't admit it. She's different since you've been around."

"Don't listen to her," Marlene said, feeling a little awkward. "We aren't dating, you know. He's my bodyguard."

Anna winked at Garrett. "Of course." Then she looked around at all the guests. "You'll have to excuse me. I need to circulate. Maybe I'll meet a gorgeous guy like you." She directed that last comment to Garrett, but he seemed to get a kick out of her.

"I hope you do, Anna. He'd be a lucky guy."

Before they could catch their breath, some of the other cast came over to chat. Everyone was in good spirits, and Marlene was having a good time. Then her costar, Michael Jamison, strode up and gave her a big hug. He was a handsome man, trim but not muscular like Garrett. It seemed that lately Marlene compared other men to her bodyguard.

"Marlene, it's so good to see you." Michael looked up at Garrett. "And Garrett, I'm happy you're here to make sure Marlene doesn't get into any trouble."

Marlene chatted with the man for a few minutes. He was an excellent actor, and it had been a pleasure working with him. Garrett kept his eyes on Michael, as if he thought the guy might grab her for a kiss. It was difficult to watch a woman you cared about kiss on screen; Marlene had heard that from other couples, anyway.

Maybe Garrett cared about her more than she thought. Or maybe it was a macho thing: he felt challenged by her relationship with another man. But acting was strictly professional; Garrett knew that. It struck Marlene that might not mean much. After all, wasn't her relationship with Garrett professional, not personal?

Marlene was on her third glass of champagne by the time they found a quiet corner, where they could sit and talk. The party was in full swing, with guests clustered in groups to talk, while others danced outdoors on the expansive terrace.

Garrett had refilled his club soda, and he sat by the fireplace facing toward the room. No one was going to get by him, that was for sure. Marlene wished it was a real date. She wanted to sit closer, even kiss in the dark when no one was looking. Her imagination was running away with her. She'd seen too many movies, or rather, starred in them.

"It occurs to me that I know hardly anything about you," Marlene said, "even though you know a lot about me."

"What would you like to know?"

It was going to be that easy? Marlene should have asked sooner. "Do you have family?"

"I have a younger sister, Adele. She works as an attorney in D.C. Her husband is in politics and they have a son and a daughter."

"So you're an uncle."

Garrett smiled, and his eyes sparkled. Marlene wondered if she was babbling, as he seemed entertained by her. But she hadn't had *that* much to drink. "Yes, I'm an uncle. And my parents live in the D.C. area too, in the suburbs."

"Do you see them often?"

"Not as much as I'd like to. Until recently, I was away a lot. When on deployment I had no contact. They got used to it, though," Garrett said. "But they know I'm working as a bodyguard now. Maybe I'll visit this year over the holidays."

"So Wyatt was how you got hooked up with Stealth?"

"Yes, we're friends, and we'd been on several missions together. He got out first and had some connections. When he heard that I had to leave the service because of my ankle, he recommended me to Travis."

"I'm sure they're glad to have you."

"I hope so."

"Your ankle doesn't seem to bother you too much."

Garrett smiled. "It's fine...unless I fall from high buildings, run marathons, or kick in doors."

"And being a SEAL was that stressful?"

"That and more."

Marlene tried to imagine all that he'd been through, but she couldn't. She knew that only the toughest men made it through the training, and into active duty as a SEAL.

"Have you ever been married?" *Where did that come from?* Marlene's cheeks warmed. She was getting terribly personal.

"No, I haven't been married," Garrett said. "I suppose I've been married to my work. Duty called, and that took precedence. Besides, when I was active, it was difficult to imagine starting a relationship. I was hardly ever home, and when I shipped out I couldn't tell anyone where I was going, or when I'd be back." He paused. "But some guys do it. They have women back home, even get married. I have to hand it to them."

That was the most he'd said all at once. Marlene felt like he was opening up to her, like she might really get to know him.

"But I hadn't found a woman that I wanted to share my life with, or even have a long-term relationship with." Garrett's blue eyes pierced straight into her heart. He'd clearly said *hadn't* found a woman, not *haven't*. Marlene might be splitting hairs, but it might mean there was hope for her.

"I haven't been married either," Marlene said. "But then, you already knew that."

She wanted to say that she hadn't found the right man before, and nearly said much more. Maybe the alcohol had gone to her head. But she was inclined to think it was because Garrett was not only the sexiest hunk she'd had the pleasure to know, he was also caring—and insanely good in bed. Why did she have to fall for a guy she couldn't have? And what had happened to her vow to avoid soldiers? Was she willing to head straight for heartbreak?

Marlene stood up. "It's probably time to go. These parties can last all night, but I'm ready for bed."

Garrett's eyes gleamed with lust, and she looked away. Oh, God, what was she doing?

After thanking their hosts, Garrett guided her back to the limo. By the time they got home it was late, so Marlene went to her room, leaving her bodyguard to check on security for the evening. She got into her nightgown and slipped under the covers. Only that wasn't where she wanted to be.

Marlene desperately wanted to be in Garrett's

arms. She heard him go to his room, then the heavy door clicked shut behind him. She waited, wondering what he was thinking. She imagined him getting undressed, sliding into bed alone. Her body responded; a shiver coursed through her and her skin warmed.

Marlene resisted for as long as she could. She even closed her eyes, reluctant to give in to desire. But she didn't want to sleep alone. It wasn't that she was afraid, exactly. Yet there was no way to predict what the future held. For all she knew, it could be their last night together.

The menace that Garrett had held at bay so far might win out against them. All Marlene wanted was to feel Garrett close to her, melt against his strength, and to be together again. Even if this was the last time, and even though it was a bad idea, she relented.

Quietly, Marlene slipped out of her bed and went to Garrett's room. The door wasn't locked. She pushed it open, and saw him stretched out on the bed, naked. A delicious tremor went through her at the sight of him, with pale moonlight streaming through the window, making him look like some sort of angel.

Garrett was all muscle and virility, utterly irresistible. Marlene walked over to the bed and lifted her nightgown off. She snuggled into Garrett's warm embrace, and felt his heat sear her skin. He pulled her close, and pressed her head against his hard chest.

Passion flooded her veins and she closed her eyes. Garrett ran his palm down her spine and cupped the back of her thigh. Then she draped one leg over him, and his mouth covered hers as he devoured her with a hot kiss. Marlene kissed back with equal fervor, sighing with pleasure.

CHAPTER EIGHTEEN

The next morning, Garrett was up early. He slipped from the warmth of the covers and went to the fitness room for a hard workout. He needed to clear his head. While he jogged on the treadmill, he thought about Marlene. She was still asleep; it had been very late before she'd gotten to sleep—and for Garrett, even later.

He'd held her in the crook of his arm, with her head on his shoulder, listening to her steady breathing. Even now he could feel the warmth of her skin, her softness, and breathe her feminine scent. He was hot for her, and with little provocation would have gone back to the bedroom to take her again. She'd ruined him for any other woman. There wouldn't be another like her.

In some ways, Garrett had made sacrifices in his life that had cost his personal happiness. He thought of other soldiers with wives back home. He'd often envied them, as they had a woman who cared about them, waiting for their return.

Garrett hadn't had that, but he hadn't complained. From all he'd seen and done, he hadn't been sure that he was capable of a close relationship. Maybe he'd been too damaged and emotionally destroyed. Yet the way he responded to Marlene gave him hope. What he felt for her was strong; it ran deep.

And he would continue to feel that way, even when their time together was over. Garrett couldn't envision Marlene as part of his life, as much as he loved her. He wasn't the kind of man for her; she'd said it herself. He was military, and she was a movie star. They couldn't be more different.

Passion had blossomed between them, and Garrett had welcomed it, despite his better instincts. Memories of the hours he had with her would be all he'd have later. Marlene would move on; she'd find a man that suited her, one who would take her arm under the bright lights of Hollywood.

Garrett wasn't that man. Although the thought of any other man putting a ring on her finger left a bitter taste in his mouth. That was his possessive nature talking. Marlene wasn't his, and he had no right to alter her life to suit him.

Also, there was information he kept from her. Garrett couldn't forget that. She'd know sooner or later. There was no way to seek redemption. What had happened was done. He could only hope she would understand, and not judge him too harshly. But he had no right to expect that of her when he was unable to forgive himself.

After Garrett showered and dressed, he found Marlene in the kitchen with the cook. Laura had made cappuccino to go with croissants. He grabbed a pastry and greeted them through a mouthful of goodness.

Laura smiled. "What would you like to drink?"

"Espresso would be good."

The cook started to prepare his drink, while Garrett said a proper good morning to Marlene. "You look lovely." And she did. In a filmy blouse over white jeans, she looked delectable.

"Did you have a good workout?"

"It was fine. You have some good equipment in there."

Marlene sipped her drink. "Yes, I have more than I really use. The yoga mats and elliptical machines are my favorite."

When Laura served the espresso, Marlene suggested they go in the library. "It will be more comfortable."

Garrett sipped his drink. "I might need another one of these. It's very good."

Marlene sat on the floor, yoga style, and reached for a photo book. She began flipping through the pages. "You haven't seen my family," she said pushing the book sideways so he could see. "Here is a recent picture of my mother."

Cynthia Parks was pretty like her daughter. She had a friendly smile and striking green eyes. "You have her eyes," Garrett said.

Marlene flipped the page. "And here's one of her with my father."

Garrett knew her history, and a lot about her family. The background on her had been thorough. But the photographs showed another side, the warmth of a close family. Dean Parks looked young. He'd only been in his late twenties when he died.

Intrigued, Garrett looked over Marlene's shoulder as she flipped through the book. She stopped at a page of photos. "Andrew," she said, pointing to one of the pictures. "We were just kids then."

The knife in Garrett's gut twisted, and dug deeper. But he kept quiet.

There were many photos of Marlene with her brother, at school, on holidays. Only now Andrew was no longer around to share in his sister's life, or look out for her. Garrett listened while Marlene shared a couple of stories, things she'd done with her brother that were memorable. She spoke of him with fondness and love.

Then she turned the page, and Garrett caught a glimpse of some baby pictures. Marlene started to close the book. "Wait," he said. "I want to see those."

"Oh, that's embarrassing. My mom took way too many baby pictures. I'm either half-naked on a blanket—mothers tend to like that kind of photo—or I'm dressed up like a baby doll."

Garrett turned the book so he could see the pictures better. There were a few of her in the cradle, and some in a highchair. Then she was a toddler, cute as a button. It struck him that he was looking at the real Marlene. The sentimental photos had been taken before she'd learned to change and shift depending on circumstances.

Prior to her acting career, Marlene hadn't needed to pretend so much. And not just on stage, but in life. She'd had the freedom to be herself. As Garrett flipped through the pages, he saw her as a teen, then all dressed up for the high school prom. It was touching, and he felt like he knew her a little better.

"My mom went overboard," Marlene said, taking the book back.

"I liked them." Garrett studied her for a moment, seeing her in a different light. Then he remembered his purpose for the day. "I have some business to attend to later. I've arranged for Wyatt to be here in my absence. I'm hoping you're planning to stay home today and relax. I'll feel better about leaving if I don't have to worry about you."

Marlene gave him a demure smile. "I rather like you worrying about me."

Garrett nearly told her how much he did worry, and what she meant to him. But he didn't. Instead he resumed his bodyguard demeanor and stood up. "He should be here shortly. I'll be at Stealth for a while this morning, then I have a few things to do. I should be back before dinner."

Marlene stuck out her lower lip in a pout. "Well, don't leave me alone for too long."

As soon as Wyatt showed up, Garrett prepared to go. "I need to use your car. It will save time."

"Sure, no problem." Wyatt tossed him the keys. "She's a sweet ride; I had the engine tuned up. Don't get any tickets."

Garrett laughed. "I'll keep that in mind." He headed for the door. "Stay close. I'll be back as soon as I can." He trusted Wyatt and didn't need to give him any instructions. His friend knew the ropes and was up to speed on Marlene's case. Wyatt was a guy that he'd trust his life with.

The Mini Cooper was silver, with a red top and red racing stripes. Garrett had driven it a few times before. It handled well and was fun to drive. He pulled out of the garage and headed down the driveway, waving at the gate guard as he exited.

It was a cold March day, but the weather was clear. The neighborhood was quiet. The green lawns were neatly trimmed, and flowers bloomed in the gardens. Roses and a variety of poppies dotted the scenery. Garrett's mind was still on Marlene. Driving along the quiet residential streets, he dwelled on thoughts of her with her brother.

Garrett was torn. He felt like a fraud. Marlene trusted him, but she didn't know all that she should. It would be best to tell her, but he couldn't bring himself to do it. With her life hanging in the balance, he didn't want to share what he'd held back for too long.

Garrett didn't want to shock her, nor did he want to see the look in her eyes when she realized what had happened. He'd taken her to his bed, and been closer to her than any woman—yet it was going to end badly. He saw no alternative.

If only there was another choice. But there wasn't. Garrett shouldn't have allowed the intimacy between them as he had; that was going to make it harder on her. He'd been greedy and now it was too late. He couldn't go back.

With Marlene in his arms, he hadn't been able to turn her away. It did no good to pretend he wasn't guilty. She was the expert at pretense, not Garrett. The knowledge that he withheld tormented him, ate away at his insides.

Garrett was in too deep now. If only he'd told her that first day, but he hadn't. And each day it was more difficult to envision revealing his sordid past. Andrew had been a young marine, full of life and purpose. He'd fought hard, and been a credit to his country.

Battle was unpredictable. One didn't know, couldn't predict every move. That day the sounds of gunfire had been deafening, and smoke from firebombs clouded the air he breathed. It had been Iraq and it had been brutal. Garrett was used to war, to death and destruction.

Yet he'd still found it rough to deal with. The hardest part was seeing one of your buddies die, losing another SEAL, or any serviceman. That day the skirmish had nearly overwhelmed them. As was sometimes the case, the marines had worked right alongside the SEAL team.

Garrett had known Andrew, and talked with him

many times. They were friends and had each other's back. Or they had. The horrifying scene came back in a blur. The roar of guns, the shouts of men, blood and anguish. Garrett's team had moved out of range and readied for action.

They'd just been stealthily progressing back toward the main unit. They'd taken cover in a partially destroyed building with the marine unit. On cue, they scurried back behind a wall. Garrett hadn't seen it, but a stray bullet had hit Andrew.

Never leave a soldier behind. Garrett lived by that motto. He'd heard a man call out, "Parks got shot." Before the other men could react, Garrett held up his hand. "I'm going back for him." He glanced out at the open space. He'd made it here; he could make it back.

"Cover me," Garrett said, then ran toward the partially destroyed building. He'd found Andrew crumbled against a wall, bleeding heavily. "I've got you. Hang on." He gently lifted the man over his shoulder and edged toward the opening. It wouldn't do to get himself killed, as Garrett was Andrew's only chance for survival.

Shots sounded in the distance; the enemy had probably retreated to a more secure position. Garrett made a break for it. He sprinted back to his men, and lowered Andrew to the ground. Quickly, he ripped off his jacket and pressed it on the open wound. It looked bad.

Andrew tried to speak, and Garrett leaned closer to hear. The man was able to get out a few words before he expired. His thoughts had been of Marlene, his beloved sister. He'd known that Garrett would tell her for him.

But he hadn't yet. Garrett was riddled with guilt. He'd failed to save the soldier, had lost Marlene's brother. He should have made sure all the guys were with them before changing position. Or he should have seen that Andrew had been hit and taken him along when they'd first moved. He might have stopped the bleeding sooner, and her brother might have lived.

Afterward, the team understood. Losing a soldier was hard to take. Garrett had felt the failure, and had taken it hard. His teammates hadn't offered any inane reassurances, like it wasn't his fault. No one said anything like that. They were soldiers. They knew. It was something Garrett would have to live with. Death was a part of war, and it didn't get any easier.

Garrett didn't know if he could have averted disaster. He'd felt responsible for the younger guys, so brave and idealistic. It did no good to wonder how it could have been different. It hadn't been, and now the failure and the guilt haunted Garrett.

How could he tell Marlene? There was no way to say that he'd failed to save Andrew without burdening her with more grief. Garrett hadn't saved him. There was no way to change it, no matter how difficult it was to live with that knowledge.

Garrett snapped back to the present with a shock. He had stopped, and was about to make a right onto Mulholland Drive. He looked left to check for oncoming traffic, and a man on a motorcycle caught his eye. The guy, slowing to turn right onto the residential street, had his helmet shield up, and briefly glanced over at Garrett.

That was all it took. Those blue eyes, icy and cold. Garrett wouldn't forget them. Those cruel eyes met his, and adrenaline surged in his veins. *Son of a bitch.*

It was Buckner.

Before Garrett could react, Buckner changed course, whipped in front of the Cooper, and sped off on his crotch rocket, heading down Mulholland. In a split second, Garrett was on his ass, hoping that Wyatt's souped-up car could keep up. "Come on, baby," he said. "Don't lose him." He floored it.

The winding road was fairly clear, making it possible for Garrett to whip around any vehicle in his way. Rage surged in his veins, and his pulse pounded. He couldn't let the asshole out of his sight; he couldn't lose him. This was his chance to nab him, and take him out of action for good.

Buckner had gotten bold, and come out in the open. He'd probably been heading for Marlene's house to case the place, or do harm. God only knew what he'd planned. It was time to stop him. Garrett pressed the gas pedal. He had to go faster.

The motorcycle had the advantage, but Garrett kept him in sight. He sped along the winding road, flying past anything in his way. Buckner was jet-propelled along the street, weaving around cars. He was a daredevil, speeding ahead.

Buckner had made a mistake. He'd gotten brave, but he was going to regret it. Garrett was in his element. The chase was on and he had the enemy in his sights. He tailed the guy with a fury, and the car had more pep than he'd thought.

Gliding down the street at a high rate of speed, leaning into the curves, Buckner stayed ahead. But Garrett pressed the car to its limits, holding tight as he swept over the road. He swore under his breath. He couldn't lose him, not now.

It appeared that Buckner knew this road, and had likely driven Mulholland Drive many times before.

The guy didn't slow or hesitate. He drove like he knew where he was going, like he knew every curve, dip, and bend like the back of his hand.

But Garrett stayed with him. He hadn't caught him, and Buckner had gained on him, but he was still visible up ahead. The road was long, with wide sweeps to it, so Garrett was able to keep his quarry in his line of vision. If the guy misjudged a corner, or hit a wet patch, he might go down.

Anything could happen. Garrett pursued with a vengeance, ruthlessly focused on catching the madman, almost within reach. There was a signal at Beverly Glen, just above the Hollywood Hills, but the motorcycle raced through the red light. And Garrett did the same, watching and prepared to swerve to miss traffic. He made it through.

Buckner flew down Mulholland, then made a right on Cahuenga, another long boulevard, and Garrett followed. The Cooper was low to the ground, and hugged the road, so Garrett gave it more gas. He put on the pressure, hoping that Buckner would make a mistake. He prayed to see him skid over the pavement, the motorcycle out of control at high speed.

But Buckner and the motorcycle slid over the road without slowing. Just past Franklin, there was a bend in the road, and for a moment Garrett couldn't see him. He raced ahead and reached the curve but was unable to spot the motorcycle.

Franklin veered west and Garrett went that direction, then slowed. He couldn't see Buckner, couldn't tell where he'd gone. Hillcrest Road was to his right. If the guy had sped up there, Garrett wouldn't be able to catch him. Buckner might have continued on Franklin and not turned at all.

It was impossible to tell. Garrett had lost him. He slammed his fist into the dash. "Dammit." There was no way to find the guy now. He'd had his chance and missed it. If only he'd been in a faster vehicle...but he hadn't been. Garrett was furious.

The only good thing was that Garrett's training had kicked in, and he'd memorized the motorcycle license plate when Buckner had initially skirted in front of him and taken off at the Mulholland intersection. There was little chance that running the plate would reveal Buckner's address. The guy wouldn't be that stupid.

It was probably a stolen plate, but Garrett had to try. He called Travis to let him know he was running late, and filled him in on chasing Buckner. It was evident that the creep was close and getting confident, which was good to know. It was only a matter of time until he tripped up, and Garrett had him in his grasp. That couldn't come soon enough.

CHAPTER NINETEEN

Buckner was enraged. How dare that loser chase him? Shaking with anger, he'd pulled onto a narrow side street to wait. He'd turned up Hillcrest, and hadn't seen Flynn go by. He'd lost him.

There hadn't been a chance that small car could catch him, but it was annoying. He had every right to drive by Marlene's home. It was a public street. Yet he'd been pursued like some common criminal.

Buckner edged out onto a residential street then headed back to Franklin. He observed traffic but saw no sign of Flynn. So he rode to Santa Monica Boulevard and went home.

He needed to exhibit self-control. His neighbors were used to seeing him on the bike, but he couldn't allow his distress to show. The garage door opened, and Buckner drove inside. He lifted off his helmet and threw it against the wall, then peeled off his jacket and dropped it on the floor.

Once he was in the house, he swore. That traitor had balls chasing him.

If he'd had his gun, Buckner would have ended it right there. But it had only been a reconnaissance trip. Still, he shouldn't have gone near the place without a weapon. He wouldn't make that mistake again.

All it would take was one clear shot and Flynn would be out of the picture. It would happen. Justice would be served. And Marlene was beginning to piss him off too.

She should know better. He was the hero, not that flaky ex-SEAL. But it seemed Marlene believed the guy's lies. Buckner had seen them together, and he seethed with the unfairness of it all. There she was in photos next to her bodyguard. They were all over the media like they were some romantic couple.

Bodyguard my ass. The guy was a fake, a fraud. Why couldn't Marlene see it? She was too gullible, too ready to believe whatever she was told. If only Buckner could get close enough, he could convince her, make her see how it really was.

He sank into a chair and stared at the framed photograph of Marlene. Her false smile irritated him. Grabbing the frame, he dashed the picture to the floor, and watched the glass crack then come free of the frame. He was in control; he was calling the shots.

Buckner reached down and lifted the picture, shaking off a few shards of glass. "You owe me," he said. "It's taking you too fucking long to figure it out, though."

He remembered it all, every tiny detail, as if it had just happened yesterday. It had been Iraq, during one of the many battles he'd fought as a marine. Andrew Parks was in his unit, and he'd spoken with him. He knew about his sister, the movie star. And he knew how fond her older brother was of her.

It was touching, really, and it had been a shame that anything happened to Andrew. It shouldn't have. War had been brutal, but Buckner had been a capable soldier, one of the best. He'd been tough and well trained. His unit had counted on him, and he wouldn't have let a teammate down.

Fear hadn't ruled, only courage. In the heat of battle, Buckner felt strong, invincible. He hadn't cowered to save his own life. He'd been there to protect others, and he would have saved Andrew.

Guns, smoke, shouting to near-deafening levels had ensued. But it hadn't distracted Buckner from his duty. He'd fought bravely, and killed many of the enemy. He'd been an asset to his team. Yet he hadn't fought for the glory. He'd fought for honor, and had done all he could for his country.

Then the units had pulled back, scurrying from one crumbling building to the next. Buckner had checked to make sure all the guys were together. He hadn't seen Andrew, and looked around. They'd been fighting alongside the SEALs that day.

Flynn had shouted, "Move. Now." And the men had gone in the direction he'd been waving his arm.

Buckner had lagged. "Where's Parks? I don't see him."

But the SEAL had refused to be defied, and shoved him ahead. "Get moving."

Buckner resisted. "I don't see him. I'm going back."

Flynn had slammed his hand into his back, making Buckner fall forward. He slid onto the ground and there had been gunfire all around, leaving no choice but to scramble to the next building. The SEAL had fucked up. Parks still wasn't with them, and Flynn had refused to let anyone go back.

Buckner had fought, and finally shoved Flynn aside. He'd run back, looking for his teammate. And he'd found him. Andrew had been shot. He'd been shot because Flynn had left him behind. Never leave a soldier behind. But the traitor had done so.

It had cost Parks his life. Buckner dragged him back to the unit, but the marine was already dead—because of Flynn's cowardice and stupidity. If the traitor hadn't gotten in his way, Buckner would have saved Andrew.

But it had been too late.

Marlene was deluded if she thought Flynn was a hero. He couldn't be trusted, and she might find that out too late. Just like her brother had. But the guy must have told her a different story, one that suited him, and painted him as the macho protector.

Why hadn't she seen through Flynn's lies? Buckner had to get to her, needed to get close enough to shed light on the truth. He was the man she could count on, and once Marlene knew, she'd be grateful. That was the only way it could turn out. She'd be indebted to Bucker, and then he'd have her for his own.

Marlene couldn't possibly choose to be with the man who'd betrayed her brother and left him to die. As soon as she knew that Buckner had been willing to risk his own life to save Andrew, and learned that he could have saved him if not for Flynn, she'd fall into his arms.

Instead, she was still with her bodyguard. But that would soon change. Buckner wasn't jealous. He couldn't envy a weak-principled man like Garrett Flynn. Yet the injustice of the situation irked him. As the real hero, he should be treated with more respect, and recognized for his deeds.

Marlene belonged to Buckner, and he was going to take her. All he had to do was get Flynn out of the way. He didn't have his unit with him this time. He was the lone wolf, but he was up to the task.

It would happen soon. Fun and games were over. Flynn had dicked around with him for the last time. The asshole would regret interfering, and he'd be forced to admit that Buckner was the real hero. Before he took the SEAL out for good, he wanted to see the guy's face when Marlene discovered the truth. And she would. Buckner would see to that.

CHAPTER TWENTY

Wyatt didn't hover; he went about his business checking on security, not taking it for granted. "I'll check in with the team," he called over his shoulder. "If you need anything, I'm not far."

When he left, Marlene went to do a yoga workout. It calmed her mind, and gave her the strength for the long days of filming. Plus she had to stay in shape. Her trainer wasn't scheduled, but would come by if she called.

Instead, Marlene did a workout on her own, preferring the quiet. One section of her fitness room was set up for yoga. The floor had cushy mats, and she had a variety of equipment. After turning on some classical music, she began her stretching.

The warmup felt good, and relaxed her. Marlene's thoughts drifted to Garrett. As she moved through her routine, limbering her body, she remembered how he touched her. His hands were big and strong, and there was power in his body. A delicious tingle raced over her skin, and she felt so alive.

The intimacy drew her toward a future that she wasn't sure she could handle. Garrett had allowed her to get close, move into a personal bond that her heart was caught up in. Marlene couldn't let go, and wasn't sure she wanted to.

Butterflies fought in her stomach when she considered the future. It was all so unpredictable, but it was more than that. The military had been the source of joy, as well as grief. Having lost two men in her life, she didn't want to lose another.

It would be better not to have Garrett at all than to have him and endure the loss. Surely that's what would happen. His career would mandate that. Some women were willing to live that way, always wondering. But Marlene wasn't certain she was up to the task.

She'd sworn that type of man was off-limits. Then she'd met Garrett. Her heart was pulling her toward a relationship that her head told her could only lead to disappointment. Yet she was torn. If she hadn't met him, then Marlene wouldn't have sought out such a man.

But she had met him; that was the problem. And it was difficult to ignore the effect he had on her. Try as she might, Marlene wasn't able to brush aside her feelings. She couldn't pretend not to care. Maybe she could put on a show of insensitivity, but she couldn't hide the truth from herself.

Marlene loved Garrett. Yet the question remained: what was she going to do about it? Each day, she struggled to convince herself that it would be over soon. When the crisis resolved, for good or bad, Garrett would be gone. Then she'd get over him.

But would she? Marlene was no longer sure. There was no other man like Garrett. He was special to her. And when he went, there was every possibility that she wouldn't fall in love again. She wasn't even thirty yet, so that seemed extreme.

But the heart had a mind of its own. Marlene couldn't pick the man to love, or she'd have shut Garrett out from the start. They were wrong for each other, but their feelings weren't. They couldn't be.

When she was in his arms, it felt so right.

Conflicted, she finished her workout. It had physically revitalized her, but hadn't soothed her emotionally. After showering and changing, Marlene went to the living room to stare out at the city view. It gave her an expansive feeling, made her feel that she could overcome challenges that had seemed insurmountable before.

Laura brought her some tea, so Marlene sat for a while sipping and meditating on her dilemma. Yet she wasn't able to get any clearer about the resolution. She reached for her phone to dial her mother, needing to talk it out, and glad she got an answer on the first ring.

"It's good to hear from you. I just got back from a walk. How are you, honey?"

Marlene poured out all that had happened since they'd last spoken. She skipped any details that might be too upsetting, but there was plenty to talk about. Her mother listened while she described the issue she'd had with filming. "I just hadn't been able to get it right."

"So what changed?"

"I talked to Garrett and...the emotion opened up for me. I was able to connect with it, finally."

"I can't wait to see the film when it's out. I'm sure you are wonderful in it."

Marlene's mother was her most loyal supporter. "I'll let you know as soon as they announce the date. We're nearing the end of filming, but it will still be a while before it's in the theaters.

"You know, Mom, my career is challenging. You've seen me go through a lot. But it does have its rewards. And it is a way for me to make the kind of money I need to, in order to support the charities that matter to me so much."

"That's true," her mother said. "But also, you are a star and you love the stage. You've loved it since you were a little girl, performing in school plays. I can't envision you giving it up."

"I can't either. There's always a way to get through something, if I don't give up." Marlene shared most things with her mother, and knew she'd understand about Garrett. "Dating is difficult for me as a celebrity, though. You know better than anyone about my history of relationship failures. Then there were the producers who wanted to take me to bed, promising me the sky if I did so."

"You're too smart for that."

Marlene didn't mention the abusive relationships she'd been in. There were some things it was best not to share with her mother. She'd escaped and put that behind her. "I'm not sure what to do, Mom." She shared how she felt about Garrett, and confessed that she loved him.

"I really do love him, but I'm not sure we have a chance together," Marlene said. "It's not right for me to lead him on if we don't."

"Of course you have a chance together...if you love him."

"I just can't...allow myself to be vulnerable like that. He's a former SEAL; he's military. That's exactly the type of man I should steer clear of. Yet I'm drawn to him."

Her mother talked for a few minutes about her brother. "He was a good man, a loving son, and a wonderful brother. I grieve for him too, honey. But would he want you to let what happened destroy your life?"

"I know what you're saying, but what about you

and Dad, then? He was your childhood sweetheart, and he meant everything to you," Marlene said. "Yet he was taken away from you at such a young age. You didn't have the life together you'd dreamed of." She swallowed hard, tears welling in her eyes. "I know this sounds awful to say, but wouldn't you be happier if you'd married a man that you could grow old with?"

For a moment, her mother was silent, and Marlene could sense the emotion on the other end of the line. "There are no easy answers. The loss of the man I loved was devastating; I won't deny that." Her mother took a breath. "But it would have been worse if I hadn't known your father's love. We were together for as long as was possible, and I haven't stopped loving him. I wouldn't trade the time we shared for anything."

Marlene wiped away the tears.

"So you have to ask yourself, honey...would you prefer not to have grown up with Andrew? Do you wish that you hadn't been close, that he hadn't been part of your life, so you wouldn't endure the grief now that he's gone?"

"Of course not," Marlene said with no hesitation. "I wouldn't wish that at all."

"I know you wouldn't." After a moment of silence, her mother said, "I love you, honey."

"I love you too, Mom. When this is all over, I'll come for a visit. I miss you."

When she hung up, Marlene stared out the window. The conversation had helped to put things in perspective, and she took time to sort out her emotions. She'd been so afraid of loss that she'd nearly made a huge mistake and turned away from the right man.

Beneath her resistance to love, Marlene knew what

she'd really been afraid of. She realized that something inside her had changed. She wanted to be with Garrett, wanted to share her life with him, and finally, felt strong enough to face whatever came. Love was a risk, but it was a risk worth taking. Now she needed to talk with Garrett, because she didn't know if he felt the same way.

Marlene ate an early lunch, then sat at her desk to check emails. There was one from her manager about an upcoming project for her to consider. And there were a couple from her event coordinator with details of the next fundraiser. There were others, but they weren't urgent.

After finishing work, Marlene got up to stretch her legs. She picked up her phone to check her social media accounts. It was fun to see how many followers she had. Despite her fame, it amazed her how many fans liked to interact with her. She was careful to keep it professional, as she'd heard too many horror stories.

A photo had gone viral, and the threads had exploded with comments. It was all very alarming, so Marlene looked closer. Scanning further, she was stunned. There was a picture of her brother Andrew, one that had been published in the news following his death.

Since she was a celebrity, even the most private parts of her life were open to scrutiny. It had been even more horrible at the time, as she'd been so raw with grief. Now the picture had circulated again, for no reason she knew of.

It seemed that someone was intent on reminding her about what had happened—as if there was any chance she'd forget. But the comments weren't like the ones before. There was a different tone to them, hurtful and unfeeling.

Marlene stared at the screen. *Andrew could have been saved. He was allowed to die.* The thought of such a thing, the mere idea that his premature death might have been avoided, upset her. Surely, whoever had written those cruel statements had made them up.

Was the person trying to hurt her? Marlene had no idea why. Then she saw, written in bold letters: *YOU ARE MINE MARLENE. YOU BELONG TO ME. YOUR BODYGUARD WILL SOON BE GONE.*

Marlene's pulse pounded, and she felt faint. That had to be Buckner. Anxiety riddled her stomach. Had something happened to Garrett? He hadn't returned yet, and she feared the worst.

She prayed that Garrett was okay. This was all because of her. Yet Marlene still didn't know what Buckner wanted with her. He didn't fit the profile of an average stalker. He had some sort of vendetta, but she didn't have a clue what it was.

Buckner's obsession was dangerous. But at that moment, it wasn't her life Marlene was worried about. She rushed outside and looked around for Wyatt. He was talking to one of the other guards. As Marlene rushed toward him, he looked up and frowned. "What is it?"

She handed over the phone. "Look at this message," she said breathlessly. "It's Buckner. It has to be. He's after Garrett."

Wyatt's expression was all business. He scrolled on her phone, reading the messages, and looking at the photo. "He's trying to intimidate you. It's pure harassment. We're not going to buy into his scare tactics."

Wyatt held her phone in one hand, while he made a call on his own. She held her breath. "Garrett, are you at the office? Oh, really. Okay, can't wait to hear about it. Yeah, I'm calling because Buckner has been busy on social media. Wait until you see what he's up to." Then he clicked off.

"He's not hurt? Is he still downtown?"

"Buckner's all hot air. Garrett is fine, and he's on his way back. We can show him this stuff as soon as he gets here." Wyatt handed her phone back to her. "He'll be here shortly, so don't worry."

Marlene went back inside, with Wyatt right behind her. The threatening comments had rattled her, but Garrett hadn't been injured or worse. Marlene could breathe again. The social media attack had been a reminder that a dark threat still loomed over her, and that her pursuer was getting impatient.

When Garrett walked in, he looked angry. "Let me see what we've got," he said, and Marlene handed over her phone. He read the malicious comments, then looked at her. "Are you okay?"

She shook her head. "It was alarming, but Wyatt was here. I didn't know what to think. I thought that something might have happened to you."

Wyatt looked at her too. "Believe me, Garrett is not an easy target. This fool doesn't know who he's messing with."

Garrett sat in a chair. "I need to get my hands on this guy."

"I don't understand," Marlene said. "My brother died in action. Why won't this lunatic let it go? What's the point in reopening the wound?" She noticed a look cloud Garrett's features, but wasn't sure what she'd seen. It was likely that he was as upset as she was. Using her brother's death to terrorize her was a heartless act.

Garrett let out a long sigh. "Buckner's been busy today. I ran into him earlier."

Marlene's eyes widened. "You what?"

Wyatt didn't comment.

"On my way out this morning, I nearly ran the guy down. I'm sure he was heading here." Garrett proceeded to tell them about chasing the guy for miles, but losing him. "It really ticks me off. I nearly had him. If I had gotten my hands on him, I'd have squeezed the life out of him. He'd have been in no shape to post pictures or type any comments."

"Shit, you were so close," Wyatt said. "My car is fast, but not that fast."

"I couldn't even get close enough to shoot the son of a bitch," Garrett said. "By the time I realized it was him, he'd already taken off. I had a visual, but was too far back to even shoot a tire out. I had no stable shooting position, and Buckner was definitely not a motionless target."

"Hell, in a situation like that it would be pure luck to hit a moving target at any kind of distance," Wyatt said.

"I couldn't risk it. There were other cars around, and some pedestrians crossing the street," Garrett said. "But this game isn't over, and Buckner will get what's coming to him. It will only be worse for him the longer he avoids me."

Wyatt leaned forward. "What did you find out at the office?"

Garrett threw up his hands. "They're close. It's only a matter of time. They'll find this guy." He sighed. "I'm tired of waiting, and I'm not a patient man to start with."

Wyatt stood up. "Well, I'll check in with you later. I've got some stuff to do. But I'll stay available, just in case."

After his teammate left, Garrett turned to her. "Travis ran the plate on the motorcycle. It was a dead end, like I thought it would be. The vehicle isn't registered to Buckner, but they're checking it out anyway."

"Buckner is vicious. It worries me. What will he do next?"

Garrett came over and put his arm around her. "He's getting careless. He came out in the open today, and got a little too bold. It was nearly his undoing. The guy blusters and threatens, but he's a coward. We'll find him. I'm sure of it."

Marlene rested her head on Garrett's shoulder. It was a comfort to have him so close. She wanted to tell him so, and to tell him so much more. Now was not the time, but maybe soon. The crisis had escalated, but she had faith that it would resolve before too much longer.

The question was how it would end, and whether they'd be able to escape harm. Marlene hoped they would, but so much had happened. She was rattled, and didn't know what to expect—but she didn't say that to Garrett.

CHAPTER TWENTY-ONE

The following week on the set, morale was high. The filming would soon be finished, and the director seemed pleased with the result. Post-production would take another six months or so, before the Christmas release. Marlene congratulated her costar, other members of the cast, and spoke with Nicholas. He'd been an amazing director to work with, and she hoped to do so again.

That week there hadn't been any more incidents with Buckner, but there was no doubt in Marlene's mind that there would be. She wasn't naïve enough to think that the man had gone away. The situation annoyed as well as frightened her.

Marlene felt violated, because the guy had the ability to dramatically affect her life. Now that she was doing so well, and had overcome the recent challenges in her career, it was aggravating that she hadn't been able to slip from the maniac's grasp.

On one of the last days, Marlene had a chance to talk with Anna about the premier. It wasn't too early to plan what to wear, since creating a unique design took time. "My designer is working on my dress, but it's in the beginning stages," Marlene said.

Anna sat on the sofa in the dressing room, with her legs crossed, drinking mineral water. "What do you have in mind?"

"I'd love to have a dress like I saw once; sheer fabric covered the arms and draped down to the floor.

Red silk in a floral pattern concealed the important areas, so the dress wasn't entirely see-through." Marlene wrinkled her nose. "But it had a long train that dragged on the floor, like a wedding dress sort of thing. I'm sure I'd trip over it and embarrass myself."

"No kidding. But it sounds beautiful."

"The dress can't be too weird, or overly sexy, either. I don't want everyone staring at my cleavage while I'm trying to talk."

Anna swung her ponytail over her shoulder. "Yes, that is so irritating."

"So I need something classy, yet stunning. I want to stand out, yet not have the audience snickering about some odd aspect of my dress," Marlene said.

Anna shrugged. "That sounds simple enough."

"Uh huh, well, we'll see what he comes up with. So what about you? What kind of dress are you going to wear?"

"I'm going with a weirdly designed, overly sexy, backless dress with a plunging neckline, so all eyeballs are glued to my breasts."

Marlene burst out laughing, along with Anna. "You'll be on the front page. No one will stop talking about your dress."

"Yep, that's the idea." Anna grinned. "But then, we both know I wouldn't have the guts." She swigged her drink. "Hey, is Garrett going with you?"

"It depends," Marlene said, and gave her friend a brief update of recent events.

"Geez, this Buckner guy doesn't quit." Anna frowned. "Should I be worried?"

"I hope not, since I have Garrett to protect me. But there's no way to predict the outcome." The mention of her bodyguard shifted Marlene's focus. "I have to tell you, though, that I feel more than just professional fondness for him."

"Talk to me," Anna said with renewed interest. "I told you he was irresistible."

"I confess...I'm really in love with Garrett."

"When did this happen?"

"It's been happening for a while. I just couldn't deal with it. But I can't deny how I feel." Marlene sighed. "Yet with all that's been going on, there's been no chance to discuss the future."

"And does Garrett feel the same way you do?"

"That's the thing. I don't know for sure. He hasn't said he loves me."

Anna pointed a finger at her. "I'm sure he does. I've seen how he looks at you." She leaned forward. "He's trained to be professional, and you're a client. You might have to be the first to say it. You have to tell him that you love him."

"I want to," Marlene said. "But it has to be the right time."

"Well, don't wait too long." Anna stood up. "He might take off, thinking that he's saving you from God knows what, or some macho thing like that. And you don't want to lose him...not Garrett." She put her hand on the door handle. "So I'll see you at the press conference on Friday, then?"

"Of course, we can give each other support. Those things are always unnerving." Marlene hugged her friend goodbye.

It was routine to allow the media onto the set after filming, so they could interview the cast and the director. They'd also photograph the set and see clips of the movie before release. Marlene had been the center of attention before, and would be this time too. There were already rumors about her winning an award for her performance.

That evening, Marlene had the pleasure of going out to dinner, instead of staying home. She had cause to celebrate, and Garrett didn't voice too much objection. After all, the phones were secure now, and he'd made sure there were no trackers on the limo. He had his team covering, so they wouldn't be followed.

Marlene didn't think about all of that. She just wanted to go out and have a good time. Garrett was firm about dining at a restaurant inside a major hotel. That made access for any attacker more difficult. It was more secure than the bistro with the sidewalk patio had been.

The Ritz-Carlton was a good choice, and met with Garrett's approval. An evening out meant dressing up, so Marlene wore a silver cocktail dress, but kept the jewelry to a minimum. There was no sense in attracting trouble, or the eye of potential thieves.

She wasn't sneaking out in disguise, so would be recognized. But Garrett assured her that he wouldn't allow fans to interrupt their evening, and the hotel had a policy against paparazzi. It was the best she could hope for.

They stopped at the bar for a drink before dinner, or Marlene did, anyway. Garrett ordered a non-alcoholic beer, and sipped it while she had a glass of champagne. She was on a high from finishing the film, and looking across at her date made her feel even better.

Garrett wore a slate-gray shirt, open at the neck, underneath a charcoal blazer. He had a thin silver chain around his throat, adding to his sex appeal. His hair had been trimmed shorter and was attractively spiked, making her want to run her fingers through it. "If you ever get tired of the protection business," Marlene said, "you could be a model."

The lusty look in Garrett's eyes sent a twinge of pleasure straight to her core. "I don't see that happening. I only wear this stuff for you."

"Speaking of which…at the premiere you'll need to dress appropriately. So be prepared to wear a designer suit. You have plenty of time to have one tailored for you."

Garrett sipped his drink, and Marlene focused on his kissable lips. "I could see that one coming." He leaned back in the chair. "So you're done filming?"

"Yes, I'm not expecting any more retakes. Nicholas released us, so it looks good." Marlene tasted her champagne, liking the dryness and the sensation of the bubbles on her tongue. "I don't want to be overly confident, but there has been talk of awards."

"It's a good movie. I can tell, even though I've only seen it in pieces."

"I agree, and I think it will be a hit at the box office."

"Plus you're the star," Garrett said, his blue eyes sparkling in the candlelight. "You did a great job; you should be proud."

"It was very rewarding," Marlene said. "I'm crossing my fingers. There's a chance I'll receive an award, which would do wonders for my career." She smiled. "And for my ego."

In the darkened room, Marlene couldn't take her eyes off Garrett. He was so handsome and such a gentleman. It was no wonder that he'd stolen her heart. She drank her champagne, enjoying his company, and they talked about trivial things.

When they finished their drinks, Garrett took her

up to Wolfgang Puck's for dinner. Located in the heart of Los Angeles, the hotel's restaurant had panoramic skyline views. Tinted blue windows wrapped around the dining room, giving a sky-blue hue to the city's vista. The lights on all the tall buildings glittered against the dark evening.

It wasn't Marlene's first time at the restaurant. "I think you'll enjoy what the chef does here." After being seated at a table by the window, they studied their menus. "The halibut is good; I've had that before. But I'm in the mood to try something different."

When Marlene looked up, Garrett had already put his menu aside and was watching her. Despite knowing him intimately, his gaze made her as nervous as a schoolgirl. The waiter came by and Marlene ordered the Japanese black cod. Garrett chose the beef tenderloin.

She ordered white wine, a label she recognized, and Garrett switched to soda water with lime. Then they gazed out at the view. "The city looks amazing from here, doesn't it?"

"It does, and I like being up high."

Marlene thought about how many times he must have jumped from helicopters, so certainly heights didn't freak him out. And from the top floor of the hotel, the view of the city was breathtaking. She twirled her wine glass, then glanced at Garrett.

He looked awfully good under the soft lights. Of course, he looked good in any lighting. Marlene stared out the window for a moment. Where was this going? There was no disputing that this was a romantic date, bodyguard or not.

Yet Garrett held back. He didn't hold her hand, or better yet, lean over to kiss her. Marlene wished he would, but understood why he hadn't. He wasn't pushing her into anything; they hadn't made any commitment. And she wasn't certain of his feelings.

It was one thing to sleep together, but that didn't mean that Garrett wanted to spend his life with her. Or even continue to see her once the danger had passed—provided she came through it safely.

He was congenial and polite, but not more than that. Certainly Buckner was a concern. That was one explanation for Garrett's mood. Sneaking out for a dinner one evening and ignoring the threat didn't mean it had gone away.

Garrett seemed a bit reserved, and that might be why. Yet his eyes gave away what was in his heart. When he looked over at her, Marlene sensed a deep emotion that remained unspoken. She nearly blurted out how much she loved him, but the words locked up in her throat.

Marlene loved him too much to hear that he didn't feel the same, or to face the reality that they were so wrong for each other. Just for this evening, she'd forget about circumstances and be grateful for the time she had with him.

At the end of the meal, any feeling of awkwardness vanished when Garrett took charge. He'd gotten a room for the night. "I know how stressful all of this has been for you," he said, taking her hand. "A night away will be good."

In the elevator, Garrett put his arm around her and held her close. Marlene's pulse raced, then she leaned against him, feeling his strength and his warmth. The scent of his maleness ignited her desire and the rest of the world seemed to drop away.

When the door to their suite clicked shut, Garrett lifted her into his arms and carried her to the bedroom. Light filtered through the windows, casting a soft glow over the room. He lowered her to the bed and placed his palms on her cheeks.

Leaning down, Garrett kissed her ravenously, and Marlene wrapped her arms around his waist. When he released her, and she gazed into his eyes, her heart swelled with emotion. "Garrett...I..."

"It's okay, sweetheart. I don't want you to worry. Trust me." Then Garrett slowly undressed her, adoring her as he went. As he peeled off garments, he caressed her skin with hot kisses. When he took a bare nipple in his mouth, Marlene arched her back in pleasure.

Garrett stripped off his clothes, and Marlene reached out to hold his heat in her fist. He was so virile and strong. She admired his rock-hard muscle, flat abs, and lean thighs. Stroking his erection sent molten heat to her belly. There wouldn't be another man like him; he was the one for her.

Garrett scooped her onto the pillows and straddled her, then held her hands over her head, pinning her to the bed. Marlene wrapped her legs around his waist to hold tight. He dipped into her, making her moan with the sensation. All she wanted was for him to take her, to feel him filling her, and to get lost in his arms.

Garrett made love to her—as she did to him— sometimes tenderly, other times with passionate abandon. Each interlude was delicious, and Marlene craved more. His hot kisses and powerful body melted her from the inside out. She wanted to wake up beside him forever more, but accepted the special night together, no matter what the future held.

CHAPTER TWENTY-TWO

Garrett had made love to Marlene long into the night. He'd sensed a change in their relationship, but couldn't put it into words. All he'd been able to do was to hold her and love her. That would have to be enough for now.

Marlene was his woman, the only woman he wanted. Yet having her seemed impossible. There were too many strikes against them, too many reasons it was a bad idea.

Plus he was still keeping something important from her. Garrett cursed himself for not telling her at the first opportunity. Having had her in his arms, his gut wrenched at the thought of losing her. Yet that was a very real possibility once she learned the truth.

In the still of the morning, Garrett reached under the sheet and raked his hand over the curve of Marlene's hip. She stirred with a sigh, and opened her eyes. She was soft and warm, and he was aroused by the feel of her. When she snuggled closer, he pulled her against him.

Garrett gently kissed her temple, then her jaw. Marlene's green eyes met his and passion surged. With his hand on the back of her head, he pressed her into a deep kiss. Breathing her in and nestling against her feminine curves ignited a fire within him.

As he kissed down her body, Garrett's lips lingered on her silky skin. She was so sweet, so sexy. He pressed his lips to her belly, then over her sex.

Marlene purred like a kitten, and Garrett put his palms on her thighs, slowly parting them.

Reaching underneath, Garrett cupped her round buttocks, lifting her to his mouth. He sucked and licked, tasting her sweet cream. Marlene panted, and her hips rose to meet his lips. With a flick of his tongue, he drove her crazy. She whimpered, and Garrett spiraled the tip of his tongue around her most sensitive area.

When she shuddered against his lips and cried out, Garrett pressed his mouth to her sex, relishing her pleasure. Then she collapsed to the bed, and he kissed his way back up to her lips. Rubbing his nose against her ear, he whispered, "I want you, sweetheart...like I haven't wanted any other woman."

Then Marlene grasped his heavy erection and stroked with steady pressure. Reaching for the side table, Garrett found a condom and rolled it on. Then he dipped into her heat, sliding deep. She wrapped her legs around the back of his thighs and raked her hands through his hair.

Garrett plunged into her with a steady rhythm, trying to hold back from exploding too soon. But Marlene felt good and was so hot. She gripped tightly around him, making a tiny sound in the back of her throat. It was his undoing. He kissed her with a wildness he couldn't control, then his body stiffened.

Marlene rocked into him and cried out, coming apart underneath him. Garrett released hard, and ecstasy swamped him. She was his; they were together as one. His breathing was ragged, and his heart pounded. He rested his head beside hers, taking a moment to recover as his body hummed with satisfaction.

Then Garrett slid next to her on the bed and enclosed

her in his arms. She was quiet, cuddled against him. Marlene was a dream, more than he deserved. It couldn't last, but he held her tighter anyway. A man could hope, even if there wasn't a shred of reality to base it on. Marlene was special, and he dared to conceive that somehow it all might work out.

On the way to the studio that morning, they stopped at Marlene's home to shower and dress. The filming had ended, but there was a press conference scheduled that afternoon. Garrett needed to go to Stealth for a status on the situation. He'd had a text from Cooper that indicated they were following up on a lead.

Once Garrett ensured that Marlene was safely in the studio, he'd take care of business. It was the safest place for her, due to all the security on site. And he'd be back by the time the media arrived.

When Garrett left Marlene, he sensed some tension. She'd said that press events were stressful, but a necessary evil. At least she'd be among the cast, and had her friend Anna with her. Maybe it wouldn't be too bad, and he'd return soon to give her moral support.

For the sake of efficiency, Garrett used one of security's vehicles. He'd gotten away from using public transportation since traveling around in the limo; plus driving would get him back faster. Traffic was slow, as was usual for a Friday in Los Angeles, even though it wasn't rush hour.

He parked the car in the garage across from the building where Stealth occupied one of the upper floors, and headed toward the elevator. A sixth sense put him on alert. There had been times overseas, in the desert or the thick of a forest, where that was all that had saved him.

Hypervigilance was like a superpower that could be learned. Over time, Garrett had honed his. It wasn't anything he could put his finger on, but the hair on the back of his neck pricked at the silence of the multi-level garage.

Then a glint of metal caught his eye. Without hesitation, Garrett dropped to the floor and in rapid motion rolled behind a wide concrete pillar. The rifle shot echoed in the cavernous space and a bullet impacted an exterior wall.

"Shit." Adrenaline pumped through Garrett's veins and he shifted into attack mode. That had been a rifle shot, but his Glock didn't have as much range. He yanked it from the holster and held the gun in both hands, waiting, listening.

Then there was a roar of an engine and the squeal of a tire. Garrett wasn't foolhardy enough to stick his head around the pillar to see. At close range a shooter could hit a target even from a moving vehicle. He held his gun in position, ready to shoot the head off anyone who peered around.

Then the sound of the vehicle faded. Garrett stood up, still concealed behind the pillar, and leaned over the wall to look down to the street. Like a flash, a motorcycle shot out of the parking lot and sped away. It was a black motorcycle, and even from above Garrett recognized Buckner's build, how he straddled the bike.

There was no use shooting. Garrett was too high up; Buckner was moving too fast. Then the bike disappeared. "Goddammit to hell." He lowered the gun and kicked the wall. The shooter had nearly shot his head off. And now he'd escaped.

How long had the asshole been in the garage? Buckner had waited for him, ambush style, intending to pick him off with a well-aimed rifle shot. Garrett didn't have time to wonder how the guy had known he'd be there. Maybe he got his jollies hanging out there as a routine, hoping for the right moment.

It didn't matter. Buckner had shot at him like a hired sniper, and Garrett was pissed off. He stabbed at the elevator button. Impatient when it didn't open fast enough, he jogged to the stairs and took them two at a time.

Garrett strode into the building as if he hadn't nearly been killed a minute before. His training had taught him to control his reactions. He'd slowed his breathing and heart rate, ready to face the enemy to conquer any opposition. On the way up to the office, rage bubbled to the surface. *That creep has taken his last shot at me.*

When Garrett walked past Tessa, she gave him a glance but didn't say anything. He went straight down the hall and into the office. Travis looked up and, without flinching, said, "What happened to you?"

"Buckner shot at me...that's what."

Travis narrowed his eyes. "Son of a bitch."

"Yeah, that's what I said." Garrett paced the floor in front of the desk. "He missed, as you can see...I saw the glint of his gun just before he pulled the trigger."

"You'll be relieved to hear that we've located Buckner."

That had Garrett's attention. "I need that information." He leaned closer to the desk. "I'm taking that guy out."

Travis punched an intercom button. "Coop, get in here pronto. Garrett is storming around my office like a fire-breathing dragon."

The computer tech appeared in the doorway, unruffled. "Got something for you...it looks like we have an address for Buckner."

Garrett lowered into a chair. "Don't keep me in suspense."

Cooper sat down. "The license plate on the motorcycle panned out, after all. When I traced it, the name it was registered to didn't match, and the address was falsified. But I just had a hunch, so I sent a guy to check things out."

Garrett listened, anxious for the punch line.

"I got a driver's license photo of the guy the vehicle is registered to, and had it shown around," Coop said. "Eventually, we found a mechanic who recognized our guy. 'Oh, that's Christopher Ulridge,' the guy says. 'He's a regular...loves that little Suzuki of his. It's his baby. Comes by often to get it tuned up. Nice guy, a retired marine.'"

"Marine my ass," Travis said.

"So we got an address on the owner, Christopher Ulridge, who is really Buckner lying low." Coop grinned. "Everybody messes up, even bad guys. Buckner's blind spot was his prize motorcycle. He gave a home address when he took it to the shop...overlooked the possibility that it could be traced back to him."

Garrett held out his hand, and Coop gave him a slip of paper with the address typed on it. "I just got that an hour ago. It's better that you're here anyway. I have an aversion to texting sensitive data."

Travis watched Garrett bounce out of the chair. "I'll send someone with you."

"No need. He's just one asshole; I can handle it," Garrett said, waving the piece of paper. "When I find this rat, it will be my pleasure to take care of him. He won't have any clear shots again. I'm gunning for *him* now."

Travis looked like he was about to say something, but Garrett cut him off. "I'm not afraid of Glenn Buckner. I just can't wait to get my hands on him."

Without giving his boss a chance to argue, Garrett made a fast exit, in a hurry to get to Buckner's place. The guy had gotten a head start, and would be there first. That was just as well. Garrett would have the advantage, so he could sneak up on the weasel and trap him.

The residence was in West Hollywood, a bit of a drive from downtown, but conveniently located near Beverly Hills. It gave Garrett pause to think of how close Buckner lived to Marlene, no doubt by design. Yet he didn't dwell on that. Garrett was focused, single-minded in purpose.

When he pulled onto Buckner's street, he slowed. It was a quiet residential area, deceptively so. The neighbors had no idea who'd moved in down the street. The guy had pawned himself off as retired military, faked the honorable designation. That ticked Garrett off, just like everything else.

Garrett pulled off the street a couple of houses away, next to a grassy area between two homes. That way no one would wonder why a strange car was parked in front of their house. Each would figure it was a visitor to the neighbor's home.

Once on his feet, Garrett strolled along the sidewalk, purposely looking bored so as not to attract attention. He didn't see anyone outdoors, but it didn't mean that prying eyes weren't watching him from a window. When he reached Buckner's place, he took stock of the situation.

The house appeared quiet, and the drapes were drawn. If he didn't know better, he'd think the resident was sleeping in. Garrett had come prepared. Standing to the left of the front door, he retrieved a lockpick from his inside pocket, and within seconds he had the door unlocked.

Garrett had made as little noise as possible, but waited to see if the occupant had noticed. Then he drew his gun, keeping it hidden behind his jacket, and opened the door. He was met with silence. Stepping inside, he let his eyes adjust to the interior lighting.

There were no signs that anyone was home. Without making a sound, Garrett crept farther into the interior. He scanned each room, finding it empty. Then he went to the garage. The motorcycle wasn't there. Buckner was gone.

Cautiously walking through the house, Garrett took in the scene. The place was a mess; trash littered the carpet and the air smelled of rotten food, mingled with other noxious odors. A map of the city was tacked up to the living room wall where a homeowner would have normally hung a painting.

Looking closer, Garrett saw red pins marking Marlene's home, the studio, and Garrett's apartment. He'd been there so infrequently that he'd nearly forgotten he had his own place. But Buckner hadn't. There was even a pin in downtown at the Stealth Security office, and another right across from it at the garage.

Turning, Garrett saw piles of papers on the coffee table and, leaning over, he read some cryptic notes. Yet they were clear enough. They were plans, details of missions, imaginary missions that Buckner had concocted.

On the floor was a picture frame, its glass shattered. A photograph of Marlene hovered near the edge of the table, having been salvaged from the broken frame. For some reason, the scrawl of her signature caught his attention, and Garrett realized that Buckner must have obtained the picture at one of her charity events.

It was all very creepy. Some weirdo had Marlene's photo and spent endless hours plotting her demise—if that was Buckner's goal. It wasn't yet clear what the guy had in mind. Garrett's skin crawled. That had to be it. Buckner wanted Garrett out of the way so he could have Marlene.

Did Buckner really believe she'd go with him under any circumstances? Or did Buckner plan to kill Marlene too?

As mentally unstable as the guy was, it was impossible to know what went on in his mind. Garrett walked through some other rooms, and checked out the kitchen. He wasn't looking for anything specific, but thought he might find a clue.

What he learned was that Buckner lived in a self-made delusion, devoted to strategizing and complying with orders that didn't exist, *hadn't* existed. From the looks of the place, Buckner did little else but fancy himself as a soldier. The circumstance wouldn't have been worthy of Garrett's notice, if it hadn't been deadly.

Whatever wild idea entered Buckner's skull became his reality, or so it seemed. And he didn't dream away his idle days, instead seeking to make his version of reality come true. The magnitude of what Garrett faced was grim. A man who didn't live in the real world was capable of just about anything.

Garrett had to get to Marlene. He didn't intend to wait around until Buckner returned. Now that he knew where he lived, Garrett would be back.

He retraced his steps through the house, having

avoided disturbing anything. Buckner wouldn't know that he'd been there, and wouldn't realize they had his address. Covering his fingers with his shirt, Garrett locked the front door and pulled it shut.

The street was still quiet; the chirp of a bird was the only sound.

Garrett went back to the car and got behind the wheel. He turned the key and checked the time. It was getting late. The press conference would start soon, and he intended to be there when it did. The media weren't dangerous, just annoying. Still, he preferred to be with Marlene when she faced them.

He edged away from the curb and gave the car some gas. Halfway down the block, he tapped the brake to keep his speed down. The brake pressure was a bit weak, but he'd let them know when he returned the car. At the intersection farther down, he signaled to make a right turn, but when he put his foot on the brake, it went all the way to the floor. He pumped it, but it was useless.

The car rolled through the intersection and crested a slight hill. Garrett yanked on the emergency brake, but that did no good. It must have been disabled when the brake lines had been cut. He was on residential streets and didn't want to swerve into a kid or a dog, so he focused on steering to keep the car straight.

At the next corner, Garrett turned onto a broader highway, pulling in front of oncoming traffic. It was a near miss, but the other driver honked and swerved around him. If only he'd been driving a stick shift, but he couldn't downshift an automatic.

Putting the car into neutral, Garrett looked ahead, needing a quick solution. The car was gaining speed down the hill, even without being in gear. Then he saw a park not far ahead. Unfortunately, the signal coming up was red. He scanned for traffic, and deftly missed a car crossing the intersection on the green light.

Garrett steered up over the curb, across the grass, and into a massive tree trunk. The airbags exploded, knocking him in the chest—but the car had stopped. He shoved at the airbag and managed to get out of the car. Then he turned and sprinted toward the main thoroughfare.

Once the accident was spotted, the police would be called. Garrett wasn't about to stick around for that. Buckner was on a rampage. Cutting the brake lines hadn't propelled the car into a fatal accident, but it had slowed Garrett down.

He needed to get to the studio. With Buckner on the loose, there was no time to waste. Running faster, he made it to the busy street, but there were no taxis in sight. It wasn't New York, after all. Garrett thought quickly. He could call Travis and have him send one of the team to pick him up.

That would take too long. By the time a ride got there, it could be too late. The car ride had gotten him closer to Hollywood, thus closer to Marlene. He considered running, but again, too slow. Garrett spotted the street car a block over and sprinted to catch it.

When he hopped on board, his ankle complained as a result of the fast jogging. The nagging ache was the least of his concerns. Once in his seat, Garrett dialed Marlene. He needed to hear her voice, and know that she was okay. Buckner would be blocked at the studio from seeing her, but that didn't put Garrett's mind at ease.

Buckner was desperate. His actions showed it.

When Garrett got her voicemail, he dialed security at the studio. He knew the guard who answered. "Steve, this is Garrett...can you put Marlene on the phone?"

"That might be difficult," the guard said. "It's a zoo here right now. The media is swarming the place. The cast are giving interviews."

"Have you seen Marlene?"

"Sure, I saw her. She was talking to a media guy. I'm sure she's the center of attention."

"Do me a favor. It's important. Go and find her. Have her call, no matter what's she's doing. It's an emergency," Garrett said.

"She can't be far. Anna was right beside her. They can't be hard to find. I'll tell her to call you."

Garrett's veins flooded with adrenaline, and his pulse raced. This wasn't good. He had to get there fast. Leaning to look out the window, he could see the street was in the distance, not far up ahead. He'd be there soon, probably, before Marlene even called him back.

He sent a text to Travis, keeping it brief: *Buckner not home. Cut my brake lines. No injury. On way to studio.*

When the street car stopped at a light, Garrett hopped off and took off running. He prayed he'd find Marlene knee-deep in journalists, looking radiant and charming them with her witty replies. He wanted nothing more than to feel foolish for having imagined the worst.

CHAPTER TWENTY-THREE

The press junket was one of the most exhausting but important parts of releasing a feature film. Marlene knew that a large percentage of the film's budget was designated for promotion, so she intended to give it her all. She wore a nice dress with leather pumps. The event was fairly casual, the atmosphere designed to make friends.

The distributors and publishers of the upcoming film had planned an afternoon press junket at the studio. The promotion of the movie involved advertising campaigns, including everything from magazines to conversations in chat rooms.

The press would be allowed to visit the movie set and gain insight into how some of the special effects were done. Interviews with the director, producers, and stars of the film were especially popular, so would be the pinnacle of the event. Even a few private interviews had been authorized, and one was scheduled for Marlene, as well as a separate one for her director.

The public relations firm provided food and drinks, along with goodie bags, posters, and keepsakes. The journalists would circulate and interact, then have the opportunity to ask the cast questions. The questions avoided anything too serious. *Why did you become involved in this production?* or *Which actor is most like their character?* were the types of things the public wanted to know.

The studio had been spruced up for the occasion, and many rooms were opened up so the press could look around. Security was tight, but the guards knew how to remain in the background and not ruin the mood of the event—although a junket was often a stressful experience anyway.

Marlene had been to more of these types of events than she could count. The journalists were herded around like speed daters and could only ask basic questions, none that were of a personal nature. She was determined to make it a pleasurable event. After all, the point was to stir up excitement about the film, and there was no better way than to create rapport with the actors. Fans loved hearing about their favorite stars.

Anna escaped a band of reporters and went to Marlene's side. "How you doing?"

After giving a brilliant smile to the two journalists who'd been hanging around, Marlene turned to her friend. "I wish Garrett was here. He's late."

"What happened to him?"

"I'm sure he got delayed at the office or something, but I haven't had a moment to call him. My phone's in the dressing room, and there's no way to slip away." Marlene admonished herself for needing her bodyguard's support. It wasn't as if there was a lack of security. She admitted that she really just wanted to see his handsome face, and know he was there during the interviews.

"He'll be here," Anna said. "I know he won't miss it." Then a group of journalists spotted her and Marlene lost her friend's attention.

As the minutes ticked by, Marlene began to wish she'd worn more comfortable shoes. Maybe she could sit down during her private interview, away from the hub of the main group. That should be soon.

Marlene chatted with members of the press when they approached her. She was friendly and answered their questions, adding some humor when appropriate. It was best to keep things light. The hallways wound around to various sets so the press could take photographs.

Relieved to have the crowd move ahead of her, Marlene held back near the main area. Her interview was coming up, and she didn't want to miss the reporter. It was someone from a prominent entertainment channel.

Marlene watched the crowd filter down the hall. She turned, hoping to see Garrett, but he hadn't arrived yet. Security dotted the vast studio, and some stragglers lingered to look at movie posters or read material about the upcoming film release.

Then a man appeared beside her. He wore tinted glasses, so she couldn't see his eyes. A press pass dangled around his neck, and he had a camera over one shoulder. "Hello, Marlene."

Instinctively, Marlene smiled. This must be the journalist who'd arrived for the personal interview. She'd thought that she'd be called to the director's office, but maybe not. Before she could inquire about where he planned to conduct the interview, or to verify his name, the man leaned closer.

Marlene felt a prick at her waist and glanced down to see the sharp tip of a knife at the base of her ribs. She froze, unable to make sense of the situation.

"Don't show any reaction. This stiletto can slice into you before you can scream. Turn around as if everything is normal, and walk down that hallway to your right. Make everyone think you are on your way to do an interview," the man said.

Marlene hesitated, trying to think of a way out. If she screamed loudly, then security would rush to save her. But she might be dead by then. The knife glinted under the lights, and she had no doubt the man would make good on his threat.

To buy some time, Marlene did as he asked. She turned and walked slowly down the hallway with the stranger beside her. *Breathe, breathe*, she thought. *I have to get away.*

Getting inside hadn't been a problem. Faking press credentials had been simple. And people were so easy to fool. All Buckner had to do was look the part, and he'd been accepted as one of the journalists welcomed with open arms.

He'd known the studio would have security, so he'd prepared. Metal detectors were used to screen each arrival for weapons, but his ceramic gun had gone unnoticed. Its glass fibers hadn't so much as caused a blip on the scanner.

The thin stiletto had been concealed up his sleeve, taped to his forearm. It had given Buckner pause when the detector had indicated there was metal on his body. But he'd just smiled and lifted his arm. In a bored voice, he'd said, "Sorry, it's my watch."

Buckner had worn a Swiss Army watch with lots of fancy dials. The guard had checked out the watch, saying he'd like to get one of those, then waved him through. That had been a close call, but Buckner hadn't been seriously concerned. This mission was meant to be, and he wasn't going to be tripped up by something as trivial as studio security.

For a while, Buckner had blended in, getting used

to the surroundings. His plan had been mapped out some time before, but it was too early to execute it. From a distance, he'd watched Marlene without being obvious about it.

Security roamed about, so Buckner had made an effort to ask a few questions of the cast and express interest in the film. He had been interested, but not in the movie. His focus had been on the star, and Marlene had looked lovely as she entertained the visitors.

It had done his heart good to watch her. Marlene was beautiful, admired by fans and press. She was talented and charming. Best of all, she was *his*. Buckner had waited much too long to make that reality come to pass.

The time had finally arrived, and he knew Marlene would be pleased when she finally understood the situation. She'd be relieved to know that a man like Buckner was willing to look after her, care for her. She shouldn't have to be on her own. What had happened to her brother hadn't been her fault.

Buckner would rescue her. It was too bad that Marlene hadn't seen the light sooner. But then Flynn had most certainly lied to her. That could be dealt with, though. Buckner was the stronger man, the more efficient soldier, and he'd win this battle.

When Buckner had approached her, he'd been surprisingly calm, considering how long he'd strategized and looked forward to that moment. Yet it was to be expected. He'd been trained for battle, and had learned how to control his reactions.

Yet standing close to Marlene had its effect. Her perfume wafted around him like a hypnotic drug. With her so near, Buckner's desire for her surged. But he shouldn't jump the gun. There was plenty of time.

He had to do this right.

Her long blond hair curled down her back, and the dress she wore accentuated her best features. In fact, all of Marlene's features were her best. If she had any flaw, Buckner didn't see it. It would really be too bad if he had to kill her.

Marlene's shoes clicked on the floor as she walked slowly down the hallway. They were out of sight now, safe from anyone's curiosity. She stalled, leaning away from his knife.

"Don't make a sound," Buckner said in a low voice, "or you'll be dead in an instant. This blade can go straight through your heart."

Marlene began to walk again. He could see her trembling, and it made him feel good, boosted his ego. She knew who was in control. Buckner had been looking forward to this. Now things would change. He'd finally get the respect he deserved.

The demeaning attitude that Marlene had displayed the one time he'd spoken to her wasn't evident now. At that event, she'd been haughty, like she was above it all. Without any consideration for him, she'd brushed him off. Now Buckner had the upper hand, and she realized his power. That thought produced a high like no drug ever had.

It would all be over soon, and justice would be served. *You're mine, Marlene. We belong together.* The thought seemed so real that he wondered if he'd spoken the words aloud. Buckner guided her down the hallway to their destination, knowing the outcome. There wasn't anything she could do about it. He was in charge, and her bodyguard had no chance of saving her.

Marlene was terrified. The tip of the knife pricked at the fabric of her dress. Involuntarily, she held her breath, afraid that she might accidentally lean into it. Without needing confirmation, she knew the guy was Buckner. It had to be. And facing him in person was so much worse than being the victim of his attacks from afar.

Her senses were heightened. Buckner was unpredictable, and she had no experience dealing with such a man.

With one hand on her arm, Buckner guided her down the empty hallway. She smelled a mothball odor, as though his clothes had been stored in a trunk, long past their usefulness. His body odor was repulsive, and a wave of nausea hit her.

Buckner's rough handling, his threats, and his gritty voice served to intimidate her. Marlene didn't intend to be his victim, and swore she'd discover a way to escape. Yet panic gripped her at the knowledge that he might kill her before she got her chance.

If only Marlene could call for security, but that was impossible. She didn't have her phone, and if she screamed, she'd be dead. The studio walls were thick, and the chance of anyone hearing her was remote. She was too far away now.

She prayed that Garrett would get there and save her. But her heart fell when she realized he might not make it in time. Buckner was frightening, an evil that she wasn't sure how to fight. She feared that he had no mercy in his heart.

If only she knew what he wanted from her. If Buckner's goal was to kill her, then why not just do so? What was he waiting for? What was this really all about?

The movie studio was like a huge maze, with

various areas assigned to different sets. Buckner forced her down the hallway, turning right then left, as if he knew where he was going.

Confused and scared, Marlene steeled herself not to give in. There had to be a way. She couldn't have come this far only to lose in the last moment. She waited for her opportunity.

At the end of a dark corridor, Buckner stopped. Marlene considered running, but he still held the knife on her. With his other hand, he removed the tinted glasses, folded them, and put them in a pocket. Then an evil grin distorted his features, his cold eyes freezing her soul. The glacial blue of his eyes was nearly transparent. A chill raced up her spine.

Buckner retrieved a thin device from his pants and waved it over her, checking for trackers. Marlene's pulse pounded. She wondered how he would react when he discovered the devices, and whether he'd fly into a rage.

But he didn't. Buckner smirked. "The shoes...that's kind of obvious," he said. "Take them off."

Marlene removed her shoes and held them in her hand. When he reached for them, she handed them over.

"Flynn thought he was so clever, did he? Well, let's leave him a trail and make him worry." Buckner dropped one of her shoes in the hall, and, holding the other, he motioned for her to start moving again. When the shoe on the floor was out of sight, he dropped the other one. "That should do it."

Marlene didn't like this one bit. Garrett had put trackers on her as a precaution. It would have been useful, except it appeared that Buckner wanted to be found. He was leading Garrett to them.

Garrett was in danger, and might be caught off

guard with these tactics. Buckner wanted him out of the way. She knew that much, but she didn't know exactly what her captor had in mind. Yet she had no choice but to go with him.

They went a bit farther, then stopped again. The look in Buckner's eyes wasn't at all reassuring. His expression was riddled with evil, his eyes narrowed, and his lips stretched thin. He was a horror to look at, but Marlene couldn't turn away.

Buckner spoke in an eerie voice that echoed in the empty space. "You'll be fine, Marlene, if you do as I tell you to." But his next action seemed to contradict that. He grabbed her wrist and held the tip of the knife over her hand.

Marlene suddenly felt faint.

"I'm not going to slit your wrist. That would be too messy," Buckner said. "I just need some blood." He pricked her finger, barely touching it but drawing a good amount of blood—evidence of how sharp the knife was. Then he let it drip onto the floor, making bright red spots.

Marlene stared in shock.

"Let's put your bodyguard in the right mood, and make him wonder what's happened to you," Buckner said. "You'll lead him right to us." Farther down the hall, he pricked another finger...more blood.

Marlene pressed her fingertips against the palm of her hand to stop the bleeding. The minor pain in Marlene's fingers paled in comparison to the dread that was building inside her. She was in the hands of a psycho with a knife, and Garrett was going to walk into some sort of trap. She could sense it.

Then Buckner turned a corner and opened a door. He shoved Marlene inside. The darkness nearly pushed her to the breaking point, but she refused to allow any weakness. After he shut the door behind them, he flipped on some low ceiling lights.

There was just enough light to enable Marlene to see into the room. Buckner pushed her forward. They were inside a sound studio. It was a room that hadn't been used in a while, in a part of the building that wasn't likely to be visited anytime soon. Items were strewn around and cables were piled up. The air smelled stale.

"No one will hear us in here," Buckner said.

Marlene looked around, trying not to reveal how frantic she was. They were in a soundproof room, designed for recording. Once that door closed, there wasn't a chance that anyone in the hall would hear them—even if someone happened to walk by.

The situation seemed to grow worse by the minute. Marlene had the impulse to run for the door; maybe she could make it out before getting caught. But it was hopeless. That knife would plunge into her back before she made it three steps.

Stepping deeper into the interior, Marlene took in the details of the environment—what Garrett had referred to as situational awareness. It was a long room with padded walls and an acoustic ceiling. There was a variety of equipment and control panels. On the floor were a bunch of tangled cables attached to an electrical box.

But there were no weapons, not even something that would serve as a club. No sharp items, and no furniture except a couple of stools in front of one of the control panels. Marlene actually considered lifting one of the stools and cracking it over Buckner's head.

Bad idea. She figured she'd get as far as grabbing the stool before her life was over.

There had been times when Garrett had spoken

about preparedness, but Marlene was vague about that. She seemed to recall that even when they functioned in civilian jobs, ex-SEALs did stuff like put razor blades in the tongues of their shoes, or carried some kind of cord that could be used as rope.

The thought of strangling Buckner gave her a flicker of perverse satisfaction. But it was fleeting. She was alone in a sealed room with a madman, and her best weapon was her fingernails. If he came any closer, she'd scratch his eyes out—even if she did bleed to death from a stab wound. At least he'd remember her, and suffer at her hand as much as she could manage.

Buckner sauntered up to her, wielding the knife as a reminder. "I'm sorry, Marlene."

Her ears pricked up. Did he have a soft spot after all? Could she exploit it?

"I understand your grief over losing your older brother. That shouldn't have happened. But it did." Buckner frowned, but his effort at sympathy came across as grotesque.

Marlene didn't trust herself to speak. Whatever she said might set him off, have the reverse effect of what she intended. So she listened, trying to make sense of it, looking for a way to manipulate things to her advantage.

In a sort of disjointed discourse, Buckner spoke of Andrew as if he'd known him. He called him a man of valor, one of the silent heroes. He cited events that seemed disconnected, except in his warped mind. And he mentioned his own bravery through the telling of weird anecdotes. Marlene watched in amazement, studying the strange look in his eyes, observing his awkward body movements.

"You're all alone now," Buckner said, "with no one

to protect you."

Marlene stiffened, her thoughts muddled. *What does he mean by that?*

"But I sought you out." Buckner's eyes were glassy. "I'm responsible for you now. You've been so foolish to trust Flynn." Then he seemed to remember something else. His cold eyes went vacant.

"I was there for you, Marlene. I went to your charity events. I supported you. But you don't recall do you? You couldn't be bothered." Buckner's chest heaved, as if he couldn't get enough air. "I spoke to you...but you brushed me off. I wasn't worthy of your notice. But you will learn...you will find out just how important I am."

Marlene struggled to recall ever seeing him before. The fundraisers were crowded. If he'd worn the tinted glasses, she wouldn't have noticed him. It was his stark blue eyes. Once seeing his brittle gaze, no other feature was as memorable. The hatred behind those eyes blocked out any possibility of seeing beyond them.

Buckner leaned toward her, his rancid breath choking her. "I'm an ex-marine, you know. You should treat me better, show some respect."

When Buckner grabbed her arm, Marlene's heart pounded so hard that she thought it would leap out of her chest. The guy was nuts. And she was in grave danger.

The cold peril of facing a killer was more than Marlene could tolerate. She willed her body to move, to run, to do something...anything. But her limbs were heavy, her feet like anchors, weighting her to the floor. Any hope of escape evaporated—if it had been there in the first place.

Looking into the unfeeling eyes of a psychotic, all

seemed surreal. Then fear arrowed into her heart. But it wasn't fear for her own safety.

Garrett was honor bound to protect, especially women, and most of all—*her*. He would put his life on the line without hesitation. Dark foreboding blossomed in the pit of her stomach.

Because of her, Garrett would follow the trail of blood and play into Buckner's hand. His life was at risk. Marlene might lose him, watch him die at the hand of a lunatic. She had to save him...but how?

CHAPTER TWENTY-FOUR

Garrett arrived with the press conference in full swing. He surveyed the main room, but there was no sign of Marlene. He had to find her, to see for himself that she was fine. He'd overreacted. The event had plenty of security. It wasn't a place Buckner was likely to try anything.

Or so he attempted to convince himself.

The place was thick with journalists, and noisy. Cameras flashed as photographs were taken. Garrett spotted a few of the cast. There was her costar Michael surrounded by a group of reporters. Nicholas was having a conversation that looked intense.

But Marlene was not in sight.

Then Garrett saw Anna looking rather bored, as she chatted with a well-dressed woman who had to be an interviewer. He strode over and interrupted. "I need to speak with you for a minute." Garrett glanced at the reporter. "*Privately.*"

"I appreciate the interview, Anna." The woman waved across the room and headed toward someone she seemed to know.

Garrett said, "Where's Marlene?"

"She's here. I was with her not long ago, but then I got swept up in all the activity," Anna said. "She was wondering about you. You're late. She was worried."

"Yeah, that's a long story," Garrett said, "for another time. I really need to speak with Marlene. Any ideas?"

Anna shook her head. "Not really. I went down the hall with the studio tour, so the press could get some photos of the sets. But Marlene wasn't with us. She's very popular today. I'm sure she was accosted by some reporter." Just then an enthusiastic young woman interrupted them.

Garrett spotted the security guard he'd spoken to on the phone, and briskly walked over to him. "Steve...hey. Do you know where Marlene is?"

"She can't be far," the guard said. "She was making the rounds. This crowd can't get enough of her."

Garrett frowned. It seemed that Marlene had been there, but it was driving him crazy that she seemed to have vanished. "Did you give her my message? Ask her to call me?"

"Sorry, I didn't get the chance," Steve said. "I did see her after you called, but a reporter was deep in conversation with her. There was a private interview scheduled, so that's probably where they went."

For a moment, Garrett breathed a sigh of relief. That was it; Marlene was in an interview. "Where was the private interview supposed to happen?"

"That's the thing," Steve said. "At the security briefing this morning, we were told it would take place in the director's office."

Garrett stared at him.

"But she went the other direction with the journalist. I guess she was going to show him around, give him a tour or something."

"Which way did they go?"

Steve pointed toward a hallway, and Garrett took off at a sprint. The hallway was empty, outside the scope of the event. No one else was going that way. Enough messing around. Something was definitely wrong.

Garrett retrieved his phone from his pocket and activated the tracking app. It was a good thing that he'd insisted that Marlene wear devices so he'd be able to find her. Glancing at the screen, he frowned. She was too far away for comfort.

There wasn't a second to spare. He jogged down the hall, his rubber-soled shoes hardly making a sound. He didn't want to alert anyone ahead of him; surprise was on his side. The studio was as large as a hotel, and the hallways seemed to go on and on.

He followed the light on his phone, leading him to Marlene, thankful that he hadn't left locating her to chance. Moving as fast as he could, he headed toward her. Garrett had a sick feeling in his gut.

Marlene meant so much to him. It seemed like an odd time to be struck by how much he loved her—but then, maybe not. Panic gripped his stomach at the very real possibility of losing her. He'd sworn to protect her, and was determined to do so.

Then the device flashed, indicating he was close. Garrett slowed at a corner, listening for any sound. It was quiet. He pulled his Glock from the holster and, holding it in both hands, entered the adjacent hall. No one was there. Then his eyes went to the floor...Marlene's shoe.

Garrett picked it up. "Shit." If he'd had any hope that he'd find Marlene strolling through the halls giving an interview, it was dashed. It had to be Buckner. He had her and had found the tracking device. This was bad.

The tracker light indicated they were farther ahead. Garrett would need to approach cautiously, not knowing what he would find. *Hold on, sweetheart. I'm coming for you.*

The trail led him to Marlene's other shoe. Buckner

was playing games with him. Well, playtime was over. *I'm on my way, asshole.*

Garrett moved through the hallways with purpose. He listened for any sound, and looked for any sign of Marlene. Glancing down, he slowed his pace, then stooped to the floor. *Blood.* This was worse than he'd anticipated.

Buckner was with Marlene, and she'd been hurt. He might be too late; there was no time to waste. Moving ahead quickly, Garrett kept his eyes and ears open. The silence was unnerving.

Then there was more blood...and more. Buckner was luring him in with Marlene's blood. He'd harmed her, and that was unpardonable; he'd pay for his crime. Garrett's heart raced. He had to find her without further delay.

Garrett jogged down the hall, following the trail of blood. It stopped in front of a closed door. He stood to the side and listened, but didn't hear anything. Marlene had to be in there.

With his gun ready, Garrett turned the knob then pushed the door open. The interior was semi-dark, so he took a moment for his eyes to adjust to the dim lighting. The low sound of a male voice could be heard, causing adrenaline to surge in his veins.

Garrett went into fight mode: calm, focused, unafraid. The enemy was within reach. He could hear the conversation, but he couldn't see them.

There was a fabric panel blocking his view. Garrett approached, holding his gun in front of him. He peeked around to see what was happening. Rage filled him at the sight of Buckner with Marlene. The creep had his arm around her waist, holding her back to his chest, and he looked directly at Garrett.

Instantly, Garrett assessed the situation. The room

was an old sound studio with a bunch of abandoned equipment. At the far side was an electrical box with a bunch of cables intertwined in a pile on the floor. There wasn't much else of significance in the room.

Buckner was in range, but Garrett couldn't shoot. With one wrong move, Marlene could get hit. And there was another problem: her captor held a knife to her throat. If he could get his hands on the attacker, he'd wring the life out of him with his bare hands. Yet Buckner had the advantage.

Aiming the gun at Buckner's head, Garrett stepped into the room. He looked into the man's icy-blue eyes. "Let her go."

Buckner's haughty laugh was the only sound in the room.

"You can't get out of here without being seen," Garrett said. "You won't get away with this."

"What makes you think so?" Buckner smirked. "I've planned this down to the last detail. I'll get out, and I'm taking Marlene with me."

Garrett considered blowing the man's brains out, but that knife was too close for comfort. One slice could cut Marlene's jugular, making it next to impossible to save her.

"I knew you'd come for her." Buckner shoved the flat side of the knife under Marlene's chin. Her eyes were wide with fear. "Drop the gun, Flynn."

Garrett hesitated.

"Now," Buckner said, "or I *will* use this knife. It would certainly mar your reputation as a bodyguard. Not that it will matter soon."

Garrett knew the man was insane enough to kill Marlene, so he lowered the gun and dropped it to the floor.

"Kick it over," Buckner said.

Taking the small advantage offered, Garrett swung his foot to slide the gun across the floor, and in doing so, moved two steps closer. He'd succeeded in closing some of the distance between them. Marlene looked at him, and Garrett gave her a look of confidence, to convey that it was going to be okay.

"Don't come any closer," Marlene said. "That's what he wants. He'll kill you."

"I'd advise you to listen to the lady," Buckner said, then kicked the gun into the darkness. "I'm in control now."

Garrett was wholly unprepared for what came next. Buckner tightened his grip on Marlene, and she gasped. On high alert, Garrett was ready for a fight. If only the guy would fight like a man, and not use an innocent woman as a barrier.

Then Buckner smirked, as if he was privy to some secret. He appeared a bit too pleased with himself, which put Garrett more on guard.

"You haven't told her, have you?" Buckner said with a fake smile. When Garrett didn't respond, the guy emitted an evil laugh.

Marlene was motionless in the madman's grasp.

Buckner launched into a tirade, barely taking a breath. He described Andrew's death in detail, including a battle scene and an attempted rescue. It was a story that appeared to be true to Buckner as he recited it—only it was pure fiction. "You're a traitor, Flynn. Why don't you come clean with her? You were the one who killed her brother, or you might as well have been."

Garrett died a little inside when he saw the shocked look on Marlene's face. But he said nothing.

"I am a man of valor," Buckner said, "not you. I would have saved Andrew's life, and Marlene would

266

be with him today. But you got in my way. You shoved me to the ground; you stopped me from rescuing him."

Marlene looked into Garrett's eyes. "Is that true?" she said in a voice filled with emotion. It was the worst possible time for her to find out about his involvement in Andrew's death.

Before Garrett could think of what to say, or a way to alleviate the shocking effect of the news, Buckner cut in. "So you see, I'm the man you want, Marlene. Don't believe Flynn's lies; don't let him come between us."

Garrett realized the man's goal all along had been to possess Marlene. As if Buckner believed Marlene would fall into his arms, he released her but held the knife in position. The man was crazed, with a distorted concept of himself. He really thought that they'd view him as powerful and intimidating.

Buckner held the knife in his left hand and gripped Marlene's arm in his other. With the sharp point at the base of her ribs, he hardly looked like a suitor about to make a plea for her affection.

Yet in his frenzy, Buckner forged ahead. "Don't believe his lies. You know the truth now. We can run away together. I'll take care of you, because your older brother isn't alive to do it."

Buckner looked lasciviously at Marlene. "Don't worry about Flynn. I'll take care of him for you. He's not a problem."

"You're demented," Garrett said in an authoritative voice. "You have an overblown ego. But all you can do is terrorize. You don't have the guts to face me like a man."

Buckner's face turned red, as if he'd been slapped.

"You're not a soldier," Garrett said. "You weren't in

battle...*ever*. You're a reject. No one wanted you."

The veins in Buckner's neck popped out, and his jaw locked.

"Your view of the world is complete delusion, just like your assumption that Marlene will go with you," Garrett said. "You're a screw-up, an impotent son of a bitch. You failed to be a soldier...and you've failed to be a man."

With the lies thrown in his face, Garrett saw the man crack. Called out, he reacted violently. He seethed with hatred; his expression was that of a killer. In his emotional state, he might slip up. Garrett watched, waiting for the opportunity to take him out.

Yet Buckner seemed to cling to false hope. "Marlene, this is your chance. You're mine. You won't regret it. Tell me that you'll leave with me."

Marlene's green eyes flamed. "Go to hell...you're insane. Take your hands off me."

"If you care about her, as you claim, you'll release her," Garrett said. "This is between you and me."

Buckner's certainty that Marlene would view him as a hero was clearly shattered. "No, you bitch," he spat. "You don't see how it is. After all you know you'd stay with that idiot. You deserve to be with me. I can't leave you to a life not worth living."

The man was seething, as the ultimate glory of having Marlene had been taken away. "I'll have to kill you both." He glared at Marlene. "If I can't have you, then no one can. I'm the only man who has a right to you. Your life without me to guard and keep you safe would be too unbearable to endure." He took a raspy breath. "I'll have to end your life. It's the kindest thing to do."

Buckner stood to the right of Marlene. While holding the knife to the base of her ribs, he reached inside the left flap of his jacket and pulled his gun from a holster. He pointed it at Garrett.

"Don't move or you're dead. You think you're so macho," Buckner said. "You really thought you could save her. What a joke."

Garrett didn't flinch. Just one chance; that was all he needed.

Then Buckner spoke to Marlene in a cold, calculated tone. "I'm going to kill your boyfriend first, so you can watch. I want you to know what a mistake you've made." He sneered. "You'll grovel at my feet before this is over."

Buckner narrowed his eyes, then cocked the gun with the barrel aimed at Garrett's heart. Without warning, Marlene lurched forward, then propelled her body over Buckner's hand and the gun. It went off and she dropped to the ground, just as the knife clattered to the floor. She was facedown, and blood seeped out around her.

Garrett leapt forward and fell to his knees beside her. "Marlene..."

But the response was from Buckner. With his hands on Marlene's shoulders, Garrett looked up to see a Taser pointed at him. The asshole was a fucking one-man armory.

"It's over. You lost," Buckner said. In a split second, Garrett assessed the man's expression. It was one thing to threaten to kill, but it was quite another thing to do it. The man was no soldier, and his shock was evident. He'd killed the woman he'd wanted, the one he'd done all of this for. Buckner was stunned, with a desperate glint in his eyes.

But there was no going back. Buckner was crazed, and in his moment of hesitation, Garrett attacked.

Growling like an animal, Garrett grabbed the

man's ankle and yanked hard. Then he let go, like he'd touched a hot stove.

As if in slow motion, Buckner's body flew up as his feet went out from under him, then tipped backward and fell into the electrical box. The Taser clanged against the metal then tangled in the cables. The energy from the Taser shorted out the electrical wires, and the man's body was zapped—electrocuting him in an instant.

Garrett hardly paused to look at the dead man. This was no time to feel relieved. Guilt about his part in all of this swamped him. He loved Marlene more than life itself, and now he may not be given the chance to tell her. All he wanted was for her to live. His gaze fell to her motionless form in a pool of blood.

CHAPTER TWENTY-FIVE

Garrett turned Marlene onto her back, and pressed his jacket against the wound to slow the bleeding. Her eyes were partially open, and her breathing was shallow. But she was conscious. "Stay with me, sweetheart."

Footsteps sounded in the hallway, then Wyatt appeared in the room. Without asking any questions, he dialed his phone. "She's here, but bleeding heavily...move fast." He told the paramedics how to find the room, and they showed up quickly.

Garrett spoke to Marlene to keep her awake, and maintained pressure on the wound. The medics took over the instant they arrived, and worked swiftly. Moving back, Garrett let them tend to her, but he continued to talk, letting her know he was there. It was a good sign that she was conscious, but he knew she hurt like hell.

Once Marlene was on a stretcher with the bleeding under control, an IV was started and she was given oxygen. Her eyes fluttered opened and closed, so Garrett wasn't sure how much she was aware of.

Wyatt stood next to him. "Once you booted up the tracker app, we knew you were in trouble. Travis sent me, and had an ambulance waiting out front. He expected the worst."

"That might save her life," Garrett said. "Without immediate medical attention, the gunshot wound might have been fatal."

When the medics began to wheel Marlene out of the room, Garrett followed to ride in the ambulance.

Wyatt was on his phone again. "I'll take care of this mess," he said, standing near Buckner's lifeless body. "I can deal with the police and let Travis know what's happening. I'll check in with you later at the hospital."

Once Marlene was in the ambulance, the medics hooked her up to equipment and took her vitals again. They maintained communication with the emergency room.

Garrett watched, with his heart breaking. Marlene's eyes were closed, and he didn't know the extent of the internal damage. The medics weren't able to tell him too much; that would be up to the emergency room staff and the doctor.

Sitting as close as he was able, Garrett held her hand, hoping she knew he was there. The immediate and aggressive intervention by the paramedic crew was probably all that had saved her. Any delay could have been fatal. He was grateful for the backup from his team, and it hadn't come a moment too soon.

Upon arrival, Marlene was rushed to emergency and Garrett was left to wait. After what seemed like an eternity, a nurse came out to tell him that Marlene was in critical condition and would be in surgery for a while.

Garrett sat in a nearby chair and put his head in his hands. "God, please let her live."

Hours passed without any word, and Garrett watched the clock, anxious for the doctor to come out to give him an update. Marlene had to survive the surgery; she just had to.

When Wyatt entered Garrett was pacing the floor. "Any news?" his teammate said.

"Not yet."

Wyatt sat down. "What happened back there? Do you want to talk about it?"

Garrett gave him a brief rundown of the incident. Near the end, his eyes were moist. "She threw her body on the gun...to save *me*. If she dies it will be because of me. I'm the one that should have taken the bullet for her."

"Marlene was very brave. She risked her life to protect you."

Garrett looked at his friend. "Buckner would have killed me. At close range like that, he wouldn't have missed."

Neither said anything for a minute.

Then Garrett spoke. "She has to make it through this; she *has* to."

Wyatt stayed for a while, then left Garrett to continue to wait. There was no way to know how long it would be. Eventually, the surgeon came out and talked to him.

"Marlene will come through this," the surgeon said. "She's a strong young woman."

It seemed that the bullet had entered at an angle, not straight on. That was fortunate, and as a result there was less damage than there might have been. The speed of the bullet had propelled it right through her, since it had been fired at such close range.

"I've done what I can for her," the surgeon said. "She's in the recovery room."

"When can I see her?"

"I'll have the nurse come get you when Marlene is taken to a room. She will be sleeping for a while, but you can visit briefly."

Garrett breathed a sigh of relief. It wasn't over yet.

Marlene was in serious condition and had a long recovery ahead of her. But she was going to make it.

Not long after, Wyatt reappeared to check on things, and Garrett relayed what the surgeon had said.

"Well, it's a damn good thing that the shooter didn't use the armor-piercing bullets this time," Wyatt said. "That would have been a fucking disaster."

"What did he use? I didn't recognize the gun."

"Travis has been in touch with the police about the incident. This time Buckner used a polymer gun, non-metal so it would get by the metal detectors," Wyatt said.

"Undetectable guns have been illegal for years, if they can even be found."

"I'm guessing he nabbed one on the black market," Wyatt said. "The guy was smart and resourceful; I'll give him that."

Garrett gritted his teeth. "And look where it got him."

"The one good thing about using that ceramic gun was that the cartridges didn't have metal casings. The charge was bonded to the bullet without any brass shell. I'm not saying they didn't do a lot of damage...but it could have been worse."

Garrett frowned. "So how did he get that little stun gun inside the studio? That sure wasn't plastic."

Wyatt shrugged. "The Taser? We may not find out. It's possible he'd hidden it in the sound studio earlier. He was a slimy bastard."

Garrett raked both hands through his hair, then stood up when the nurse came in. "You can see Marlene now," she said. "But only for a few minutes."

Wyatt stayed behind, while the nurse led Garrett to the room in intensive care. She pushed open the door for him. "I'll be back in five minutes," she said.

Marlene was hooked up to a bunch of machines. She looked fragile and pale, but was beautiful. Her blond hair fell over the white pillowcase, making her look like an angel in the snow. Her breathing was steady, and when Garrett took her hand, it was warm. "Thank God you're alive," he whispered.

He pulled a chair close to the bed and continued to hold Marlene's hand. Remorse filled him. Garrett wished he would have told her about everything sooner—before Buckner had used the knowledge for his own purposes.

Garrett hadn't expected her to forgive him, but he had hoped to tell her in a way that she could deal with. He'd waited for the right time, but that hadn't come. Instead, Marlene had discovered the secret from the mouth of a madman.

Whatever resentment Marlene felt for him, Garrett deserved. And how he felt didn't mean a thing. All that mattered was that she recovered from the trauma, so in the future she'd be healthy and happy. He'd move aside once he was certain Marlene was okay—if that was what she wanted.

Garrett loved her deeply, but that was selfish on his part. He had no right to her, although he knew, without a doubt, there wouldn't be any other woman for him.

Marlene opened her eyes to a room full of flowers. Bouquets with well wishes had been sent from friends, cast members, the director, and even the producer. She breathed in the floral aroma, so glad to be alive. She'd survived the ordeal and would be allowed to go home soon.

The first few hours had been rugged. Marlene had vague memories of doctors and nurses fussing over her. The pain and discomfort reminded her of just how close she'd come to dying. She felt like she'd been hit by a truck, but she was breathing. And the doctor had said she would fully recover.

It would be a long road of rehab, but the bullet hadn't damaged any major organs. It had arrowed through her, missing her heart and lungs. Marlene was lucky, and she knew it. But it had been worth it all, because the alternative was too gruesome to consider.

She shuddered to think what would have happened to Garrett if she hadn't reacted as she had. The thought that he could have died brought tears to her eyes. She loved him so much.

The days in intensive care were rather hazy. She knew Garrett had been there, had heard his voice and felt his touch. But she'd been too weak to speak, and her vision had been blurry. Yet knowing he was there had been a comfort.

But recently, he hadn't been to see her, and Marlene didn't have much trouble guessing why.

She'd had many other visitors, although not for long as she was still quite weak. Her mother had flown out and was staying at a hotel close to the hospital. Anna had been by twice a day. Even Wyatt had come by to check on her. Nicholas and some of the cast wanted to visit, but had been told to give her a few more days to recover first.

It would be so good to get out, to get some fresh air, and see something besides the inside of a hospital room. The doctor said he would release her today if her condition remained stable. She'd hired a nurse for home care, and her rehab appointments were scheduled.

Marlene scooted up a bit higher on her pillow, and winced with pain. It was going to be a while before she was normal again. But her life was her own. The evil that had threatened her was gone. Anna had spoken with Garrett about how it had ended, then relayed the story to her.

Buckner was dead. It was finally over, and Marlene could move on with her life.

But she didn't want to plan a future without Garrett. He'd been scarce the last few days, and she missed him. The bodyguard job was over, but she didn't want him to go.

Marlene knew how she felt about him, and that wasn't going to change. Yet she didn't know how he felt. She didn't know what she'd do without him. She didn't need him like she had when she'd been in danger. It was better than that. She *wanted* him, and had trouble envisioning her life without him.

Anna opened the door and came in, disrupting her thoughts. "You're awake." Her friend gave her a gentle hug. "I'd squeeze you hard, but I might crush a rib."

Marlene laughed. "I'm supposed to get out of here today."

"I heard. That's great news."

"I'll be up and around soon. We're long overdue for some shopping."

Anna grinned. "I'll say. Between filming a war movie and fighting off a real-life villain, you've been a bit busy."

"I just want to lie by the pool and drink piña coladas for a while."

"Sounds perfect," Anna said.

"Have you seen Garrett? He hasn't been in to see

me. I'm starting to think I look worse than I thought."

Anna giggled. "You look lovely. You even have some color back in your face. For a while you were ghostly pale."

"Maybe I scared him away," Marlene said.

"I don't think that's possible. Garrett had been in the hospital so much, I think the staff is going to give him a white coat and put him to work."

"He'd look sexy," Marlene said, then sighed. "I love him so much."

"I know you do, honey." Anna patted the bed. "Tell you what, since the doctor is springing you from this joint today, how about if I assist you with hair and makeup? You are a star, after all. There might be a photographer just waiting for a chance to get a photograph of the awesome Marlene Parks as she's wheeled out to the car."

"I certainly hope not," Marlene said. "But you need to make me presentable anyway."

Marlene was weak, so Anna propped a few pillows under her head and worked her magic. When she was finished and Marlene looked in a hand mirror, she decided she didn't look half bad. "The dark circles under my eyes are a nice touch."

"That's not my doing," Anna said. "I brought you some clothes, too. The nurse said she'd help you put them on."

"Thanks, Anna. I feel better already."

Once her friend left, the doctor arrived to make his final check. What he found met with his approval, so he signed the release papers. The nurse assisted Marlene to get dressed and then brought the wheelchair to escort her out.

Marlene fully expected to see Samuel pull up in the limo, but she didn't. After waiting a minute, a luxury sedan pulled up to the curb with Garrett at the wheel. "That's your ride," the nurse said.

"You and Anna knew, didn't you?"

The nurse just smiled.

Garrett hopped out of the car and came around to help her in. He wore faded jeans with a thermal shirt, and hadn't looked more drool-worthy. His hair had grown and was a little shaggy, making her want to run her fingers through it. He smiled, and Marlene's eyes went to his kissable lips.

"You really know how to make a girl feel better," Marlene said as he lifted her into his arms.

"That's the idea." Garrett gently put her in the front seat, then jogged around to the driver's side.

"Where did you get the car?"

Garrett started up the engine. "I bought it. I can't have you riding home on the bus now, can I?"

"Um, what about the limo?"

"I thought you'd rather ride in a vehicle that doesn't have bulletproof windows." Garrett glanced at her. "Although I might have those installed later."

Marlene looked out the window. It was a lovely April day and flowers were in bloom. "Can we stop by the park? I'm just so sick of being cooped up...just for a few minutes?"

"Of course, sweetheart."

She did love it when Garrett called her that. It made her warm all over, and touched her heart.

While he navigated the streets, Marlene leaned back. She was stiff and uncomfortable, but hadn't felt better. She was with Garrett, and the future was theirs. Maybe.

At the park, Garrett pulled up to the curb so she had a nice view of the lawn and the flowers. He lowered the windows to let in some fresh air.

"It's so pretty," she said. "It's so good just to be alive."

Marlene studied Garrett for a moment. He was as handsome as ever, but there was a crease in his forehead that hadn't been there before. She could detect the worry in his expression, although he did his best to hide it.

"So...were you going to tell me?" Marlene said.

Garrett turned in the seat to face her. "I meant to, so many times. I should have said something much sooner."

"Yes, you should have." Marlene had felt betrayed, and had been shocked at discovering Garrett's secret. But in the hospital she'd had time to think. Life was precious, and the most important thing was those she loved. She just needed to understand, to be able to put it all in perspective.

Marlene took a breath. "Now I know why you were there that first day."

"I had no idea it was to help you dodge a bullet," Garrett said. "But it's fortunate that I showed up."

Marlene admired his strong figure, the hero he was, through and through. Any reason she might have for rejecting him faded when she looked into his eyes. "You saved my life...more than once."

Garrett's eyes filled with emotion. "And you saved mine."

"I don't know what I would have done if anything had happened to you," Marlene said.

Garrett took her hand in his. "You scared me to death, taking a bullet like that."

"So why did you come to my charity event that day? I know you weren't just a fan, that you came for *me*. But why?"

Before speaking, Garrett looked down. He rubbed

his thumb over the top of her hand. "Your brother died in my arms." He paused. "His last thoughts were of you and your mother. With his dying breath, he made me promise to tell you that he was proud to serve his country, that he had no regret."

Tears streamed down Marlene's cheeks, smearing the carefully applied mascara. But she wasn't sad. Honor and duty were familiar to her; she respected a soldier's dedication. She'd mourned the loss of her brother, as she had her father, but she was filled with pride for their sacrifice.

"It means so much to hear Andrew's last words."

Garrett squeezed her hand. "I did what I could to save him...I failed."

Marlene knew the guilt haunted him, but there were no words that could make it go away. "I'm glad to know the truth. I don't hold it against you. I know if you could have died in his place, you would have."

They were silent, holding hands. Leaves rustled in a light breeze, birds chirped, and the sound of children laughing could be heard in the park. Life was precious, and so was Garrett.

"I should get you home before you tire out on me." Garrett started up the car.

Marlene had a pang of loss. Home meant empty rooms, a quiet space...without Garrett. She closed her eyes, and deep exhaustion overcame her. Dull pain filled her chest, but it wasn't just the physical healing. The prospect of losing Garrett made her ache, and left a gaping hole inside her.

At her home, Garrett carried her inside, but didn't immediately leave. "Where will you be most comfortable?"

"Take me to the lounge chair by the windows. I want to look out. I'm just so tired of confinement."

Garrett placed her on the chair and got plenty of pillows. Marlene didn't want to close her eyes, afraid that Garrett would be gone when she opened them. But she couldn't fight the heavy feeling in her limbs, and she drifted off.

CHAPTER TWENTY-SIX

When Marlene woke up, she had no idea what time it was. She opened her eyes to see the sun low in the sky, and shadows on the buildings. It was quiet, and she thought she was alone except for her domestic staff. And tomorrow she'd have the nurse.

With effort, she pushed upright and draped her legs over the side of the lounge so her feet touched the carpet. She was relieved to see that she hadn't been abandoned.

"Going someplace?" Garrett said, his blue eyes sparkling.

"How long was I sleeping?"

"A while. It's good for you." Garrett pulled a chair closer so he could hold her hand. "Do you need anything?"

"Water would be good."

Garrett filled a glass with water from a pitcher that was nearby. He handed it to her.

The water tasted good, and Marlene felt better after the rest. "You're still here." She dug her hand through her hair and made an effort to fluff it out. "I must look like a wreck."

"You look beautiful, sweetheart." Garrett sat next to her on the lounge, then lifted her hand and tenderly kissed her wrist. "You always look beautiful."

Marlene's heart skipped a beat. If she'd had more strength, she might have fallen into his arms.

"I have something I want to say." Garrett looked into her eyes. "I waited too long before to tell you the truth, to bare my soul to you. I won't make that mistake again."

Marlene nibbled at her lower lip, wondering what was coming.

"I used to envy guys who had a woman back home, someone to fight to return to. I didn't have that," Garrett said. "There was more to it, that day I first saw you at the event."

Marlene held her breath.

"Your brother had talked about you a lot, and had shown me pictures...not your movie star pictures, but childhood photos. I know it sounds strange, but I felt as if I knew you. There was a connection when he spoke of you, told me stories of your family and of your youth."

Garrett continued, as though he feared if he hesitated he might not get a chance to say it all. "The thing is...you're special. Not because you are a movie star. Any red-blooded male in the country has likely fallen for you. But it was different for me.

"I love you, Marlene. I think I loved you before I ever met you that day. You are the only woman for me," Garrett said. "And I want you to be mine."

Before her eyes, Garrett dropped to one knee beside the chair. He reached in his pocket and pulled out a diamond engagement ring. "I would be honored to have you as my wife. I want to share my life with you, if you'll have me." He paused, choked up. "Will you marry me?"

Marlene's eyes clouded with tears. She was so happy that she thought she'd burst. Garrett loved her. He wanted to marry her.

Garrett held the ring out to her. "Please say yes,

sweetheart. Will you marry me?"

"I love you so much. I have for a while. I wanted to tell you, but everything happened so fast. And I wasn't sure..." Marlene's gaze locked with his. The love she saw in Garrett's eyes made her heart swell with emotion. "Yes, I will marry you. You've made me so happy."

Garrett leaned close, and when his lips touched hers, he kissed her sweetly, passionately. In that kiss, Marlene sensed the pent-up need, the unbounded love, and the sincerity of his desire for her. She kissed back, drinking him in, wanting all of him.

"I love you," Marlene whispered, her lips against his.

Garrett grinned. "I'm the happiest man alive."

Ten months later, Marlene was fully recovered from her injury and she felt fabulous. The movie had released in December with rave reviews. It had been a box office hit.

At the Golden Globe awards ceremony the following January, excitement was high. Marlene had been nominated for an award and anticipated the evening with great hope. Garrett escorted her, dressed in a tuxedo, which, not surprisingly, suited him quite well. His hair was short, and his closely-trimmed beard was sexy. She was sure the attendees would think that he was an aspiring actor. He certainly had the looks for it.

Anna attended dressed in a glittery blue dress that fit her so well it looked like it had been painted on. Her wavy brown hair gleamed under the lights, and her bright smile captivated the fans. Marlene was pleased for her. Great things were in her friend's future, and her brilliant performance in a supporting role had helped make the film stand out.

Marlene arrived in her limo with Garrett by her side. They strode along the red carpet together, while the photographers snapped pictures. It was a big night, and one that Marlene had long awaited. She slipped her arm through Garrett's and looked at the diamonds glittering on her finger. The photos of her with her fiancé would make quite a splash.

She'd offered to let Garrett sit it out, but he'd refused. "This is a big night. I'm going to be there with you."

They'd talked about it, how it would work. Garrett assured her that he could be on the Stealth team, even while married to a movie star. It wasn't usually done, but Travis would make an exception. There were many assignments that didn't require staying out of sight. He assured Marlene that he'd been on plenty of clandestine missions. He wasn't clamoring for the limelight, but if being married meant tolerating photographers, then so be it.

Marlene had wrestled with her own internal conflict, but not for long. Her career demanded that she travel, and often film on location. She'd be away, unavoidably. In Hollywood, marriages tended to have a short life for all kinds of reasons. It was one of the things that had caused her to avoid relationships.

But Garrett wasn't just any man. He was unique in too many ways to count. After all they'd overcome, he assured her that whatever they faced, they'd figure it out. "We love each other. We'll make it work."

Marlene didn't argue. Being with Garrett was effortless; it was right. She felt like she'd known him much longer than she had. She was madly in love, and had no intention of letting anything break them apart.

Garrett's career had inherent risk, and involved danger on a regular basis. For so long, Marlene had vowed to avoid falling for a man that could so easily be taken away from her, but she had changed. She no longer feared; she only loved.

That night Marlene proudly walked the red carpet on Garrett's arm. Another bodyguard, recently hired, followed behind and kept the crowd under control. He wouldn't live at her home; that was Garrett's territory. But the new bodyguard would ensure her protection in public, and since he was a Stealth team member, Marlene felt very safe.

The event was thrilling, as well as entertaining. Marlene was anxious, but in a good way. Whether she won the award or not, she was happy. Garrett looked over and smiled at her, then squeezed her hand. The announcer began to preface the award for best performance by an actress in a drama.

Marlene trembled with excitement, and her heart pounded. The nominees were listed and the crowd rumbled with enthusiasm for each star. When the announcer read her name, she mentally pinched herself that this was really happening.

After a grand pause, the announcer proudly gave the name of that year's winner: *Marlene Parks*. Tears of joy filled her eyes, and she stood to go up and receive her award. Garrett hugged her before he let her go. She managed to make it up the few steps to the podium on trembling legs.

The recognition meant a lot to Marlene, and she thanked everyone involved. She shared how much the film meant to her personally, and expressed her gratitude for the award. Then she looked out into the audience to find Garrett. When their eyes met, he beamed at her.

After the awards, there were parties to attend but Marlene bowed out. She wanted to be alone with Garrett, and share her special moment. Yet they didn't go home. Instead they went to a late night feature and sat in the dark, eating popcorn and drinking Coke.

Surely she would have been recognized, but Garrett had reserved the entire theater just for her. Marlene thought of the time they'd sneaked out in disguise to go to the movies. It had been a memorable day. There had been one thing she'd wanted to do that day that she hadn't.

In a private moment, Marlene had shared her wish with Garrett. It had seemed silly, but he hadn't thought so.

That day at the movies, Marlene had wished she was just a woman at the movies with her boyfriend, making out in the darkened theater. Garrett put his arm around her, and they watched the coming features. Then he held her tighter and leaned over to nuzzle her temple.

Marlene pressed closer. "I don't know how much of this movie we're going to see."

"What movie?" Garrett dug his hand in her hair and kissed her deeply. He raked his tongue next to hers and breathed her in, as if she was the air itself. Marlene's hands roved over his rounded shoulders and down his rock hard chest.

"I can't wait until I have you alone later," Marlene whispered when he released her.

"Greedy, aren't you?" But Garrett didn't wait for an answer. He kissed her again, harder this time, and Marlene whimpered. His arms went around her and he held her tight. His kisses were hot, a temptation that was hard to turn away from.

But Marlene wouldn't have to. She was going to be his wife, and could look forward to being in his arms every night and every morning. It was a wickedly delicious thought.

Garrett nibbled on her earlobe and brushed his mouth over her cheek. "I love you," he whispered, then pulled back to look into her eyes. "You mean everything to me."

"I love you with all my heart," Marlene said, then gave him a teasing look. "And right now...I need more kisses."

ABOUT THE AUTHOR

Emily Jane Trent writes romantic suspense and steamy romances about characters you'll get to know and love. If you are a fan of stories with a heroine that's got spunk and a hunk of a hero that you'd like to take home with you, these stories are what you're looking for. Emily's romantic tales will let you escape into a fantasy – and you won't want it to end - ever.